CW01033252

Copyright © 2024 by RJ Kinner

All rights reserved.

No portion of this book or included artwork may be reproduced in any form without written permission from the publisher or author, except as permitted by U.S. copyright law.

Interior and Cover design by RJ Kinner

ISBN Paperback 979-8-9880683-3-4

ISBN Hardcover 979-8-9880683-4-1

THE OTHERWORLDS
Book Two
RJ Kinner

RJ Kinner Art

For Stewart.
Till again, my love.

"The most merciful thing in the world, I think, is the inability of the human mind to correlate all its contents. We live on a placid island of ignorance in the midst of black seas of infinity, and it was not meant that we should voyage far."

H.P. Lovecraft

Prologue

<u>Bang</u>

Rhythmic drips of moisture echoed in the dim tunnel.

Square light bulbs illuminated the puddles of stagnant water dotting the flat stone path. The stale air reeked of brine and mildew. Rats scurried to the shadows as two men walked at a brisk pace into the flickering dimness. Their footsteps slapped against the wet floor.

The taller man was in his fifties now, his rigid posture erect as he strode forward with confidence. Various puckered scars and branded symbols covered his bald head. A tattoo on the back of his neck stood out against his pale waxy skin: a single black circle. He had inscribed it decades ago, but the dark ink showed no signs of fading.

He nodded to the man walking beside him. "Does she know who we are?"

The younger man shook his head. Although his features were undeniably attractive, people usually kept their distance. His bright golden eyes seemed too occupied, too frantic, too knowing and eidolic to be called anything but insane.

"No," he said, smiling. "She hasn't been able to tell anyone we're coming."

"What about the book?"

The young man's smile widened into a sharklike grin. "Now *that*, she knew. This is it, Declan. This is the exact moment we've been waiting for." He inhaled a shuddering breath. "And we're going to do it this time. They've told me we will."

"You're sure?"

The young man's smile wavered. "They've *told* me."

The pair turned onto another corridor lined with pipes leaking streams of rust. A metal door stood cracked open at the end of the hall. Muffled screams came from behind it. The older man pushed open the screeching metal hinges, stepping into the dimly lit room.

A woman lay hunched on the ground, hands cuffed behind her back with a plastic tie. Blood and sweat matted her long brown hair into tangled knots. A man wearing a black rubber apron leaned nonchalantly against the wall, using a metal file to round off his fingernails. His eyes, devoid of emotion, flicked to the two men who'd entered.

The younger man closed the door behind him and stood with folded arms. The steady dripping of water masked the gasps of the woman on the floor.

"Tell them what you told me," commanded the man against the wall.

"Go to hell." She spat.

The man removed a remote from his belt and flipped a switch. The woman screamed and fell to her side, body convulsing in spastic bursts.

An almost imperceptible electric hum sputtered and sparked from a small metal disc attached to her neck.

He released the button. She stopped screaming. Blood leaked from her ears.

"Let's try that again," said the man, stowing the remote. He grabbed a fistful of matted hair and pulled her to a kneeling position. "Tell them what you know about the book."

She spat out a glob of blood and hung her head. "All I know . . . is . . . a rumor. The book was found in . . ."

She faltered, eyes glazing over as she struggled to stay conscious. She shook her head. "Antarctica. They found it in the ice. Years ago." She bowed her head and closed her eyes. "It's in the . . . the archives now."

"Where?"

She pressed her lips together. Another yank of her hair broke her silence.

"Rome!" she yelped. "The . . . the Vatican."

It was silent.

The two men started laughing.

The older man clapped the younger man on the shoulder and flashed a rare broad smile. "You may be right about one thing; this is our chance to do it right this time. We're bringing Him back. All of them back."

He pulled open the door. It screeched. "I'm going to tell your father about this. Deal with her, and meet me when you're ready. We're going to need you for this one. You and your friends."

The young man smiled. His wild gaze brightened as he tilted his head to listen to something no one in the room could hear.

Voices almost no one else in the world could understand.

"They say we should leave in three days. That's when security will be the lowest. There's a"—he closed his eyes. "There's a guard who's struggling to pay her bills this month. She's our way in."

3

The older man waved to the man still holding the woman's hair. "Get everyone ready."

The man wearing the rubber apron let go of the woman and disappeared through the door. The older man nodded once before shutting the rusty slab behind him.

The younger man pulled a black handgun from his back pocket. Silver scratches covered the outside mechanisms. No, not scratches. Notches. He cocked it in one fluid motion and pointed it at the gasping woman on the floor.

Her eyes locked onto the barrel, filling with fear and panic. She replaced it with resolve, spitting out another mouthful of blood and phlegm. "The book . . . you don't know what it is. You don't know what it's capable of. I hope for your sake the others get it before you do."

The man chuckled.

"You don't stand a chance against them," she continued, her voice cracking. "I don't care who you are. There are people protecting this world, and they're stronger than you'll ever be."

The young man knelt next to the woman, wrapping his arm around her shoulders. She recoiled. His fingers dug into her skin as she resisted. "Laura, Laura, Laura. Like everyone else you've abandoned, you disappoint me. You know who we are by now, don't you?"

He pulled her head close to his mouth and uttered four words.

Her eyes widened in horror, her already pale face turning green with disgust.

"Oh my God," she whispered.

The man grinned. "There you go. I love seeing those dots connect."

She glared at him. "It was you all this time, wasn't it? I suspected, but I never thought . . . you . . . you bastards."

"How rude." He stood. "Is that any way to treat someone who's about to let you go?"

"W-what?"

"I'm sending you back to your friends." He shrugged, circling the woman and bending down to untie her hands. "Call it an early Christmas present."

She pulled away as soon as she was free, but her legs buckled when she tried to stand. Her hands shook as she rubbed her bleeding wrists. "Why are you doing this?"

"Because I want you to take them a message. I want them to *know* we're coming. I want them to realize who we are before their whole world comes crashing down." He sucked in a rapturous breath, lips curling into a wobbly smile. "I want them to be *afraid*."

The woman's shaking hands wiped blood from her forehead.

"Give them a message they won't ever forget," he said. "Tell them we're back, and things will be different this time."

She looked down. "I . . . I'll tell them."

"Good."

The young man tilted his head to look down at her with a sympathetic smile, one a parent would give a child. He reached down and cradled her cheek, moving his thumb back and forth.

The smile vanished. He placed the gun against her forehead. Her eyes widened.

"For we are many," he whispered.

BANG.

ONE

Growing Pains

"Come on, Lily! Only a few more jumps!"

I tried to slow my breathing, balancing against the rough bark of the pine tree. The platform swayed and buckled in the wind as the cold air dried the beads of sweat from my face. I swallowed. This obstacle course had looked easy from the ground. Well, easy-ish.

That was before the wind had picked up, making it progressively harder to stay upright. Though I had to agree with Roger and Cliff; in the last few weeks, I'd gotten better at the whole "being a Jumper" thing.

Not great, but better.

I crouched and readied myself to jump to the next rope. The wind pushed it out of reach, twisting the sturdy cord into loose knots. I waited until it swung back before springing for it. My numb hands clamped onto the coarse fibers, and I fell forward. I jerked my legs up and let go.

Landing on the next platform, I hopped to the next obstacle: thin strips of wood spaced out in a horizontal ladder. My foot slipped on the last wrung. Wheeling my arms to keep steady, I grabbed onto another hanging rope and swung backward into the air. My stomach dropped, but my hands stayed firmly clasped on the rope.

I panted, my arms burning as I glanced below. My dangling feet hung above the soggy ground. Luckily, a net separated me from the distant forest floor. It didn't make it any less terrifying.

"Come on, Lil!" a voice called below me. "You're almost there!"

I looked down. Roger squinted against the increasing raindrops. The blue plastic tarp shielding him and Cliff flapped in the wind. Roger's expression was neutral, but even from here, the white-knuckled grip on his elbows was obvious.

My breathing slowed. Though we saw each other almost every day, his presence was still reassuring. Since the events of October, living by myself had become dangerous and unpredictable. Nightmares, flashbacks, and worst of all, unplanned trips to the Collective were everyday occurrences.

So Roger had moved into Terry and Susan's house, bunking in the guest room downstairs. Henry and Cliff thought it was a great idea, as it took care of two problems at once. I had someone to talk to, and they had someone to watch the Gate in the barn. Roger had since made a habit of attending my training sessions when he had a free shift. He said it was just to see my progress, but I suspected he wanted to make sure I didn't kill myself.

Given my current situation, he had a point.

He gave a double thumbs-up and smiled, rain pelting his face. "You got this!"

I shifted my grip on the rope and wrapped my feet around the knot at the end. Swinging back and forth, I pivoted toward the next cord, catching my foot on the platform. The wind blew rain into my face as I arched my back and pulled myself to safety.

Shaking out my arms and catching my breath again, I heard cheers below me. I wiped the water droplets from my eyes.

A small crowd had gathered with Roger and Cliff underneath the tarp. My heart leapt. The excited faces of Bea, Bryn, Bunny, and Henry peered up at me through the rain. What were they all doing here?

I hurried forward to the last obstacle. The zip line was technically the most dangerous obstacle, as there wasn't a net, but it was also the easiest. I grabbed hold of the slick metal bar and pulled my feet onto the footrest. Stepping off the platform, I tried to keep the smile off my face as my brain screamed, *Wheeee!*

The scuffed blue mat grew larger as I approached. After waiting a few seconds, I let go, rolling into a somersault before skidding to a stop. Tucking some stray strands of hair behind my ear, I steadied myself and stood.

I heard cheers and turned to see the small crowd approaching. Bryn reached me first and threw her arms around me, her red scarf bobbing behind her. "Congratulations, Lily." She laughed. "You did it!"

Bea jogged up beside me, her dark skin contrasted by her bright smile. "Well done! And not a bad time, either."

I looked around at the group as Bryn unlatched her arms from around my neck. Henry, Cliff, Bunny, and Roger advanced with smiles on their faces, their hoods drawn against the rain.

"What's . . . going on?" I asked.

"Well . . ." Henry cracked a smile, softening his intimidating presence. "You just finished the endurance portion of training. Congratulations, Lily, the worst of it's over."

I blinked. "I—what?"

"Today was your last day. Sorry we didn't tell you." Cliff chuckled. "But Rog thought you'd do better if you thought it was just another training course."

My gaze shifted to Roger, who tried to wipe the smirk off his face. He seemed more relaxed now that I was back on the ground.

I glared at him. "Thanks for the confidence."

He shrugged. "What? You get nervous. Now the worst of it's over, and you didn't have to stress."

I rolled my eyes. "The stress is my *motivation*. I could've completely flunked today without it. What would you have done if I totally blew it?"

"Um." He chewed the side of his lip. "Well, you didn't. So . . . nothing."

Everyone laughed.

"Wait, really?" I asked. "I'm done with training? For real? I didn't expect it to end, like . . . ever."

"Believe me, I know what you mean," Cliff said. "It feels like it takes an eternity. But you're done with the preliminary three weeks of endurance training. Now, we get to the fun stuff."

My stomach sank. By Jumper standards, "fun stuff" usually meant "near-death and very painful experiences."

Roger nudged my arm. "You don't have to look so scared. You've already gotten a head start."

I swallowed. "A head start on what?"

Bryn gave a wide smile. "Combat training!"

I groaned. They weren't wrong. I *had* received a bit of training a few weeks ago. I could scrape by on basic self-defense, but that was where my knowledge took a running leap into a brick wall.

"Don't worry," Bunny said. "You don't start today. We'll make sure you get a break. Twelve hours, at the very least."

I sighed. "Gee, thanks."

Everyone laughed again.

"So, is that why you all came out here?" I asked. "Just to watch me finish?"

"Well... mostly," Bea admitted. "I was relocating a few civilians in the area and finished in time to stop by."

"The people who came out of the portal with Cliff?" I tilted my head. "I thought they were all taken care of."

Bea's shoulders hunched. "No. Unfortunately, some cases weren't as simple as knocking on a door and rewriting some memories. These two will have to rebuild everything they've lost since The Bound took them. I'm sure you'll meet them sometime soon. They're staying at Sarah's place. Actually, you—"

She broke off as a buzzing noise interrupted her. Flipping open the copper-colored compact, she sighed at the message and shoved the Chatterbox back in her pocket. "And there's the inevitable. Sorry, but I have to go."

Cliff cocked his head. "Everything all right?"

She nodded, waving her hand. "It's nothing, just... something that I need to follow up on." She turned to me and gave a warm smile. "Congratulations, Lily. I wish you luck on your next portion of training. Till again, everyone."

The group mumbled departing words as she walked away, opening a portal to Giftshop with her Teleporter. She disappeared a moment later with an electrical *zap*.

Bryn stretched her arms behind her back. "Well, it's getting late. I better be heading out too. Henry, Bunny, you want a ride back to town?"

Henry stared at the spot where Bea had left and furrowed his eyebrows. "Thanks, but no. I think I'll head over to Giftshop and see how progress on the west side is going. Till again, and congratulations, Lily."

I waved and smiled while he pulled out a Teleporter and followed Bea to Giftshop. After the incident with The Bound, Henry had discovered a Teleporter inside his jacket pocket. It was a nonnegotiable sign that Giftshop wanted him out of retirement. He didn't seem to mind.

"I'll take that ride, Bryn," said Bunny. "Beats hitchhiking back to Stars Crossing."

Bryn raised an eyebrow. "Always the lazy one, aren't you? Some things never change."

"Always going back on your offers, then?" Bunny shook her head. "Some things never change."

Bryn playfully punched her in the shoulder.

"By the way, where's Pete and Tinker?" I asked. "Aren't they usually with you guys?"

"They're on assignment for a few weeks," Bunny said. "Some of the higher-ups wanted their help constructing boundaries around Earth's Gateways. Around the more populated areas, at least."

"Like the one in Stars Crossing?"

"Mm-hmm. Right now, they're probably covered head to toe in grease at some research bunker in the middle of nowhere."

I smiled. "I bet Tinker loves that."

"He's ecstatic," Bryn agreed. "I don't think we'll convince him to come back. He's got too many toys to play with now." She grabbed my hand and squeezed. "Congratulations again, Lily. We've got a two-hour drive ahead of us, but we'll see you around. Till again."

They waved and headed to the small dirt road that connected to the outside world. The Jumper outpost had been built deep in the woods, far away from any town or civilization. It was by design that the entrances were almost impossible to find from the main road. Security was a priority for the few hundred residents who called the small tree-house village their home.

Cliff, Roger, and I meandered back into the main hub of the outpost. The usual mumble of conversations grew closer as we approached. A group of giggling children rushed past us, one carrying a messily stitched flag up the nearest set of platforms. The icy rain fell in spattering bursts, but the children didn't seem to mind. Their ongoing game of capture the flag was too important to be ruined by a little weather.

"So . . . I'm really, actually done?" I clarified. "This isn't, like, some trick that tests me on my instincts, right?"

Roger chuckled and shook his head. "Nope, that's it for endurance training. Promise."

I exhaled a sigh of relief. Even though I'd been getting better at surviving the rigorous training schedule, every day was still a challenge. I'd lost count of the times I wanted to quit, but Roger and Cliff wouldn't let me. I appreciated their encouragement, but it left me questioning whether I'd made the right decision by becoming a Jumper. They were all brave, and athletic, and capable, and I . . . wasn't.

"Don't worry." Cliff stepped over a fallen log. "Combat training isn't half as bad as it sounds. It just takes practice and patience. You'll do fine."

I didn't respond. After running through the pouring rain all day, I didn't feel like sitting through another round of pep talks. We walked in silence before returning to another tarp-covered training area dug into a sloping hillside.

I pulled off my soaked hoodie and tugged on my rain jacket over my damp T-shirt. My arms were numb. "Same time tomorrow?" I asked Cliff.

He turned. The bags under his eyes were prominent today. He wiped some rain from his face. "How 'bout we give you an extra few hours to sleep in, okay? Let's say nine tomorrow morning at the ring."

I blinked. That was almost three hours later than usual. "Are you serious?"

He smiled. "Yes, I'm serious. I have to get going; evening check-in starts soon. See you tomorrow."

Cliff tousled Roger's hair before heading toward the main clearing of the outpost. His steps dragged through the dirt and pine needles.

"I don't think I remember how to sleep in anymore," I said.

Roger plopped on a nearby wooden bench. "At least we'll have time for breakfast before we head out."

I tilted my head. "We? Are you planning on coming out tomorrow too? What about your shift?"

He shrugged. "I have the late shift tomorrow. I can at least come in the morning and head to the station after that."

"Why?"

"Um"—he coughed—"I thought it would be nice to see you on your first day. If you don't want me there, that's fine too. I just figured, since our schedules lined up, um, I might as well . . . you know."

I sat next to him. "It's not that I don't want you to come. It would be nice to see you." I laughed. "You know, we may live in the same house, but we don't see each other much, do we?"

"I know. Weird, right?"

We watched the rain blow against the trees.

He tilted his head to the tarp above us. Small puddles of water and clusters of leaves had collected in it. "And, uh, maybe tomorrow after training we could swing by Sal's if you . . . if you wanted? I hear Rhonda's added peppermint bark to the menu now that Christmas is coming up."

I smiled. "I'd like that."

He smiled back. "Great. You ready to head out?"

I stood. My regular aches from training seemed to lessen with the knowledge it was finally over. Maybe tomorrow wouldn't be so bad.

Inhaling the familiar scent of pine, I stretched. "Let's go home."

Two

Status Quo

The pain in my shoulder sent a shock wave of nausea across my body. I screamed through my teeth. My other hand dug into the rock, the sharp edges cutting to the bone.

Leo's expressionless face watched me as he dangled over the swirling masses of multicolored clouds, his coat flapping in the wind. His hands were ice cold and clammy.

"Please! Just climb up. We can figure something out!" I yelled. "Please don't make me do this!"

He blinked, eyes empty. "Why are you waiting? You know you have to drop me."

I shook my head. "No."

"You can't change the outcome."

"Please."

"You know you have to kill me."

Stinging tears leaked into my eyes. A fresh new rush of guilt sank into my stomach and made it hard to breathe. "I can't. Please! I know you. I've lived your whole life. If you die, then so does a piece of me!"

The frigid wind whistled as I sobbed into the sleeve of my jacket. It was already wet. I pulled away and looked down. My sleeve was heavy with blood. So was the rest of me. It dripped from my clothes.

"I can't kill you," I said. "Please don't make me."

Leo reached up and patted my arm. My skin blistered at his touch. I screamed. "Poor Lily Masters." He shook his head. His face sank into itself, skin graying and rotting before my eyes. I recoiled but couldn't escape the stench of death.

"You already have."

My spine curved upward. I put a hand over my mouth to muffle the scream already gurgling in my throat, but it escaped anyway. My whole body shook. Uneven breaths came in shallow gasps.

I gripped the edge of the sofa and looked around the dark living room. Panting, I ran through my regular mantra of facts that reminded me of my place in the universe.

My name was Lily Masters.

I was twenty-one years old.

My head was pounding.

But I was still breathing.

I was inside a familiar old house that squeaked and settled every few minutes. Everything I just saw was a dream. I wasn't in bed because I had fallen asleep on the couch last night after dinner. The house was quiet. The usual pitter-patter of rain had disappeared in the last few hours. The dusty couch cushions smelled like cotton and the musty scent of perfume spilled long ago. I counted my breaths and listened to the sound of my heartbeat.

Breathe in.

And out.

The door opened down the hall. "Lil?"

The knot inside my stomach released as the familiar voice neared. I wiped my face as Roger shuffled down the hall. He was still in his pajamas, but his eyes were alert.

"Hey," he said. "Another one?"

I nodded. Pulling my knees to my chest, I unclenched my hands, echoes of pain spreading across my palms. They stung. Crescent-shaped cuts leaked smears of red from my fingernails cutting into my skin. In the moonlight, the blood looked black. Like the living tar The Bound had used to control people from the inside out. The horrible, unnatural parasite that left its mark inside me, even months later.

I blinked. It wasn't black slime. Just blood. That was a relief, though I knew it shouldn't be.

Roger sat beside me and held out a hand. "Can I see?"

I showed him my palms. He took my hands gently in his and turned on the lamp. I squinted away from the light as my eyes adjusted.

Roger tilted my hand back and forth and examined the bleeding cuts. "They're not deep. I'll get the first aid kit."

He headed to the bathroom, returning a moment later with a battered white tin box marked with a red cross. Selecting some alcohol wipes and a roll of gauze, he went to work.

I didn't notice the pain until he started cleaning. The mild stinging grew intense when he pressed the cool strip of cotton against them. I didn't complain. Pain was something I'd grown accustomed to in the last few weeks.

He ripped open a pack of sterile gauze. "So, you wanna talk about it?"

I pressed my lips together.

He wrapped one of my palms in soft white fabric. "Which one was it?"

I bowed my head and blinked away the burning in my eyes. "Leo again."

Roger sighed. "Lily—"

"I know," I said. "I *know*. I know I didn't have a choice, and I know you've told me a hundred times already, but I just—"

My voice cracked. Swallowing, I composed myself. "I know you don't understand the Collective, and frankly neither do I, but that day . . . that day I didn't just see his life. I lived it. All of it. And logically, I *know* it was only residual memories. I know his life wasn't mine, but it doesn't change what I saw. It doesn't change what I felt."

My breath caught in my throat. I shook my head. "And I just can't help feeling like . . . if only I'd been able to disrupt the Link sooner, things would be different now. Maybe I could've saved him, maybe not. But at least I could've *tried*."

Roger was quiet. He had finished wrapping my hands, but he hadn't let go.

"Listen," he said finally, "I know you probably don't want to hear me say this again, but it wasn't your fault. None of it was. Leo was already dead when we got there. He died the moment The Bound took control of him."

"Roger—"

"It'll take time to come to terms with that," he said. "Which is completely natural. But you need to move on, Lily. Begin to, at least. You can't keep replaying the past in your mind, hoping that it'll turn out differently, because it won't. What's done is done. You can't change it, and you need to stop thinking you can."

I closed my mouth and stared at the couch. No matter how hard Roger tried, I knew he wouldn't be able to fully understand what I felt when I accessed the Collective. Neither would anyone else. Navigating life connected to the storage bin of humanity's memories would be something I had to do alone. The thought terrified me. I used to wonder why Grandpa Masters turned away from hearing the Collective, but now I was beginning to understand. And I was beginning to think he'd made the right choice.

I sniffed and rubbed my eyes. "What time is it?"

"Almost midnight."

I sighed. "So much for sleeping in. I'm sorry I woke you up, too. I didn't mean to fall asleep here last night."

He shook his head. "Don't worry about it. I was . . . kind of awake, anyway."

I raised an eyebrow. "You too?"

He nodded.

"Which one?"

He bobbed his shoulders. "Couldn't tell you. I woke up 'bout half an hour ago but couldn't remember a thing."

I chuckled darkly. "Must be something in the water."

Roger flashed a rueful smile.

We drifted into silence. The lack of rain pounding the roof was almost disturbing. I'd grown so used to the constant drizzle that its absence left a hole in the background.

"Are you heading back to bed?" I asked. "You still have time to get a mostly full night's sleep."

"I'll probably try in a few hours. You?"

"Let's just say I'm not counting on it."

We both sighed.

"Well," I said, "what do you wanna do?"

Roger looked around the room before his eyes settled on the window behind us. He leaned sideways and glanced up toward the roof, smiling.

"I might have an idea."

"Careful, that part's a little slippery."

"Rog, it's *all* slippery."

"Well . . . be extra careful."

"I'll remember that when I'm plummeting to the ground."

"Don't worry, I got you."

I shifted the bundle of blankets under my arm and shuffled across the moss-covered shingles. "And we couldn't have done this on the ground because . . ."

Roger wedged his foot against a metal ventilation pipe sticking out of the roof. "You'll see in a second. Just don't look up until I tell you."

I tossed Roger the armful of blankets. The night was damp, accented by the smells of rain and chilly aromas of wintertime. We were both bundled in sweatshirts and beanies, but it was still uncomfortable to be outside. I held on to the edge of a brick chimney and stepped closer to Roger as he maneuvered to the flattest part of the roof. We sat and wrapped ourselves in blankets until the cold stopped snapping at our extremities.

"Okay," he said, "look up now."

Repositioning the beanie farther back on my head, I tilted my gaze away from the black-silhouetted tree line. A slight dizziness overtook me. The glittering waves and clusters of the Milky Way splashed the deep-blue sky.

Since we were on the roof, the trees fell away to the horizon, leaving an unobstructed view of the infinite expanse.

Unlike the viewing bay in Giftshop, the stars on Earth were familiar to me, which was somehow comforting. Even with my limited knowledge of astronomy, I recognized a few constellations.

I blinked. Despite the knowledge of the countless Otherworlds, our little corner of the universe seemed so quiet, so peaceful. At least, for the time being.

"Wow," I breathed.

"Yeah," Roger agreed. "Stars are pretty good tonight."

"Do you ever get tired of it?" I asked. "Since you've seen so many Otherworlds? I'd imagine Earth pales in comparison to some of them."

He laughed. "That's like asking if the Taj Mahal is better than the Grand Canyon. It's not better or worse, just different."

I wrapped the blanket tighter around myself. "Do you think we can see any of them?"

"Any of what?"

"The Otherworlds. Places we've been. Do you think one of those stars belongs to them? Or, you know, is close to them?"

Roger was quiet. He leaned forward onto his knees. "I've . . . never thought about that before. They're out there somewhere, that's for sure. It always felt like they were, I dunno, somewhere in another lifetime."

"Or in another-world?"

"Hardy har-har."

Shadows from the tree line caught my attention. My eyes flicked to the ground below. I stared until they moved again to make sure they really were shadows. I swallowed. This was the first time in weeks that I'd been outside after dark. It was one of many things I'd been afraid to do since The Bound invaded.

These days I always seemed to be afraid of something. Even that fact terrified me. It opened up the questions I tried not to ask myself: Was I making the right decision by becoming a Jumper? Did I belong in this kind of life? Could I learn to live with the Collective, or was I just steering myself on a path to insanity? It was a genuine fear. There were times I felt that any more secondhand memories would break me.

I tore my eyes away from the shadows and tilted my head back to the vast, starry sky. "Is this . . . how it's always going to be now? The nightmares, the guilt, the fear . . . Is this what I'm going to feel for the rest of my life now that I'm . . . part of all this?"

"Do you want the short answer or the long answer?"

"Short, please."

"For right now? Yes. There's going to be bad days, probably a lot of them. Sometimes they'll be so bad you'll think you can't take it anymore. Days where you'll want to curl up under your bed and never come out again."

I looked down.

"But eventually, things get better," he continued. "Someday, you'll wake up and feel different. Things won't ever be the same as they were before, and that's okay, because they're not supposed to. You adapt, that's all. You find a life that makes sense to you. It's just a matter of . . ." He paused, searching for the right words. "Finding a new status quo."

I closed my eyes against the cold world. He was right, and I knew what he said came straight from experience, but it was still just . . . hard. It was hard to believe that things would be all right someday when everything in the future seemed so unsteady.

Roger nudged me with his shoulder and jolted me out of my train of thought. "Hey."

I met his gaze. The warmth in his eyes told me all I needed to know.

I smiled a little. "I'm all right. Really. Sorry, I just . . . I just need to get used to it, I guess." I looked out over the dark tree line and sighed. "Because what else can I do?"

Roger put an arm around my shoulder, pulling me into a firm hug. I leaned against him and shut my eyes tight, finding myself holding back tears. We'd become so close over the last month, but it always seemed that there was something in the way of us taking that next step forward. Trying to heal from the traumatic events of The Bound made it difficult to know if what I was feeling was real or just something to keep the hurt at bay. Roger hadn't brought up the subject either, which made me wonder if he was struggling with the same thought. It seemed neither of us wanted to bring it up for fear of ruining what we already had.

Roger leaned his head against mine and let out a slow breath. I buried my head in his shoulder and forced my ears not to strain for the Collective. The wind whistled through the trees. The residual drips of rain sprinkled the ground. Roger's heartbeat was slow and even.

Roger's heartbeat. I focused on that. It calmed me.

Roger squeezed my shoulder. "We'd better get inside before we fall asleep up here." He pulled his arm from around me and stood. "Come on, up."

The sudden cold made me shiver. We gathered our blankets and shuffled to the window we'd used to enter the roof.

A few minutes later, we stood on both feet in the warm living room. Tossing the blankets back onto the blanket pile, we shrugged off our coats and hats.

"Thanks again," I said. "Sorry for keeping you up."

Roger smirked. "You need to stop saying you're sorry."

I shrugged. "Sorry."

He chuckled. It turned into a yawn. "Well, at least I can probably head back to sleep now. What about you?"

I nodded.

After glancing around the living room, his eyes settled on the ground. "Hey, um, I was wondering, after Sal's tomorrow, do you think we could talk?"

"About what?"

"Just . . . about things. Um, catch up, I mean, on a few things. You said it yourself, we live in the same house but don't get to see each other much."

"I guess that's . . . true."

Roger's gaze stayed fixed on the carpet, which I knew for a fact wasn't that interesting. A pink tinge settled across his cheeks.

I swallowed. "Sure. We can talk tomorrow."

He turned toward the hallway. "Okay. Great. Um, I'll see you in the morning. Come get me if you have another nightmare, all right?"

". . . Okay. You too."

"Goodnight, Lily."

I sighed as the door to his room clicked closed. "Goodnight, Roger."

THREE

<u>Margot</u>

My eyes cracked open at the furious shriek of a beeping alarm. I glared at the cheap digital clock on the nightstand. A few hours ago, after pained concentration, I could finally get to sleep without slipping into the Collective. Those hours seemed short, to say the least.

I sat up and stretched. The Collective wasn't an inherently bad place, but it was sometimes dangerous to get stuck in. If I spent too much time trying to decipher the voices around the swirling orange clouds, I lost track of important things in the real world. For instance, my name, identity, or sometimes even more important things like breathing, my heart beating, and how to wake up again.

Bea and Henry (who'd known someone linked with the Collective) said that it was natural for me to struggle in the beginning.

"Constance always had an alarm to help her wake up," Bea had explained, "just in case she got into trouble. Don't worry too much, just let things develop naturally. That's what Connie did."

I had nodded and assured her I'd try, but that wasn't a very comforting thought, seeing as how Constance shot herself in the head.

I got dressed and moseyed down to the kitchen to grab a bowl of cereal. I ate quickly and set the bowl in the sink, glancing down the hall. Roger hadn't come out yet, which was odd.

After knocking on his door, I eased it open when I got no response.

"Rog?" I whispered.

The room was dark. Roger was still fast asleep, his breathing slow and steady. He didn't stir when the door squeaked open, and I frowned. He usually woke at the slightest noise. It was a good indication that he was as exhausted as I was.

I stepped forward to nudge his shoulder, but paused. I knew he wanted to come with me today, but maybe it would be better for him to catch up on some sleep. All the late shifts he'd accrued in the last few weeks had taken their toll, and he was heading into another one tonight.

Closing the door gently, I headed back to the kitchen and grabbed a piece of paper from a notepad. I scribbled a note:

> Roger
> I didn't want to wake you this morning so I just went to the outpost alone. Sorry, but I figured you needed to catch up on your sleep.
> I'll still meet you at Sal's before your evening shift starts. We can talk then.
> Hope you have a good day. Don't die.
> -Lily

I tucked the folded note under his door and took the Teleporter out of my jacket pocket. Opening a portal to the outpost, I inhaled a slow breath.

My stomach churned as I stepped onto the muddy path of the training area. The events of last night had made me forget what was in store today; my first day of real defensive training. Maybe it wouldn't be so bad.

It was raining here at the outpost, too. Assembling teams huddled around flickering campfires, soaking up the last moments of warmth before heading out to their assignments. A few groups bustled past me, conversing loudly about mapping plans. As I skirted around them, some shuffling steps behind me piqued my interest.

"I beg your pardon, miss," came a soft voice.

I turned. A man in his mid-thirties trotted toward me. He sported a mustache, pale brown eyes, and a ripped but clean suit. A watch chain hung from his old vest and disappeared into his rumpled black suit coat.

I smiled politely. "Yes?"

He returned the smile. "I apologize for the intrusion." He inclined his head into a little bow. "Nicholas Spaulding, at your service. I believe we have met before?"

I tilted my head. "Oh, you were one of the people held captive by The Bound, weren't you?"

He nudged a broken stick with his foot. "I can't say I'm pleased that my reputation hinges solely on that fact."

I froze. He gave a sly smile and held out his hand.

Laughing, I took his hand and shook it. "Sorry, I didn't mean it like that."

He chuckled. It was a pleasant sound, reminding me of an echoing library. "Worry not, miss. I was only having a gag. Beatrice has instructed us to meet as many people as we can while we're here, and so naturally when I spotted you . . . well, anyway. I believe I've failed to ask for your name?"

"Lily. Lily Masters."

His grip on my hand increased. It became uncomfortably tight.

I was used to people having a reaction when I told them my last name; being a descendant of a longtime Jumper family, I expected it. But I'd never seen someone act almost . . . hateful.

I swallowed. "Um, you're hurting my hand."

Nicholas let go immediately. He stepped back and tugged on the cuffs of his worn sleeves. "Oh dear, I . . . I beg your pardon."

I flexed my hand. "That's okay, no harm done. Is something wrong?"

His expression became guarded. "Of course not. However, I really must be going." He inclined his head and gave a tight-lipped smile. "It was a pleasure to make your acquaintance, Lily. I hope our paths cross again. Good day."

Without waiting for a response, he hurried past me onto another path. I stared in puzzlement as he disappeared behind a stack of green storage containers. Turning on my heel, I headed to the sparring ring and glanced back over my shoulder. Nicholas was nowhere in sight.

The sparring ring was empty as I approached. I frowned and checked the time. No, I wasn't early. In fact, the detour with Nicholas had me running a little late.

A few minutes passed. I paced around, eventually climbing onto the wooden fence and tucking my feet behind the railing. Looking around to see that no one was near, I closed my eyes and inhaled deeply.

After a moment of concentration, a tug pulled my field of view from my head. My vision drifted outward, lifting into the low branches of the pines. My translucent form hovered around the area, and I squinted through the patchy fog. I couldn't see anyone approaching yet. Something must have come up during the morning debrief. Hopefully, it wasn't an emergency.

I drifted back to my body and opened my eyes. A wave of dizziness washed over me, and I clamped onto the wooden railing. It passed in seconds.

A gust of wind swept through the trees. I pulled my jacket more securely around my neck and closed my eyes, thinking of warm summer days. The wind blew again, carrying a strange echo. No, it wasn't an echo; it was a hiss. The air crackled. The hiss moved close to my ear.

"Lily."

I slid off the railing, whipping around to see who was behind me.

There was nothing there. I was used to hearing voices on the wind, but this was different. I scanned the area, my eyes flicking to the dim shadows. My immediate thought was The Bound, but it didn't sound like their scratchy whispers.

This was a wheeze. A rasp. An invisible growl that didn't feel human. And . . . something else. A strange feeling. Fear. A deep fear. An old fear. The sickening sensation of something hidden far below the surface, oozing up through the cracks.

"Lily."

I stepped toward the swirling fog. "Who's there?"

"I will be your salvation."

I strained my ears, but the voice was so faint.

"I know your doubts. I know your mind. I have answers to the things you seek. Find me. Find them. Find . . . us."

"What?" I whispered.

"Find me."

"Lily?"

I whirled around.

It was Cliff. He stared at me with a puzzled expression, accompanied by a girl in her late twenties with dark hair. He looked behind me and cocked his head. "You okay?"

I turned and stared back at the trees. Did I really just hear that, or was that just my imagination? The feeling of immense unease was gone. Maybe I was still on edge from the nightmares last night.

When I didn't respond, Cliff stepped forward. "Lily, what's wrong? Did you hear something?"

I shook my head and cleared my throat. It was probably just residual conversations from the Collective. No need to worry him over nothing; he had plenty on his plate without me raising a false alarm.

"No, it's nothing," I said.

He glanced back at the dark-haired girl, who raised an eyebrow. "You sure? You look like you've seen a ghost."

I shook my head again. "No, it was nothing. I'm just a little tired, that's all."

I could tell he didn't believe me, but he didn't press the issue. "All right, whatever you say. Sorry I'm late. I had some trouble finding her." He held out a hand to the girl, who strode forward. "Lily, I'd like you to meet Margot. She'll be your sparring partner and teacher for defensive training."

Margot nodded once and looked at me. Or, I supposed, "looked me over" would be more accurate. Her dark hair hung in curtains around her striking face. She had a strange eye color, one I'd never seen before. I would say they were almost green, but that wouldn't be right. More like the color of steel, or clouds. Maybe it was just the lighting.

"She was good enough to take a leave from the East Coast community to help with clean up from October's . . . incident," Cliff continued. "Now that we have that under control, I asked her to help with your training."

Margot's eyes flicked over my face, appearing to calculate how easy it would be to dismember me.

I cleared my throat and held out a hand. "Um, it's nice to meet you. My name's Lily."

Glancing at my hand, she flashed a small smile. "Margot."

She shook my hand once before wrenching my arm behind my back and flipping me onto the ground. It happened so fast, I barely had time to register pain.

"Hm." She knelt on my back. "You're too trusting. We'll have to work on that."

I spent the rest of the day getting thrown in every direction except the one I was going for. The side of my cheek stung from getting elbowed in the face. The rest of me ached from the constant flailing and falling. I panted as I dragged myself up off the dirt. Again.

"Come on, flower girl," Margot said. "Show me what you got."

To say that she was getting on my nerves was an understatement. No matter what I tried, I hadn't been able to block a single hit or even avoid getting tripped. She had gone over some basics before we started, but nothing she taught me actually seemed to help.

I stood up for the hundredth time and wiped some dirt from my forehead. Streaks of red were mixed in with the mud. A fresh cut on my temple stung.

"Again," she said.

I sniffed and crouched, attempting to catch her off balance. She sidestepped me expertly, wrenching my arms back. I cried out through my teeth and stumbled back a step. That was all the leverage she needed, and soon I was on my knees with both my arms pinned behind me.

She released her grip and sent me sprawling face-first into the dirt. "You're too indecisive. You need to come up with a plan and stick with it. If you keep second-guessing yourself, you're going to get you or someone around you killed."

Wiping away some more blood and sweat, I turned to face Margot. She looked up at the clouded sky and flipped some hair over her shoulder. I was sweating, panting, and covered in dirt, but she looked the same as when we started, like a model just out for a photo shoot.

She checked a chunky black watch on her wrist. "We're done for today. Meet me here at six tomorrow morning. You got a weapon?"

I rubbed my shoulder and thought about the arm piece I found in the basement back at the house. I hadn't touched it since its discovery, but at least I knew it worked. I nodded.

"Bring it tomorrow," she said, hopping out of the ring. "We'll see if you're any better with that."

She strode away without another word, leaving me dirty, bruised, and doubting that I would ever be better at anything again.

Four

Something Old

It took forever to find someone with a connection to Sal's. Eventually, I caught a ride back with an older man named Jackson with a Scottish accent and a thick, bushy beard.

"You get in a brawl or something?" he asked as he opened a portal in the air. The dim basement of Sal's lay beyond it.

I smiled as much as I could without my lip splitting open. "Something like that. Thanks for the connection."

"My pleasure." He gave a small bow. "You'll want to head to Giftshop soon unless you want that black eye to get any worse."

So I had a black eye.

Great.

"Thanks," I mumbled, stepping into the basement of the diner. With a shuddering flash, the portal closed behind me.

The old stone floor was as dusty as always, and even more so that the nearby trapdoor was no longer in use. A month and a half ago, that trapdoor led to a Connector linked to Giftshop for quick access. Since the Gate switch on Halloween, the Gateway would be closed for the next year until the rotation switched again. It made access to the popular Jumper hangout somewhat challenging.

Walking up the narrow stairway, I rubbed my shoulder again and tried to brush away some of the dirt clinging to most of my body. Hearing the mumble of people and the clatter of silverware, I eased the door open.

Sal's was, as usual, crowded, noisy, full of Jumpers whose demeanors ranged from exuberant to exhausted. Based on the number of people, it looked like everyone had just come off the day shift, which was a good sign. I knew I was late, but I didn't know by how much. Hopefully, Roger hadn't left yet.

Sweeping my eyes around the busy diner, I spotted the back of Roger's head at our regular booth in the back. I passed Rhonda on the way, but she was too busy taking orders from a disheveled-looking team to strike up a conversation.

Roger leaned on one hand and scrunched up a paper straw wrapper with the other. Judging from the depleted water glass and empty plate, he'd been there for a while.

I cleared my throat. "Um, hey."

He inclined his head back toward me but didn't turn around. "Hey. I was starting to think you weren't coming. I've got to leave for my shift in a few minutes."

I limped forward and eased myself into the booth across from him. "I'm really sorry. Today was . . . I just got done before I came here."

He nodded and glanced up at me. "It's okay. I was just hoping you'd—" He did a double take, and his eyes widened. "Jesus *Christ*! What happened to you?"

I shook my head. Ow. "It's nothing. I just—"

"Lily, that's not nothing!"

"Roger, it's fine. It probably looks a lot worse than it is."

He reached forward to push some hair from my face. I leaned away.

"Come on, let me see."

"No."

"Lily."

I sighed, tucking my hair behind my ears. His eyebrows knit together.

"How bad is it?" I asked. "I haven't had time to look."

He leaned to look at me from another angle and winced. "Well, uh, if you want an honest answer, then it looks like you got mugged. In an alley. By a bear."

I leaned on my hand, flinching as my cheek stung. "Well, you're not that far off."

"What happened?"

Sighing again, I rubbed my shoulder. "Margot happened."

"Margot?"

"Your dad brought her by this morning; she'll be overseeing all my defensive training. I guess I learned a lot, but also . . ." I leaned back against the booth. "Ow."

Roger shook his head and stared out the window. "That's ridiculous. He shouldn't have—" He clenched his jaw. "You shouldn't have gotten this badly hurt, especially on your first day. The whole point of training is to prepare you, not beat you to death."

He ground his teeth together and stared at the table. I shifted in my seat. Somehow, I felt this was my fault.

37

"I'm going to talk to my dad about this," he said. "That was *not* okay to do to a recruit on the first day. Especially you."

I shook my head, my face burning. "No, Rog, it's okay. Please don't talk to him about this. I don't need any special treatment. It's a few bumps and bruises. I'll be fine—"

"*You are not fine!*" he exploded. A few people from the surrounding tables turned around. "Somebody kicked the shit out of you! I know accidents happen, but this"—he gestured to me—"this is just overkill. I don't care who it was, they should know better than to humiliate someone like that!"

It was quiet. The ambient mumble of voices slowly returned to normal. I watched Roger warily. It wasn't like him to snap like that. Was something wrong? Did I do something wrong?

A thought occurred to me, and I peered at Roger's face. "Rog, did you have another nightmare last night? After we came in from the roof?"

He froze. "N-no."

"Yes, you did," I said. "Come on, tell me."

He looked down.

I reached over and put a hand on his arm. "Hey."

Glancing up, his expression softened, the anger fading from his eyes.

"Did you see something in your dream?" I asked. "Something . . . about me getting hurt? Is that why you're upset?"

His shoulders hunched. "Yes."

I leaned back. "Whatever it was, it was just a dream. It doesn't make it a premonition."

Roger rubbed his eyes. I didn't realize how bloodshot they were before now. "I know, I know, it's just . . . It didn't feel like a normal nightmare."

"What happened?"

"I don't even know how to describe it. There were things I'd never seen before. Things that I..." He swallowed, gaze drifting around the diner. "Things I never want to see again. Places that didn't seem natural, and people that didn't seem like people. You were there, too. You were there, but you were ... different."

"What do you mean?"

"I don't know." He shook his head. "I can't remember a lot of the details now. Everything's all scrambled. I just remember this weird ... feeling."

I sat up. "What kind of feeling?"

"I was ... afraid of something. Something was out there, *waiting*. Something that's been lurking, or hiding, for a long time. Hiding forever. Something ..."

"Old," I finished.

His head swiveled to me. He leaned forward. "Yeah. Exactly. How did you know that?"

I watched the diner full of Jumpers and tried to ignore the unsettling weight coiling in my stomach. "It was probably nothing, but this morning, before training started, I ... I thought I heard—"

I broke off as a team walked past us, followed by the bouncing, petite, red-headed figure of Rhonda. She gave me a once-over and raised a penciled eyebrow. "Well, well, someone got into trouble. You and Rog have a spat or something?"

I returned the smile as much as I could. "Hey, Rhonda."

She laughed and pulled out a notepad and pen from her apron. "What'll you have today?"

I gave her my usual order of a ham sandwich, and she bustled away with her messy red bun bobbing behind her.

As soon as she left, Roger leaned forward again. "What did you hear this morning?"

"I . . ." I trailed off. What exactly did I hear? The faint words . . . I couldn't even remember what they were. Any details before the training session with Margot were blurry.

"Lily?"

"That's funny. I can't even remember what it was. It was so fast." I shrugged. "It was probably residual conversation from the Collective. I must've been nervous about starting combat training today, that's all."

I slid out of the booth slowly and tried to ignore the fresh wave of aches and pains. "I'm going to use the restroom. I'll be right back."

Roger frowned as I shuffled past a few people who clogged the aisle. I got a few glances from people I passed, but most of them just smiled at me with understanding. It wasn't uncommon for people to look beaten up or injured here, as this was a popular stop before continuing onto Giftshop. I guess bodily harm was one of the many joys of becoming a Jumper.

The door squeaked open to the old cramped bathroom, thankfully empty. Taking a deep breath, I peeked in the mirror.

A black eye, a split lip, a bruised cheek, and smudges of dirt and blood stared back at me. Sighing, I twisted the faucet handle. A weak trickle of water slipped down the drain as I began the painful process of cleaning myself up. Once most of the dirt had washed away, I looked a little less pathetic.

A knock came from the other side of the door as it eased open. Rhonda poked her head in. She stepped inside and pulled out a small tube from her apron pocket. "Hey. Thought you could use some help. This'll take the edge off of the sting."

I took it and managed a small smile. "Thanks, Rhonda. What is it?"

She smiled. "Just a little something I whipped up. Made from some plants that I found in Glass Woods a few years back. It doesn't do much in the way of healing, but it's a reliable painkiller."

I tilted my head. "I didn't know you made medicine."

She laughed, her glasses glinting under the bare light bulb. "We all have our specialties. You think I'm just a waitress all day long?"

I unscrewed the tube and dabbed a small amount of ointment on my lip, sighing at the relief. It didn't take all the pain away, but it masked it. A few dabs later and I could move my mouth without wincing.

"Rog told me what happened today," she said. "Sorry you had a rough training session."

I shrugged. "That's all right. It's just something I have to get used to." I exhaled slowly. "Because what else can I do?"

Rhonda tucked a hand under her chin. "I remember this girl, actually. Her name's Margot, right?"

"Yeah. How do you know her?"

"Well, I don't really *know* her, but I've seen her around. She hung with a few of the Johnson brothers' pals, maybe three or four guys Pete used to run with back in the day. I remembered her because she was so young when she joined up, barely a teenager. *And* she was hanging out with a bunch of old fogies. Odd, but I think they took her under their wing. Wanted to give her a place to belong, you know."

"I thought you couldn't join until you were eighteen?"

"Most of the time, yes," she agreed. "Sometimes circumstances dictate otherwise. Ed, for example, was only sixteen when he joined up because his father was an abusive alcoholic. He needed some way to survive on his own. He's been part of the community ever since. Or at least"—her face fell—"for the rest of his life."

I looked down. Ed was the former region leader killed in action when the incident with The Bound began. I was there when he died, which was probably one of the many reasons some people in the Pacific Northwest community avoided me. The pain was still too fresh, and I was associated with it.

"Anyway," Rhonda continued, "she stopped coming around a few years ago; I heard she got transferred to another community after an incident."

I looked up from my hands. "What kind of incident?"

"Beats me, you'd have to ask her. Unfortunately, I have to get back to work." Opening the door, she nodded to the tube in my hands. "You can have that. I've got lots more. See you around, Lily."

"Bye, Rhonda."

The door closed, and I turned back to my battered reflection. The light above the mirror flickered at an annoying pace. I tucked some hair behind my ear and heaved a breath. Whoever Margot was, I'd have to face her again tomorrow. I swung open the door to the busy diner, trying to ignore the dread settling in my stomach.

FIVE

<u>Warnings</u>

"Good God, what happened to you?"

I swiveled in my chair and faced the dusty black cat who had hopped onto a nearby stack of books. His yellow eyes bored into me as his tail swished back and forth.

"Nice to see you too, Catacombs," I said.

"Seriously, what happened? You look like you tried to take down a hornet's nest. With your face."

Sighing, I set down the book I had attempted to start. Roger had left for his shift almost an hour ago, and after a spirited debate with myself, I decided I should take everyone's advice and head to Giftshop. Even though I'd only been here a few minutes, the gentle warm hum around my cuts and bruises confirmed she slowly healed my many wounds.

"Combat training," I said. "Don't ask for more details than that."

"*No problem. I don't actually care, but I figured I should ask.*" Catacombs pounced onto the table and preened. "*Haven't seen you around here for a while. I figured you chickened out of being a Jumper.*"

I raised an eyebrow. "I could say the same thing about you. What is it you do all the time, anyway?"

"*Oh, you know, this and that. I keep an eye on things.*"

"What kinds of things?"

He flicked his tail. "*Things.*"

I rubbed my eyes. Well, I tried to. I'd forgotten about the black eye.

"Guh . . ." I mumbled. "Ow."

A draft wafted through the study, carrying the scent of peppermint and wild oranges. The warm hum on my face increased. The pain faded.

I looked up at the ceiling and smiled. "Thanks, Giftshop."

The lights brightened in response.

"Someone's picking favorites."

I turned. Margot emerged from the door leading to the viewing bay. Her colorless eyes swept around the room and settled on Catacombs. He sprang to his feet.

"*Uh, hate to deprive you of my presence*"—he jumped onto the carpet—"*but I gotta get going. You know, things to do, people to see. Later.*"

Waltzing behind a leg of the table, he vanished.

Margot strode toward me. I tried to ignore the fact that the sight of her triggered my fight-or-flight response.

"What're you doing here?" I asked.

"Came to see if you were bawling your eyes out." She pulled out a chair opposite me and plopped into it. "Ran into your boyfriend, by the way, who wasn't happy with me."

I looked down. "He's not my boyfriend."

"Whatever." She slouched into her seat and rested her feet on an empty chair. "He was all in a tizzy because he seemed to think my training methods were too much for you." She stuck a finger in her ear and pulled a face. "That boy can sure yell."

I chewed the inside of my cheek. Did he really do that? Did he go looking for Margot? I specifically asked him not to get involved, but he did it anyway. Why didn't he ever listen to me?

Margot tilted her head and smirked. "He sure has a soft spot for you, doesn't he?"

My face burned. I looked around the room. "He, I mean, I . . . we've been through a lot together, and he—"

A crinkle of static rushed past my ear. I stood up and strained my ears. Words emerged from the static, tuning in to focus like an old radio.

D . . . o . . . o . . . r . . .

Margot leaned forward to see what I was staring at. "What are you—"

Sure enough, the door behind me opened. Bea shuffled through, shoulders hunched and head hung low. She rubbed her forehead, barely paying attention to where she was going. My eyes flicked to a nearby end table. A beautiful white shining vase filled with oversized dandelions sat on top.

S . . . h . . . a . . . t . . . t . . . e . . . r . . .

I lunged forward as she ran into the table and caught the vase before it could crash to the floor, fumbling until I clamped onto the edge.

Bea steadied herself against the wobbly end table. "Oh! Lily, I wasn't expecting anyone to be in here." Her eyes flicked to Margot and then back to me when she noticed my face. "What happened to you?"

I coughed. "Oh, you know . . . training."

She pointed to the vase clutched between my hands. "How did you . . ."

"I heard it coming," I explained, setting the vase back on the table. "You know, um, in advance."

There were few people who would understand that statement without a lengthy and confusing explanation. Fortunately, Bea was one of them.

She nodded and rubbed the side of her leg absentmindedly.

"Are you okay?" I asked.

She exhaled a tired sigh. "Yes. Yes, I'm all right. There are just . . . things happening that I don't understand."

"Like what?"

She rubbed her eyes again, mouth twisting into a frown. "Do you remember Laura? From Twisting Caverns?"

I nodded. Laura's team went missing the same time I discovered the Otherworlds. The rescue mission to Twisting Caverns turned into a trap where many lost their lives, including Ed. Though Laura had been possessed by The Bound and unaware of her actions, she had ultimately been the one to kill him.

"She took a break from the community after what happened with Ed. We've been . . ." Bea paused and scowled. "Well, *I've* been checking up on her since then. As of two weeks ago, she completely dropped off the map. I've checked with other region leaders. I've asked her friends. I've sent out lines throughout the different communities, but it's like she just vanished. I thought I'd discovered a lead yesterday, but it turned into another dead end."

"Should we get the police involved or something?" I asked.

She shook her head. "I have no evidence that Laura is in any danger. As far as outside eyes are concerned, she just went on holiday. Her landlord—apparently—saw her leaving her apartment early in the morning, getting into a car with a few other people. He couldn't remember a car model, the license plate, or even the day she left."

"I'm sorry."

Shaking her head and taking out her Chatterbox, she flipped it open and typed a message. "I'm probably worrying over nothing. Maybe she just took some time to find herself. But something about the situation just rubs me the wrong way." Her fingers paused in typing as she thought. "Lily, I know it's early, but if you . . . hear anything about her, will you bring it to my attention?"

I rubbed the back of my head. "Of course, but I can't make any promises. You know . . ."

Bea waved a hand. "I know. I should get going; it's been a while since I've been home, and my mail is probably piled a kilometer high. Till again."

"Till again," I mumbled. She crossed the room to the door leading to the Guest Book and disappeared.

"So . . ." Margot began, "how'd you manage that little party trick?"

I turned. "Sorry?"

She jerked a thumb at the vase on the table. "You said you heard her coming, but I didn't. How'd you know she was going to knock that vase over?"

"Uh, well, I . . ."

I trailed off. Usually, telling people I heard voices in my head wasn't the best idea. There was a small circle of people in the community who knew the full extent of what I could do, and I wanted to keep it that way. Being able to hear the Collective already made me into a sideshow novelty. I didn't need to give them any more reasons to alienate me. But Margot was going to be overseeing my training, so maybe she should join the circle.

I cleared my throat. "Have you ever heard of the Collective?"

Margot's eyes flashed with recognition. She shifted in her seat and folded her arms. "Just rumors. It's some kind of database, right? Of people?"

I nodded. "Kind of. More like the storage bin of humanity's past thoughts, memories, and emotions. It connects to everyone, even if they don't know it. But some people have a two-way connection. They can hear and see it, and . . . sometimes the things they hear are more like predictions than memories."

"So what does that have to do with . . ." Her eyes widened. "Wait, no. That's impossible. You can't be—don't you need years of training and study to do that?"

I shook my head. "Not for me. The ability to hear the Collective can be passed down through a bloodline, not just by training. I got it from my dad's line because my grandpa could hear it. It's some kind of genetic trait. An anomaly in my brain or something."

Margot's usual brooding expression shifted. She sat up in her chair and leaned on her knees. "So, you get . . . information? Like how you knew she was going to bump into that table?"

"That's right."

She looked at the floor and played with the sleeve of her jacket. "So, can you . . . search for information about specific people? Could you find someone based on where they've been before?"

"That's an odd question." I tilted my head. "You have someone you're looking for?"

Margot shrugged. "No. I was just thinking you could make bank working for one of those psychic detective agencies."

I huffed a breath through my nose. "Hardly. I only Discovered a month and a half ago, so everything I hear isn't on purpose. It could be years until I'm able to search people on command, and even then, trying to sift through that much information is like drinking from a firehose. I may never manage it."

Margot nodded and twisted a loose thread on her sleeve.

"You Discovered a month and a half ago?" she asked.

"Yeah."

"So . . . when The Bound invaded and everything went to hell around here?"

I laughed a little. "Pretty much."

"Interesting." Margot stood and stretched. "Well, I gotta get going. I just popped by to make sure you weren't crying yourself to sleep in here. Don't forget to bring your weapon tomorrow. We'll see how well you know how to use it."

Groaning inwardly, I swallowed. "Right, I'll . . . be sure to do that."

She opened the door to the gear room and paused. "And, uh, flower girl? A piece of advice: you need to learn to block. You can't be scared of getting hit. It'll cost you too much time. And judging by the way you handled yourself today, you're going to need all the time you can get. See you tomorrow."

I sighed as she closed the door behind her. "Bye."

Six

Reality Check

The ear-shattering ring of the wall-mounted banana phone jerked me from my train of thought.

Getting up from the weathered kitchen table, I shuffled across the creaking wooden floor to answer it.

Snatching the phone off the hook, I cleared my throat and tried to ignore the screeching static assaulting me through the speaker. "Hello?"

"Hey, sweetie!"

I switched the phone to my other hand. "Hey, Mom. It's been a while since you called. I was beginning to think you forgot about me."

The speaker crackled. "Nope, I definitely haven't forgotten my favorite daughter."

I laughed. "That's good, because I'm your only daughter."

"Well, favorite-only-daughter, I have some good news for you, if you think you can handle it."

"What?"

She took a deep breath. "The lawyer's office finally found a loophole we can use. Your dad and I put the Stars Crossing house up on the market a few days ago, and I think we have a serious buyer!"

I almost dropped the phone. A horrible feeling sank into my stomach. "Y-you what?"

"I know!" she squealed. "And we have even better news! We've finally been able to get enough time off work to get things done around here. *So* the time has come to liberate you from your cold and rainy prison. We get to see you in two weeks!"

My hands turned clammy. "T-two weeks? That's . . . that's so soon."

She paused. "I thought you'd be excited, honey. You've been by yourself in that big empty house for almost two months now. Aren't you going daffy from boredom? And isn't it depressing living in a house filled with boxes?"

I tried to make sounds come out of my mouth. I failed.

"Lily? You still there?"

I cleared my throat. "Yeah, I'm still here. Sorry, you just . . . caught me off guard. I'm . . . excited to see you guys, though. Wow."

She laughed. "We're excited to see you too! I have to go; dinner's on the stove—er, most of it still is, anyway. I just wanted to tell you the good news. We'll see you real soon, honey! Love you!"

I tried to fake a laugh, but even to me, it sounded forced. "Yeah, I'll see you real soon. Love . . . love you too."

Click.

My hand dropped to my side, still clutching the phone. Full-blown panic erupted throughout my body. I felt sick.

The handle on the front door jiggled before it swung open. Roger entered the house sideways with a few bags hanging from his arms. Closing the door with his foot, he lifted the bags onto the counter and smiled.

"Hey," he called. "It was so slow tonight that they're working a skeleton crew. Jesse sent a bunch of us home early, if you can believe it. I picked up some Chinese food on the way. Hope you're hungry. They were all out of the pork lo mein you like, so I got beef instead."

Shrugging off his coat, he hung it in the closet and stretched his arms behind his back. "Man, am I glad I didn't have to do another night shift this week; I'm beat. Sorry I didn't call to ask what you wanted, but figured I'd surprise you with—" He broke off mid-stretch when he realized I was staring at the wall. "Um, are you okay?"

I turned, phone still in hand. "We have problems."

"They *what*?" Cliff yelped.

Roger and I nodded. We had rushed back to Giftshop after I had explained everything to Roger, who beelined for his dad still finishing his shift in the viewing bay. I paced as Roger talked, biting the end of my sleeve.

Things had been going so *well* since we sent The Bound back through the Tear. My parents had barely contacted me at all besides the occasional "Hello, sorry you're still there" call. Now, not only were they selling the house, but I'd have to come up with a story about why I hadn't packed anything to put into storage and why I was now living with a guy they'd never heard of.

All in two short weeks.

"They said they already have a buyer," I said. "How did that happen so fast?"

Cliff rubbed his eyes. "I don't know."

"W-what am I supposed to tell them?" I stuttered. "What am I supposed to say about *any* of this? They're not stupid, they're going to ask questions. Like why I'm dropping out of college, for starters. Or how about the guy living with me, or why I want to stay in Stars Crossing, or why they can't sell the damn *house*?" I put a hand to my head which was rapidly developing a throbbing headache. "Or . . . or . . ."

"Lily, don't panic," Cliff said.

"I'm panicking."

"Calm down," Roger reassured. "Deep breaths."

I took a few deep breaths. Now I was nauseous *and* lightheaded.

"How am I going to hide everything that's happened in the last two months? Jumpers, Giftshop, the Otherworlds, the *Collective* for God's sake. How am I supposed to lie about"—I gestured to the windows overlooking the vast reaches of space—"*this*?"

"You've got a point," Cliff mumbled. "This complicates things."

Roger folded his arms and looked at the floor. "Well . . . if they get close to discovering something, we could always . . . help them remember things a little differently."

It was quiet.

"No," I said.

Cliff stepped forward. "Lily—"

"No," I repeated. "I'm not letting you erase my parents' memory. No way."

"But we're not erasing it," Roger said. "It would be better for them, and better for you in the long run. We don't want them questioning every detail about your life now that you're a—"

"No." I rubbed my eyes. "There has to be another way."

"*You two could just get married, you know.*"

We jumped as Catacombs leapt onto a nearby table. From the red-and-blue dust coating his paws, he had been "keeping an eye on things" in some Otherworld I'd never been to.

"What did you say?" Roger asked.

Catacombs arched his back. "*I said: Why don't you and the Psychic Wonder Child just get married? It would explain a few things. Like why you'd be staying in Stars Crossing, quitting school, and why you two are living together.*"

Roger and I glanced at each other before looking down at the floor.

"Um . . ." I said, "that's not . . . we're not . . ."

"Yeah," Roger mumbled. "It's, uh . . . a different situation than that. We may live together, but it's not like—we don't *live* together."

"*I don't get it.*" Catacombs tilted his head. "*Isn't that what human marriage is? Living in the same house together?*"

My face burned. "Not exactly."

"*Oh. Then what's the difference?*"

"I think," Cliff interjected, "that we shouldn't make any hasty decisions. We still have a few weeks to think about it, so we'll consider our options and take it from there. I have to go. Someone just called for an emergency evacuation, and I need to get a team together." He nodded to me. "You should probably get some rest for tomorrow, and you"—he looked to Catacombs—"I think we need to have a little chat about . . . certain human customs. C'mon, we can walk and talk."

Catacombs hopped off the table and followed Cliff to the other side of the room. "*What's the big deal? Why are they so sweaty?*"

The door opened without Cliff touching it, and their conversation was (thankfully) taken out of earshot.

Roger and I stood in silence. We held eye contact before giving uncomfortable laughs.

Roger coughed. "Well, uh, we have a heaping pile of lo mein and curry chicken waiting for us at the house. You ready to head back?"

I nodded. "Please. I'm *so* ready for this day to be over. We're going to have to take the long way. My connection leads back to the outpost."

We shuffled through Giftshop and detoured to the Guest Book, flipping the brittle yellow pages to a fresh sheet. Signing out, we creaked open the door to the memorial hall and started down the narrow corridor. I stared at the floor and tried not to look at the many new statues carved from marble. I recognized more than I cared to count, though most of them not by name. The two statues at the end, I couldn't help but look at. Their gleaming brass plaques had been recently engraved.

Guilt twisted my insides at the sight of the two expertly carved statues. There was somewhat of an uproar when Leo's statue appeared next to Ed's. Despite my explanation, most of the community blamed Leo for the events of October, directly and indirectly. Though we stopped them from taking over the world, many possessed by The Bound didn't survive. The wounds they sustained were too great, or the actions they were forced to perform proved too much to bear.

Roger pulled open the door, and we continued through the Connector room. Squinting at the familiar pink light, we ducked under the large white vines hanging over our heads. The Gateway to Giftshop had taken a few days to locate, but the rotting stench of Tinker's genetically altered vegetation wasn't hard to follow. Within hours, it was cleared and made available for the entire community to use. Assigned teams now monitored the Connector containing the closed Tear, just in case.

It was a long walk to the Gate. The minutes passed in awkward silence.

"Um." Roger slowed his pace. "Listen, if it would be easier for you, I can always move back to the outpost. It would be one less thing to explain."

I shook my head. "I don't think that would make it any easier. Besides, you're supposed to be monitoring the Gate in the barn, remember? I think part of me thought I could escape this forever. Telling my parents, I mean. Not like I'd be able to tell them about any of this really, but . . . I don't want to lie to them."

Roger inclined his head. "I get it. Unfortunately, it's something that comes with the job. To keep them safe and to keep us safe, sometimes lying is the best option. If we told them everything, how do you think they'd handle it?"

I gave a short laugh. "Not well. *I* had a hard enough time wrapping my head around it, and let's just say I have more of an open mind than the rest of my family."

We climbed over a jumble of spongy vegetation. Roger caught my arm when I inevitably lost my footing.

He made sure I was stable and rubbed the back of his neck. "Hey, I'm sorry if I was out of line earlier about rewriting your parents' memories.

It's always been a part of life for me, but I could see how that would freak you out."

"It doesn't freak me out," I said. "I just don't know much about it. How does it work?"

He blew a breath through his nose, pausing before responding. "What do you know about nanotechnology?"

"Like tiny robots?"

"Kind of. More like a sequence of cells with a mind of their own." He held out his hands as a diagram. "We program what memories we want to tamper with, and the nanobots go in and . . . move things around. Rewire synapses that connect those memories with tangible things like sight, touch, and smell."

"You lost me."

"Say you wandered into a Gate, and the first thing you smelled was . . . let's say oranges. We'd tie that smell to something completely different. So, the next time they smell oranges, they wouldn't think of the Otherworld they stumbled into. They'd think of a grocery store, or an orchard, or something else instead."

"Huh."

He tilted his hand back and forth as a scale. "Give or take a few billion times more complicated than that, and multiply it by your other four senses. It's the opposite of what Giftshop does. Instead of reminding people of sights, smells, and sounds from their past, we help them forget. Or, I guess, *rearrange* is a better word for it."

I nodded. "So . . . have you done that to people before?"

He laughed. "Of course I have. It's not some kind of special job, not by a long shot. I got trained after I . . ." He shot me a glance. "After I came back. After . . . you know."

I gave a small smile of understanding. After his dad's disappearance, Roger left the Jumper community for a number of years. From what little he'd told me, and what I could figure out on my own, they had been a turbulent stretch of time. The track marks on his arms and other scars proved that much. One of the worst incidents cost a fifteen-year-old boy his life, and Roger his ability to sleep at night.

Nestled in the pink fluffy clouds ahead, I spotted the large orb with a pole jutting up from the ground. The way back home.

"So, apparently Catacombs doesn't know much about human social customs," I said.

Roger chuckled, hopping over a thicket of vegetation. "No kidding. You'd think with all the time he's spent on Earth, he'd pick some things up. He had a point, though. As much as that pains me to say."

"What do you mean?"

"Well." He coughed. "To the casual observer, it would look like we were . . . you know. Married. Or at least together."

I stepped over the vines and glanced up at Roger. His face had gone pink, as I was sure mine had.

"I guess," I said. "Do you think that's a bad thing?"

He shook his head. "No. No, not at all. Do you?"

"No. No, I think it's . . ." I swallowed. "I think that's fine. People can think whatever they want."

We shuffled forward a few more steps.

Roger cleared his throat again. "Look, I know things haven't been exactly stable since October. You've been adjusting to everything ahead of you. I had my dad come back from the dead, and on top of it all, we're still putting the pieces together after The Bound. It's been a lot for both of us. But I think, or at least, I feel that . . . um, that I . . ."

He trailed off as we approached the pole leading to Earth. I waited for him to resume his train of thought. He didn't.

"Rog?"

"All I'm saying is that . . . everything will work itself out." He glanced at the pole leading to the Gate and shoved his hands in his pockets. "Your parents and everything. It'll . . . it'll work out. That's all. Um, do you want me to go up first?"

I nodded, hoping my sigh of disappointment was silent.

After scrambling up the pole, we stood in the barn, shoes sticking to the spongy floor. It was dark. The lashing of rain against the window made the room seem colder.

Roger swiped a sleeve across his face and checked his watch. "Hey, we've only been gone a few minutes in Earth time. I bet the food is still warm."

"We were in Giftshop for, what, half an hour?" I asked. "How much time passed here?"

He pulled his coat tighter around him. "Five minutes, give or take. It kind of depends on the day."

I shook my head. "That's going to take some getting used to. Hey, um." I glanced at the white paint slopped into dried puddles on the wooden floor. "I'm really sorry for today. Not showing up at Sal's, I mean. I didn't do it on purpose."

Roger's expression softened. "I know you didn't."

"You're not upset?"

He shook his head. "I was looking forward to it, that's all."

"I was . . . um, looking forward to it, too. Do you—" I cleared my throat. "Do you want to try again tomorrow? Same time, same place?"

Roger seemed surprised. He smiled. My stomach lifted. "I'd love to."

SEVEN

Banditos

The magenta-colored katana swung down. I dove to the side, rolling onto the wet dirt, but I wasn't fast enough. I sucked in a breath as the blade grazed my arm.

Panting, I backed up to the edge of the ring. I grabbed my arm and watched Margot as she advanced, sword swinging by her side. She seemed bored.

"You're still wasting time." She huffed. "Defense is about analyzing your situation and calling the play before your opponent does. If you don't, it's going to cost you."

Trying to slow my breathing, I glanced down. The cut was long but shallow. It was the first time she had landed a hit, which was a minor miracle considering we'd been at this all day. The cloudy sky had turned a burned shade of orange as the invisible sun lowered to the horizon.

Margot exhaled, and the magenta blade dissolved. "We'll take the next two sets to practice with your weapon. Aim for that tree over there." She nodded to a large tree that sat just outside the sparring ring. "We'll graduate to moving targets later."

I stood and moved my wobbly legs to the other side of the ring, retrieving the strange bracelet-like weapon. Tugging the straps over my forearm, I fit the metal ring over my middle finger and shook out my arms.

Margot rolled her head from side to side. "C'mon, flower girl, we don't have all day."

Steadying myself, I held out my hand and concentrated. Eventually, small particles of light popped into existence and hardened into a purple semitransparent disc of light. I aimed as best I could.

I flicked my wrist. The purple disc careened off the back of my hand and lodged deeply into the trunk. It wasn't the tree I was aiming for, but compared to how badly I'd missed in the past, it was a victory. I kept going until I hit the tree Margot had appointed me on the fifth shot.

She pulled the hilt of her katana from her belt, forming the long, unforgiving blade of magenta light. "Not bad. Now, let's see if you can hit a moving target. Aim for me this time."

"W-what?"

She smirked, her gray eyes glinting. "You heard me. Try to get in a shot or two. I can take it."

"Are you serious?"

"Of course I'm serious."

I lowered my arm. "No way. What if you get hit? It could take off an arm, or your head!"

"What, are you saying I'm not good enough to block you?"

"I'm just saying I won't be the one to decapitate you."

She rolled her eyes and strode to a large metal storage chest outside of the sparring ring. After hopping over the railing in one fluid movement, she flung open the lid. Sets of protective padding and wooden sparring rods clattered to the ground as she rummaged through the chest.

"Aha!" she mumbled. "Here you are."

She held up a mass of clinking silver, obviously expecting me to say something. Interlocking silver rings made up a kind of jumpsuit backed with sturdy black fabric. Deep-rimmed goggles were sewn securely into the hood.

"Um." I glanced to the side. "What is that?"

Margot sighed and stepped into the clunking mass. "It's a protective suit. The kids around here use it when they first get trained." She pulled her hand into a mitt-like glove. "It displaces energy-powered weapons by a reverse magnetic reaction. So, you know, you can practice without killing someone."

She finished pulling on the baggy suit and tapped a large gold circle on her chest. The suit snapped into a formfitting shimmering ensemble.

"There." Margot's voice was muffled through the hood. "Now you don't have to be such a wimp about it." She pulled out her katana and formed it, holding it up to her arm. "See?"

"Wait, don't—"

She swung down. The magenta light puffed out of existence before it touched the suit. Her blade didn't break, it just seemed to fizzle out of reality.

I blinked. "Whoa."

Even without being able to see her face, I felt Margot's condescending smirk.

"All right, flower girl." She reformed her katana and crouched into an offensive stance. "Give me your best shot."

I backed away. "I don't know about this. What if I miss you and hit something else? Or what if I—"

Margot darted forward with blinding speed. My eyes widened as I put my right arm up to block, forming a large round disk on the back of my hand as a makeshift shield. The sudden strain on my weapon made me dizzy. I looked up into the glass of her goggles, barely able to see Margot's colorless eyes stare back at me.

"I *said*"—she shoved me back—"give me your best shot."

My eyes narrowed. Something inside me hardened.

Sliding a foot behind me, I pushed myself forward and flung my makeshift shield into her face. She fell back and blocked with the flat part of her blade. I held my arm out and took aim, backing up as she came at me again.

My first shot missed, the purple disk striking the fence post. Trying to move and aim at the same time felt sloppy. I changed tactics as I rolled to avoid a swipe, rapidly firing smaller discs.

It forced Margot to stop advancing to avoid the purple discs of light. I swung down with another shield, but Margot blocked me with my arms above my head.

"Remember," Margot said, "you're a girl. You have less muscle mass than fifty percent of your possible targets. Your best chance to get in some damage to an opponent is your knees and elbows, where all your leverage is."

She shoved my arm into my face. I stumbled back, cupping my nose. The shock of the impact sent a wave of pain through my skull.

Margot twirled her sword in a looping arc and still managed to look bored.

Her casual stance egged on the mounting frustration inside me. I sniffed back the warmth in my nose and ran at her. I waited until she pulled back before I fired. She blocked, but I was too close. I did as she suggested and threw an elbow into her side.

Margot gave a soft *oof* and staggered. It gave me enough time to get off a shot.

She couldn't block it this time, and the disc soared straight into her abdomen. It dissipated into particles before it met her, but the force sent Margot flying into the side of the railing. She bounced off and lay facedown on the ground.

She didn't get up.

I froze. "M-Margot?"

Running over, I sighed in relief as she rolled to her feet. She pulled back the hood, a huge smile on her face.

"Now *that's* what I'm talking about!" She tapped the gold circle on her chest. The suit became a clunking costume of silver rings. "Finally!"

"Are you okay?"

She laughed and shrugged off the suit. "Who cares? You actually hit me!"

I shuffled my feet. "Well, yeah, I guess so, but—"

"You were an absolute badass!"

"I don't think—"

"*Now* that I know you can rise to the occasion, we can start getting into some fun stuff."

My stomach sank. "Fun stuff?"

Margot flipped her dark hair over her shoulder. "C'mon. It should be dark enough now for this to work."

"For what to work?"

I peeked over the edge of the large plastic barrel and squinted at the bright floodlights surrounding the fenced area.

Despite my protests, Margot had dragged me through Giftshop's Connector room and shoved me through an iron door studded with rivets. Behind it was an Otherworld that I'd never been to before, an enormous cave system with walls made of jagged ice and floors made of smooth, transparent glass. Rivers of red lava bubbled beneath the clear ground.

Following her out of obligation through a crack in the ice, I found myself surrounded by tall buildings and the loud noises of traffic. The Gateway led into a dilapidated brick building scrawled with graffiti and littered with garbage. It was the last place I would expect to find a portal to another world, which was exactly how it was supposed to look. We now sat at the edge of a fenced courtyard a few blocks away.

I crinkled my nose against a sudden stench of sewage. "So . . . what are we doing here?"

Margot leaned on the chain-link fence with her fingers curled around the wire. "It's been so *boring* at the outpost. Day after day of peace and quiet . . . I couldn't take it anymore. I had to get out of there."

"Okay. And we're here because . . ."

"We're just going to have a little fun. You know how to have fun, don't you?"

I narrowed my eyes. She smirked.

"Where are we?" I asked.

"The city so nice, they named it twice. The Big Apple. The city that never sleeps. Except for Tom." She nodded at a homeless man bundled in a stained sleeping bag at the end of the alley. "He's always asleep."

"Wait, we—we're in New York?" I asked. "As in 'New York, New York'?"

She rolled her eyes. "Yes, dear pupil. Did you know about these things called 'Gateways'? They make it possible for us to be in Oregon one minute and Manhattan the next."

"Shut up," I mumbled. "Why are we hiding behind a fence like a couple of bandits?"

"Well, my *compagno bandito*"—she pointed to the shabby brick building—"this is the fine establishment of Tony's Pizzeria, known for its fluffy crust, homemade Alfredo sauce, and numerous health code violations. Overall, a hot spot hangout for the brave souls of the East Coast community. A bit like Sal's for you guys, except the owners here aren't Jumpers, and nine times out of ten their ranch dressing gives you food poisoning. But"—she held up a finger—"if they can do one thing right, it's pudding."

"Pudding?"

She gazed wistfully at the cold storage unit attached to the building. "Chocolate pudding. An old family recipe that you can't get anywhere else. They make huge batches and put them into storage. There are cans just sitting there day after day with no one to eat them. It's madness." Margot stood. "That's about to change. C'mon, Lily, let's go steal some pudding."

Before I could protest, Margot climbed onto the plastic barrel and mounted the chain-link fence.

"Margot, wait!" I hissed. "We can't just steal from people. That's illegal, not to mention morally wrong!"

Margot rolled her eyes and hopped to the other side. "Don't be so dramatic. It's one can of pudding. They won't even know it's gone."

"Margot!"

"Lily." She turned and looked me in the eye. "Sometimes you need to take risks to know what you're made of. Sometimes they'll pay off, and sometimes they won't, but at least you can sleep at night knowing you tried. You're welcome to stay where you are and let life pass you by, or you can do something with it. It's up to you, but living your life in a padded bubble is like having no life at all."

"Margot—"

She trotted toward the building, disappearing into the shadows. "Make a decision, flower girl."

I pressed myself against the chain-link fence. "Margot, wait!" I whispered.

She didn't respond. Looking around the cramped courtyard, I jumped at a horn honking in the distance. The flashing neon sign from another building cast a harsh red light every few moments. I sighed.

Climbing onto the plastic drum, I pulled myself over the fence and tripped on the landing. I blinked as my eyes adjusted to the darkness. Spotting Margot across the courtyard, I jogged to the shadowy side of the cold storage unit and crouched. She didn't turn as I approached.

"Okay," she whispered, "they're still open, which means they haven't locked up the unit for the night yet. We just need to wait until someone comes—"

The back door burst open. A lanky teenager stepped outside, straining under the weight of a water-stained box. "Well, why didn't you *tell* me we needed wheat instead of white?" he yelled behind him. "I just unpacked the whole box!"

"Quit'cha whining," a shrill voice responded. "Just get the wheat and make it fast; we got people to feed!"

"Yeah, yeah," he grumbled, balancing the heavy box against the side of the cold storage unit while he fumbled with a set of keys. "'Just make the new kid put them back, Arnie,'" he mocked in a high-pitched voice. "'He hasn't even gotten his first paycheck yet, but treat him like dirt, anyway.' What a load of crap."

Margot grabbed a piece of stray cardboard on the ground. Folding it into a tight square, she glanced up at the teenager, still fumbling with the keys. "Make a distraction on the other side of the yard."

"Like what?"

"Just throw a rock or something, but wait until he opens the freezer. Buy me a few seconds."

"Now?"

"Now!"

Margot crept from our hiding space. I shuffled to the other side of the courtyard, picking up an old beer bottle on the way. I waited until the freezer door was open and chucked the bottle. It clanged against a few rusty metal barrels before shattering against the concrete.

The guy turned toward the noise and set down the box. "Hello? Who's there?"

Margot shuffled forward and caught my eye. Motioning for me to do something else, she crouched behind the teenager, mere feet away. I looked around. The only thing I could reach was a crumpled bag of fast food and some piles of wet newspaper. The teenager turned back to the storage unit, Margot still crouched behind him.

"Meow!" I called.

His attention turned toward me. So did Margot. She clamped a hand over her mouth.

"H-hello?" he stuttered. "Mikey, is that you again? C'mon man, we've talked about this! You know I don't like comin' out here at night!"

I shuffled to find more cover on the other side of the yard and spotted Margot fiddling with the doorframe. She was only there for a second before ducking out of sight.

"Hey!" boomed a voice from the back door. "Whaddya doin' out there? Hurry up!"

The teenager jolted and scrambled to pick up the box. "I'm comin'!"

He slammed the heavy door of the cold storage unit after retrieving another crate and locked it, disappearing inside the pizzeria.

Margot and I emerged from our hiding places and met in the middle of the yard.

Margot's face was red from laughing. She bent over on her knees and heaved a few breaths. "'Meow'?" She wheezed. "Oh my *God.*"

My face burned. "You said make a distraction! What did you do to the door?"

She regained her composure and strode to the locked door, opening it with a tug. Cold, sour-tasting air washed over us.

Margot pulled out the piece of cardboard she had folded from the door-jamb. "Keeps the lock from engaging so we didn't have to break it. Now they'll never know we were here."

Ducking into the unit without another word, she returned with a large metal can labeled "Choc. Pudding" on a piece of beige masking tape and a bag of fluffy-looking breadsticks.

We hurried to the fence and scaled it again, passing the pudding between us.

I cradled the metal can in one arm and dropped, landing on both feet this time. Turning to report my success, I stopped. Margot was at the other end of the alley, handing the homeless man the bag of bread.

"Thanks, kid," he said, breaking into a toothless smile. He reached out a mitten-covered hand. "You always seem to show up when I need it most."

She took his hand. "Don't mention it. But you didn't get that from me, got it?"

He pulled back his beanie. "I dunno what you're talking about. You weren't even here, right?"

She smiled. "Good man."

They said their goodbyes, and she jogged the rest of the way to me. "Okay, let's bounce. You still got the stuff?"

I held out the heavy can as proof.

The back door to the pizzeria banged open again. We both jumped. I bumped into a wooden crate and knocked off a cluster of empty soda cans. They clattered to the ground.

A heavyset man standing in the doorway looked up and spotted the can of pudding. His face twisted into rage as he put two and two together. He pointed at us. "Hey! Stop right there!"

I froze, but Margot yanked my arm. "Run for it!"

We sprinted down the alleyway and took any turn that didn't lead to dead ends. My heart was pounding, but Margot was laughing her head off ahead of me. I struggled to keep up with her.

We ran through a maze of alleyways, feet slapping against cold concrete until Margot slowed to a stop next to a dumpster. A sudden giggle rose in my throat as the absurdity of the situation hit me. We leaned against the brick wall, laughing hysterically with our stolen chocolate trophy in hand.

EIGHT

Bonfire

"All right, you get first dibs, since you carried that thing all the way."

"Was this really worth committing a felony?"

"See for yourself."

I pried the sharp metal lid back from the can as Margot waited impatiently, clutching one of the plastic spoons she'd acquired on our way to our current hiding spot. We sat in an abandoned penthouse apartment with a view of the city below. Delayed construction, Margot had said. It seemed to be a regular hangout for her, the vacant living room furnished with old couch cushions, blankets, and various pieces of radio equipment. Cans of grape soda and empty packets of strawberry sugar wafers littered the dusty floor.

Dipping the spoon into the can, I took a bite. The cool pudding was smooth and rich. I blinked in surprise. "Wow."

She laughed. "I told you. Now pass it over. It's been ages since I've sampled this celestial nectar."

"Margot, you've only been gone for a few weeks."

She dug the spoon into the can. "Whatever."

We passed the can between us and listened to the distant sound of the city below. Grime obscured the large windows, but it didn't diminish the view of the surrounding sparkling lights and skyscrapers.

"So, was that as bad as you thought it was going to be?" she asked.

I sighed. "Well, we did just technically break the law . . ."

She raised an eyebrow.

". . . but that was still pretty fun," I admitted.

She smiled. Reverting to her usual aloof expression, she downgraded the smile to a smirk. "I think my favorite part was when you turned into a cat. That was the most pitiful 'meow' I've ever heard in my life."

I rolled my eyes. "I was trying not to let you get caught. And you should listen to Catacombs once in a while. He meows like a bus engine."

"Who's Catacombs?"

"The cat who hangs around Giftshop? Him."

"The really annoying one?"

"Is there more than one talking cat?"

Margot chuckled. "Fortunately, no. You gave him a name?"

I shrugged and grabbed another spoonful of pudding. "No one else had, and it just seemed to fit."

"Oh, I gave him a name too," Margot pointed out. "It's just not something I can repeat."

We both laughed and trailed off into silence.

I cleared my throat. "Hey, um, so I heard you were part of the Northwestern community a few years ago."

She gave me a sideways glance. "Where'd you hear that?"

I shrugged. "Just word on the street. But, uh, what's the story with that? How did you end up all the way out here?"

Licking her spoon, she thought for a minute before responding. "My . . . uncles live in Stars Crossing, so they were my way into the community. I joined up when I was about fourteen."

"Who are your uncles?"

She shook her head. "You wouldn't know them. They live in the middle of nowhere. The younger one is autistic, so his older brother looks out for him. Although I doubt either of them would make it without the other."

I sat up. "Pete and Tinker are your uncles?"

"How do you know them?"

I laughed. "We kind of saved the world together back in October."

"Huh. Small world." Shaking her head, she refocused. "I haven't seen them in . . . a while. They called me up from their assignment and mentioned Cliff was looking for someone to fill in for a teaching job. You were it."

"I didn't know they had a niece. Or any other family, for that matter. How are you related?"

"Well, as for other family, I'm the last one. There were four brothers: Pete, Ted, Perseus, who died on the job, and the youngest named Emmett."

"So they were a Jumper family, then?"

"Yep. Something . . . real bad went down between the parents and Emmett. I never found out what, but he got kicked out of the house and never spoke to them again. He got some girl pregnant a few years later and cut off contact with the community. Those . . . those were my parents."

"Wow. What did they think about you joining up so young?"

Margot dipped her spoon back into the can. "They died of a drug overdose when I was eleven. Went up to their room one night and didn't come out again."

It was quiet.

"God," I breathed. "I'm sorry."

She shrugged. "It was a long time ago."

We lapsed into silence. My stomach had turned queasy from devouring so much pudding, and Margot's depressing backstory wasn't helping.

I cleared my throat. "I, uh, also heard that you got transferred to the East Coast community after an incident."

"Yeah."

"What was that about? What happened?"

She scooped up another spoonful from the can without looking at me. "An incident."

"Well, yeah, I kind of figured. But what was the incident?"

She stood. "We should head back. It's getting late."

A jolt shot through my stomach, and I scrambled to my feet. "Wait, what time is it?"

"In Oregon? Almost seven."

I groaned and dug around in my pockets for my Teleporter. "Oh no. No, no, no, no."

"You late for something?" she asked. "Hot date?"

"Uh." The cold metal disk slipped from my hands. I caught it before it hit the floor. "No. I was supposed to meet Roger at Sal's yesterday, but I . . . missed it. And I promised to make it up to him today, and instead I'm in New York stealing pudding."

Margot put her hands on her hips. "Wow. You really *do* have a hot date."

"It's not a . . . it's not a date," I mumbled.

She threw her head back and barked a laugh. "Yeah, whatever you say. You got a connection back to Sal's?"

"No, but someone in Giftshop usually has one. I'll ask around. Do you want a lift?"

Margot looked out the window. "Nah, I'll head back in a bit. But I'll see you tomorrow, same time, same place." She smirked as I opened a portal to Giftshop. "Don't keep your boyfriend waiting."

Roger wasn't even there.

I swept my eyes around the empty diner. Rhonda was the only one in sight, wiping down tables with a rag and a spray bottle.

"Hey, Rhonda," I called. "Have you seen Rog?"

Rhonda paused on her way to the counter and looked around. She shrugged. "I guess he finally left. He was at a table for over an hour until everyone went to Bonfire. He must've gone with them."

"Bonfire?"

"It's a gathering we do every once in a while." She scrubbed a spill on the counter. "Folks bring food, play music, there's fable telling for the kids, and a huge bonfire to keep everyone warm."

Glancing at the clock on the wall, she grabbed some stray coffee mugs and bustled toward the back. "It's still going on if you want to head over; they're having it outside the outpost tonight. Just follow the singing."

She disappeared through the swinging back door, her messy bun bobbing out of sight.

I pulled out my Teleporter again, hesitating. I didn't hate Jumper gatherings, but they didn't exactly fill me with joy. It would be loud, busy, and probably full of people rehashing old times. I'd spend my time sitting awkwardly away from the group, trying in vain to believe that I belonged there. The smart thing to do was go home and get a good night's sleep. Try to, at least.

I sighed. Roger would be there. I owed him an explanation for why I left him alone at the diner. Again. The least I could do was stop by for that.

Opening a connection to the outpost, I stepped into the chilly, dim forest.

No one was there. The plentiful campfire rings had gone dark, the treehouses above me were silent and empty. It was unsettling, seeing it so quiet. Normally, the outpost was a bustling hub.

I took a few steps forward. Distant echoes floated through the trees. It came from the outskirts of town, deep in the woods.

The noises grew louder as I approached, morphing into subtle strums of acoustic guitars and mumbling voices. The sounds of laughing children interrupted the intermittent moments of silence. Pushing aside a thick mossy curtain of foliage, a warm, bright flickering light assaulted my eyes. I blinked.

A clearing the size of the main village stretched before me. The ambient mumbles became individual conversations as people milled around the central roaring bonfire. It seemed the entire village had gathered in the wide clearing, all huddled around the enormous fire pit to stave off the crisp winter air. Weathered tree stumps held an assortment of picked over pots, pans, casserole dishes, and cookie sheets. Strings of glowing bulbs illuminated the outskirts of the bonfire, bathing the entire clearing in light.

A group of excited children sprinted past me, immersed in their game of tag. I recognized a few faces in the crowd, but the majority I didn't. Stepping over a fallen log, I wandered through the clearing. Most people passed me without giving a second glance. A few pointed in my direction and huddled closer together. I ignored them.

"December, seven p.m.!" a voice rang out. "Sound off!"

The clearing quieted. I slowed my pace as the mumble of conversation turned into a hum. Adults, teenagers, children, and everyone in between stopped what they were doing and faced the bonfire. The intricate harmony of voices was beautiful. My eyes stung as the hum grew to words.

"As our story grows,
No one really knows,
What path we will believe,
And who we get to leave.

Some will go home soon,
And we will have to choose,
If we stay with them,
Or if we'll sing.

Sing, sing!
For the ones who lost their way.
Sing, sing!
For the light to break with day.
Sing, sing, sing!
And we'll patch within ourselves,
The holes of those who slipped away."

The ballad repeated as the chorus overlapped with the beginning melody. A voice near me seemed louder and fuller than the rest, hitting each note with expert clarity. I looked around to see who it was, doing a double take. It was Roger. I wouldn't have recognized him in the dim lighting.

The song ended, its echo ringing through the quiet clearing. Slowly, the spell that had captured the dark woods lifted, and the mumbled din of Jumpers resumed.

I waited until the crowd dispersed and shuffled over to Roger. He was engrossed in conversation with a group of people, laughing with a foam cup hanging loosely from one hand. A lanky guy with glasses punched Roger in the arm. Two members of the group began an impromptu sparring match and wrestled away deeper into the forest. Roger chuckled and leaned against a nearby tree.

Circling around to the front, I gave a small wave. Roger's eyes widened. Mumbling something to the guy with glasses, he stepped around the remaining group and walked to me.

"Hey," he called.

"Hey," I said.

His eyes swept around the clearing. "What're you doing here?"

I cleared my throat. "Um, Rhonda said you might be here. And I-I just came to apologize. I, um." I took a deep breath. "We were training, and Margot said that I needed to get out and do fun stuff or something. The next thing I know, we're in New York, stealing chocolate pudding from this pizza joint she goes to? Then we got caught and hid out in this old abandoned apartment building, and I didn't realize what time it was. I literally said yesterday that I wouldn't blow you off again, and I was really looking forward to it, and I—"

Roger laughed. "Whoa, easy, Lil. Take a breath."

I cleared my throat and looked down at the pine-needle-covered ground.

He sighed, transferring the foam cup to his other hand. The aroma of spiced cider wafted from it. "Look, I've been through training. Twice. I get it, trust me. Sometimes things happen you can't control, and sometimes you have to sacrifice for it."

"But I—"

"Training comes first," he said, "always. Because if you don't take things seriously, and you're not prepared, it could cost you your life one day. And making sure you stay alive is more important than skipping Sal's for a few days."

I let out a breath. The faint plume of mist disappeared almost instantly. "I just . . . I feel terrible about making you wait again. But I am taking training seriously, I promise. I'm doing the best I can."

"I know. And you don't need to worry about me." He chuckled. "I can take care of myself."

"I wouldn't go *that* far," came a voice to my right. I turned. The tall guy with glasses had joined us. Faded acne scars splashed across most of his face. "I've pulled you out of one too many tight spots, Rog."

Roger rolled his eyes. "Same goes for you, Mr. I-had-to-be-rescued-from-a-trapping-pit-when-I-was-eight."

"Hey—"

"Don't think I forgot about that."

He scowled. "Oh, you want to start this? What about that time you tried to sneak out to that party and got stuck in—"

"Okay, okay!" Roger said quickly, glancing at me. "God, you sound like Rhonda."

They both laughed. The guy with glasses held out a hand to me. "I don't think we've officially met. My name's Carl."

"Oh." I shook his hand. "You're the guy that runs the archives, right? You're Rog's friend."

Carl glanced over at Roger. "It's comforting to know that information came second. But yeah, I'm the archive guy who never sees the light of day.

And you"—he adjusted his glasses —"are Lily Masters, Psychic Wonder Child, and newest addition to the Northwestern community. I'd give you a 'welcome to the team' speech, but they'll do that when you complete all the training."

I laughed. "Wow. You sure know a lot about me; I guess having access to the community archives must be handy."

He shrugged. "I guess, but Roger hasn't shut up about you since—"

"Hey." Roger gestured toward a mass of people who were joining hands around the fire. "Um, look, they're starting another song. I think we're getting into Christmas carols now. Let's head over."

Carl shrugged, shooting Roger a smirk as he passed. Roger set down his cup on a nearby stump, and we shuffled forward with the gathering crowd.

"So, what exactly is all this?" I asked. "Rhonda called it Bonfire?"

Roger nodded. "It's something the community puts together each month. A kind of morale booster, I guess. It's a good way for everyone to check in with each other, see who's retired and who's still alive."

"What was that song for?"

Roger paused, casting his gaze downward. "We call that 'sounding off.' It happens every Bonfire at seven o'clock. It's a chance to have some closure for those who didn't make it back."

We slowed as the crowd jockeyed for positions around the fire.

I glanced at Roger. "So . . . you never told me you could sing."

He coughed and rubbed the back of his neck. "Oh. You, uh, heard that?"

"I did. You sounded really good. Where'd you learn to sing like that?"

"Um . . . thanks. I was, uh, in a band for a few years when I left the community."

A smile spread across my face. "Really?"

He rolled his eyes. "Don't make this a thing."

"I will absolutely make it a thing. How did that happen?"

He lifted his shoulders. "Just started talking to a guy on the bus one day, and he mentioned that he and a few friends were trying to start a band. We traveled around, did a few shows. Nothing big."

My smile widened. "No way! Do you have any recordings?"

Roger hung his head. "God, that was so long ago now. We sold a few CDs, but they're probably in a landfill by now."

"What was the band called?"

He raised his eyebrows and smirked. "Nope."

"What do you mean, nope?"

"I am *not* telling the girl with access to every human memory that piece of information." He nudged me with his elbow. "Nice try, though."

"Hmph," I mumbled. "I'll find out eventually."

We joined the lopsided oval around the roaring bonfire. An older lady with dark gray hair grabbed my hand, and the man to the left of her grabbed her other one. Roger held out his hand to me, smiling. Bursts of orange and yellow danced in the reflection of his eyes. I smiled back and wrapped my fingers around his.

Someone on the edge of the circle called out the first few words of "It Came Upon a Midnight Clear."

"It came upon a midnight clear, that glorious song of old!"

The circle swayed together, faces beaming.

"From angels bending near to Earth, to touch their harps of gold!"

Distantly, a crackling noise floated through the air.

"Peace on the Earth, good will to men, from Heaven's all gracious king!"

The faint crackling of static.

"The world in solemn stillness lay, to hear the angels sing!"

C . . . o . . . m . . . i . . . n . . . g . . .

I stopped swaying with the crowd as my blood turned to ice.

"Still through the cloven skies they come, with peaceful wings unfurled!"

D...a...n...g...e...r...

"And still their heavenly music floats..."

D...e...a...t...h...

"O'er all this weary world!"

I turned away from the group and stared into the dark forest. A voice called from beyond. The singing drowned it out.

"...help...!"

"Above its sad and lowly plains..."

"...please...anyone! Help...me...!"

"They bend on hov'ring wing!"

Something squeezed my right hand. "Hey, you all right, Lil?"

"And ever o'er its babel sounds..."

My head was pounding.

"The blessed angels sing!"

"Help!"

The voice crashed through the tree line, halting the song. Those closest to the sound broke the circle and watched in horror.

Bea stumbled from the darkness, face and clothes drenched in blood. Her right ear was missing. The gaping hole in the side of her head glinted sickeningly in the firelight.

Her stained hands clutched the taut folds of a drooping, occupied body bag.

Nine

Unthinkable

The gap of silence following Bea's appearance was deafening.

The gathering around the bonfire halted. The music ringing through the forest just seconds before choked, replaced by prickling shock and the pang of frozen panic.

Bea watched the crowd with wide eyes. She fell to her knees.

That was when everyone moved.

Roger and I sprinted forward but didn't reach her in time to keep her from hitting the ground. Voices yelled for med kits as people sprinted toward the outpost. Others ushered the groups of children away from the scene, their small faces confused and afraid.

Roger attempted to pull Bea's rigid, shaking body into a sitting position. "Bea, what happened?"

"Get Cliff!" she sobbed. "Get Cliff!"

Roger nodded to someone behind me. The electric zing of a portal opening tugged at the air. A few other team leaders pulled out Chatterboxes and followed through to Giftshop.

"We're getting him, Bea," Roger soothed. "It's okay, you're safe now."

She pulled herself to her knees. "No, you don't understand. I-It's th-th-them! They—"

She sank back onto the ground, her hand still wrapped around the black body bag. She clung to the crinkled plastic like it was the only thing keeping her alive.

A man with a fluffy winter coat and cowboy hat leaned down to drape a blanket over Bea's heaving shoulders. Jonesy, that was his name. "Bea, you can let go of the bag now," he said.

Bea tightened her grip. "I-I had to b-b-bring her back. I couldn't leave h-her with them! *I couldn't leave her with them!*"

Jonesy tugged at her arm. "Bea, it's okay. You can let go."

She drew the bag closer to her before releasing it. Her hand remained locked in a clawlike position. Touching the side of her face, she looked confused when her palm came away covered in blood. She gasped as she felt the hole where her ear used to be.

The older woman who'd stood next to me at the bonfire pulled the body bag away and donned some disposable gloves. She eased open the zipper and leaned away, covering her mouth with the back of her hand. Others around her did the same.

"Oh my God," someone whispered. "*Laura.*"

A tugging sensation behind my sternum signaled that someone else had used a Teleporter. Cliff entered the circle of people, followed closely by Henry. Everyone parted to let them through. A few people packed wads of gauze to the side of Bea's face to slow the steady stream of blood.

"Christ, Bea," Cliff whispered. "What the hell did you get yourself into?"

Bea latched onto his arm, her eyes wild and unfocused. "Cliff, they're back. They're all back!"

He gave her hand a comforting pat. "Take it easy. You're safe now, all right? Whatever you need to tell me can wait until you're stable." He looked up to the group. "We need to get her warmed up before she goes into shock. Jack, Chelsea, start her on fluids. Take her—"

"No!" Bea hissed. "You don't understand! Cliff, it's them. It's *them.*"

Cliff, who had been trying to pry her hand away from his arm, froze. His face drained of color. Something behind his eyes tightened.

"What?" he whispered. "You . . . you're sure?"

Bea nodded, relieved that someone finally seemed to understand.

The rest of the group seemed confused. I glanced at Roger for clarification. He didn't seem to understand either, and he shrugged.

Cliff stood. "I want everyone inside and with a headcount of their families. Now. Bonfire's over tonight."

Everyone looked confused.

"Cliff, what's going on?" asked the older woman. "Who are—"

"Just do as I say!" he barked. "We're on full lockdown. Act accordingly."

The group seemed taken aback at his suddenly harsh tone. His hands were shaking, and his jaw was clenched. I'd never seen him so upset. A darkness had entered his face that wasn't there before.

Nobody questioned him again. They dispersed toward the outpost, all muttering to each other. A group stayed to extinguish the bonfire with rakes, shovels, and hoses, while most disappeared into the trees. I recognized Irene's team tending to Bea's injuries.

Irene herself was now kneeling next to Bea, adding another blanket to her shoulders while a younger girl with blue-dyed hair held a large water bottle. Bea's sobs had subsided. She stared at the muddy ground with a vacant gaze.

Henry watched Cliff with a guarded expression. He put a hand on his shoulder.

Cliff shrugged it off. "Bea, can you stand?"

She nodded slowly.

"Then let's get inside; we need to talk."

The small medical building was cramped.

Cliff, Henry, Roger, and I barely fit around the hospital bed where Bea was now situated. After being told numerous times to leave, Cliff had apparently given up and let Roger and me stay with Bea. She had calmed down enough to speak, but the traumatized stare she slipped into every few minutes was more than a little unnerving.

The body bag was in the next room, waiting to be examined in the morning to verify it was Laura, but I had gotten a glimpse when Irene's team moved the bag. Her glazed, milky eyes and bloody pale face were now burned into my mind for the foreseeable future.

"All right." Cliff folded his arms. "I need you to tell me *exactly* what happened. Where you went, what you saw, and what you were doing there. Everything, Bea."

Bea looked up. Her head was wrapped in sterile white bandages. A series of tubes connected her IV to a beeping machine in the corner. She stared at the floor before responding.

"I've been keeping tabs on Laura since October," she began. "After what happened with Ed. A few weeks ago, she went dark. Just completely dropped off the map, and I thought the worst. Until I . . . I got a ping a few days ago in Austria from some friends of mine. I searched but didn't find a trace. I was going to give up. I thought maybe she didn't want to be found. But—"

Bea broke off and reached into her pocket, pulling out a small silver flash drive. "Yesterday, I got a letter from Laura, postmarked a few days ago. This was inside. No note, no explanation, just this flash drive."

She handed it to Henry, who plugged it into a nearby computer monitor displaying Bea's medical information. Cliff couldn't seem to stand still. He paced a few steps, rubbed his eyes, and shuffled his feet. I glanced at Roger, who eyed him warily. His face mirrored my concern and confusion.

A black video player appeared on the monitor, and the small speaker crackled to life. The camera shifted from being pointed down at the asphalt below to showing an upturned view of Laura. Her long dark hair was tucked into a beanie, framing her attractive face. Her eyes looked tired, dark circles causing her to seem much older. The watermarked date in the corner of the screen indicated the video was taken almost two weeks ago.

She shifted a large backpack on her shoulders and waved at the camera. "Hey, Bea. Sorry I haven't contacted you before now. Look, I know you've been tracking me since I left, and yes, I have been trying to shake you. It's sweet of you to want to help me, but I just need time, okay? I just need to . . . I just need to figure some things out right now. On my own. I need to focus on something other than the community for a while."

She looked away from the camera. "I've had a pet project that I've been wanting to research, so that's what I'm going to throw myself into. I figured, I have time now, so why not? Some friends in Europe wanted to join, too, so I'm meeting up with them for some intensive research. I think it'll be good if I spend some time out of the States. Somewhere unfamiliar. Somewhere new."

A voice off camera called her name. She nodded and waved. "Yeah, I'll be there in a minute." She glanced back at the camera. "Okay, I gotta go. I'm heading to the airport now. I'll try to mail this off to you before I get on the plane, but if I don't, I'll only be gone for a few weeks. We'll talk when I get back, all right? Till again."

Laura flashed a smile before the video went black. It resumed a few seconds later with a dark image, barely in focus. The inside of a tent, illuminated by a small battery-powered lantern, warped in the wind. The shadows of backlit tree branches scratched against the fabric walls. Frenzied screams echoed in the distance. The watermarked date was only a few days ago.

The camera shook before it was picked up. Laura's bruised and sweaty face looked gaunt and harsh in the dim lighting. Her panicked eyes widened as she crouched against a battered green cot. She didn't seem to notice that the camera was recording.

Voices outside the tent barked a series of indistinguishable orders. Laura dropped to the ground. She clamped a hand over her mouth as a beam of light passed over the tent walls. My stomach recoiled when the camera fell sideways. Dark shapes surrounded Laura on all sides. Dark shapes leaking puddles of dark liquid onto the dark floor.

Bodies.

The beam of light vanished. A few distant gunshots, followed by more screams, filled the air. Laura didn't move until the light had faded from view. She inched forward on her stomach and dragged herself toward the tent door.

Grabbing a backpack from under the cot, she set down the camera and pulled her shaking arms through the straps. The next few minutes of footage were a blur of colors and the sounds of crunching footsteps. Laura tripped as she slid down a muddy embankment, rolling to a stop a few feet away from the camera. She crawled toward it and cradled it in her hands.

She turned the camera up to her face again, breath coming in ragged gasps. "Bea," she whispered. "Bea, I don't know if you'll get this, but we—the research camp was attacked. I don't know by who, or why, but they came in the night and they . . . they—"

Her voice broke. She held her fist to her mouth to stifle her sobs. "God, Bea, everyone's dead. All of them. They must've thought I was dead, too. I think I'm the only one who got away. I just had time to hide the camera with the flash drive when they came in and ransacked everything. Oh God, they're all . . . all of them. It happened so fast, there was nothing I could do. I couldn't do *anything*."

The reality of what she said seemed to hit her. Snapping back to attention, she gripped the camera with both hands. "Bea, you need to listen to me. I'm going to try to get this video to you, because I don't know if I'm going to make it back to tell you in person."

The camera shook. "These people are after something. Something big. My pet project I mentioned before? It was a book. I was looking for a book. *The* book. And . . . we found it. Or at least, we found out where it is. I'll send my research notes with this video; they're encrypted, so you'll have to decode them."

She sucked in a shuddering breath. "I've been keeping tabs on the book for a few years, just out of curiosity, but I swear to God I didn't know what it would lead to. I thought it was just a story. I thought it was a myth." She closed her eyes. "I was wrong."

A shout in the distance grew closer. A sweeping beam of light lit up the trees. Laura jumped, pressing herself to the edge of the embankment. "*Shit.* I-I have to move. But Bea"—she looked back to the camera—"whatever happens to me, and *whoever* these people are, you cannot let them get the book. Do you understand? If they know what it is, and they know how to use it, it's over. It's all over. I'm enacting an extinction event watch. I repeat, this is a priority alpha *extinction event watch*."

The screen went black.

Henry leaned forward and exited out of the video player. Hidden behind it was a large assortment of open files, one by one downloading to the desktop.

Roger twisted in his seat and squinted. "What are those?"

We leaned forward collectively.

They were notes. Papers. Scraps. Scans upon scans of timeworn intricate illustrations and scribbled paragraphs. Scrambled lines of letters surrounded them. Yellowed illuminated manuscript pages mixed with quickly jotted ideas on white printer paper. Most of the drawings were sketches of creatures, strange symbols, and twisted landscapes of barren rock. Others displayed disturbing diagrams of muscles, sinew, and bone. Whole sheets of paper were almost black from the lines of jumbled letters and numbers. Another page consisted of red splotches labeled with graphs and tissue samples taped together.

There was only one blurry photograph.

It showed a book. A huge ornate tome inlaid with strips of tarnished gold, gems, and thin pieces of something white. Bones. Splintered chips of bone. I swallowed, the sudden uneasiness gripping my insides. There was something *wrong* about the way the brittle starched bones laced themselves into the thick pale cover. Something unnatural about the stretched skin of leather binding it all together. It was sickening. Disgusting. Unnatural.

It made me feel . . .

Old.

"So, what happened?" Roger asked Bea. "You got the flash drive last night, and then what?"

She cleared her throat. "I saw the videos and went back to Austria to poke around. Someone approached me, claiming to be from the research team. They told me they were hiding out with Laura, and they'd take me to her." She closed her eyes and shook her head. "I was so *stupid*. I should've realized it was a trap. They drugged me. I woke up in a tunnel when they were carrying me."

"Any clue where you were?" Henry asked.

Bea shook her head. "It was dark and wet, but that's all I can tell you. They must've thought I was still unconscious, because they left me alone. By the time they came back, I was gone. Those tunnels were like a maze. I didn't think I'd ever make it out."

"Why didn't you use your Teleporter?" Roger asked.

"I tried," she said. "It wouldn't work, so I looked for another way out. There was . . ." She trailed off, eyes glazing over before she refocused. "There was a room. An entire room fashioned like a morgue with . . . God, with bodies *everywhere*. And the body on the . . . on the table was—"

She pressed her hand against her mouth and sucked in a muted sob. I reached forward and squeezed her arm.

Bea gave me a small smile and nodded. "Thank you, Lily. I'll be all right. After I found Laura, I . . . I knew I couldn't leave her with them. We almost made it out unseen until someone spotted us. I turned a corner, and my Teleporter worked. I barely made it back to the outpost. It didn't occur to me that tonight was Bonfire, otherwise, I would've gone to Giftshop."

Bea touched the side of her bandaged head where her ear used to be. "I don't know when this happened. I guess when I was escaping? I was so scared I didn't even feel the pain."

Henry put a bracing hand on her shoulder. "We're just happy that you came back alive." He turned and clicked through Laura's seemingly endless supply of research notes. "She was right; these are all in code of some sort, but given the illustrations and the context of what she told us in the video, I think they're—"

He froze as a scanned page flicked into view. The handwriting and circles devolved into violent scribbles. A single empty black circle was all that remained, and a word. A question scrawled on the bottom in heavy black ink.

The temperature of the room seemed to drop.

Cliff took one step toward the screen, his jaw locked. Slowly, he turned to Bea. "When did you get this flash drive?"

Bea looked up. "L-last night."

"So you knew," he continued. "You knew about their involvement, and you didn't report it to me until now."

Bea opened and closed her mouth a few times. "I . . . I wasn't completely sure it was them. I didn't think I should raise the alarm if this was just a copycat group. And . . . and Laura was my primary concern. I just had to—"

"You just had to . . . what? You just had to risk your life, and the security of the *entire* community, so you didn't have to deal with it?"

She lowered her head. "I'm sorry, Cliff. I wasn't trying to—"

"What if they followed you through to the outpost?" he hissed. "What if you led them right to our front door? Do you have *any* idea how many people you could've killed by coming back here? Not to mention that you could've just cost us our one and only chance of finding them!"

Henry stepped forward. "Cliff, that's enough. Go take a walk and cool off. Come back when you've got your head together."

"No, you're not listening!" Cliff shouted. "If they're after this book, then it could be our only chance to get their position. After almost twenty-five years, we could wipe them out for good!"

"That's not what we do, and you know it," Henry said. "You heard Laura. This needs to be handled with the highest priority."

"They took *everything* from me!" Cliff yelled. "You can't expect me to—"

"*Owens!*" Henry barked. "Take a walk. *Now.*"

Cliff's wild expression broke down. He seemed to realize he was shouting and composed himself. He glanced at Roger, who stared at his father in shock. Cliff grabbed the handle of the door and turned to close it behind him, making eye contact with me on the way out.

A flash of transferred pain shot across my insides. Sometimes, when there was enough tangible emotion, I could feel it. I figured it had something to do with my connection to the Collective, but it didn't make it any less jarring.

I kept myself from staggering. The feeling left me breathless and nauseated. It was an old pain. Deep, suffocating, and cold.

The kind of pain that leaves a festering wound in its path.

TEN

The Book of Bones

Roger stared at the door as it clicked shut. His mouth hung open. "All right, what the hell is going on?"

Bea and Henry shared a sideways glance.

"What's my dad's problem?" Roger continued. "I've never seen him act like that. What's this book that Laura was looking for?"

Henry braced himself against a chair and looked at the floor. Bea stared at her folded hands. Neither of them said anything.

Roger heaved an exasperated sigh. "Will someone explain what the *fu—*"

"Rog," Henry muttered. "The book . . . it's the *Ossabrium*."

Roger's face twisted in confusion before he laughed. "I'm not a kid anymore, Henry. You can't scare me with ghost stories like you used to."

"Henry's right," Bea chimed in. "I don't know how it's still around or why it's surfacing now, but it's back. And everything that comes with it."

Roger pinched the bridge of his nose. "Wait, that can't—the *Ossabrium* isn't *real*. It was just a story we heard as kids. A legend that was made up to make us listen to our elders and . . ."

He trailed off as Henry slowly shook his head.

Roger's eyes widened. "Are we still talking about the same thing? The book that 'melts your eyes from your skull' and 'turns your blood to ink lest you forget its power' and all that? The book of monsters and demons from 'the deepest pits of the abyss'?"

"Yes and no," Bea said. "Parts of those stories are fiction, but they were based on an actual object."

Roger leaned on his knees. "Oh my God. I . . . can't believe it. That thing gave me nightmares when I thought it was just a story." His head jerked up. "Wait, if the *Ossabrium* is real, does that mean . . . stuff like the Screaming Chasm, Black Eyed Goat, and the Before Man are real? What *other* legends are out there?"

"To save your ability to sleep at night, I'm not going to tell you," Henry said.

I raised my hand. Everyone turned to look at me.

"Hi," I said. "As the only person here who didn't grow up as a Jumper, can you please explain what you're talking about? What legends?"

There was a collective glance between them, and Henry cleared his throat. "Sorry, Lily, I forget you're still new to this. Er, Roger, you probably remember this story more than we do. You're . . . a little younger than us."

"Wha—that was still almost twenty years ago!" he complained. "How young do you think I am?"

Henry cracked a smile. "Young enough. Go on."

Shooting Henry a look, Roger sighed. "All right fine. Let's see . . . the *Ossabrium*, or 'the Book of Bones,' as we called it when I was little, has existed forever."

"Like, actually forever?" I asked.

"'Longer than the mountains, the seas, and the snow-covered peaks,'" he recited. "Or . . . something like that. Some say there are prehistoric cave paintings that depict the book. Some say there are stone tablets carved with copied passages of its pages, and they bring death to those who read them. I've even heard it said that the book wasn't written by humans."

I tilted my head. "What does that mean? Like . . . aliens? Other intelligent life like The Bound?"

"Er, no. Well, kind of. Some think that it was written by something . . . more than that. Something not of this dimension. Something . . . else."

I glanced at Bea and Henry. They nodded.

"When I was a kid," Roger continued, "they said if you read any of the pages out loud, you would call . . . things, terrible things, to awaken. Things that are so terrifying they can't even have names, because their names would die just by being attached to them. Creatures bigger than continents. Monsters. Beasts. Gods."

"So . . ." I said slowly, "is it a—and I can't believe that I'm about to say this—is it some kind of . . . spell book?"

"Not exactly," Bea said. "It's more like a . . ."

"An index," Henry finished. "A catalog, or record, I guess you'd call it. A phone book."

"A . . . phone book?"

Bea heaved a sigh. "Somehow, the book has power. It can call things to it. It can wake things up. Things that have been asleep for a very long time. As the story goes, if you know how to use it, you could summon them. You could literally speak the end of the world into existence."

It was quiet.

"Like Roger, I thought the *Ossabrium* was just a story," Henry said, "but when searching for evidence of The Bound, I heard rumors of it. Eventually, I put the pieces together, and realized that some stories, no matter how outlandish, are based in fact." He heaved a sigh. "Like the Book of Bones."

"So, why haven't I heard of this before?" I asked. "I can't imagine Jumpers were the only ones to find out about it."

"You probably have heard of it, in a way," Bea said. "The *Necronomicon*, *Pseudomonarchia Daemonum*, *The Lesser Key of Solomon*, *Dictionnaire Infernal*, and countless other references. These works were based on the *Ossabrium*, in one form or another."

"Wait, hang on," I said. "The *Necronomicon*? As in H. P. Lovecraft? The book in *The Evil Dead* that turns people into zombies?"

Roger huffed a breath through his nose. "Besides the whole 'zombie' part. I think Lovecraft heard rumors of the *Ossabrium* and used them as inspiration for it. Along with a lot of his stories. Lovecraft actually spent some time in the Otherworlds, right, Bea?"

Bea inclined her head, tugging at the bandages encasing her. "That's right, in the 1920s, I think. As the story goes, he stumbled upon a Gate and was so enamored by what he saw, he begged the rescue team to let him keep his memories. I guess they took pity on him, because they broke all protocol and let him go. I suppose it was for the best, as he became one of the most notable fiction writers of all time. Or . . . supposedly fiction."

I tilted my head. "Don't all Wanders get their memory wiped?"

"They're supposed to," Henry said, "but back in the day . . . some didn't follow protocol as closely as they should have."

"I don't believe for a second that Lovecraft stayed out of that Gate any more than we do," Bea said. "His illness at the end of his life proved that much."

"What do you mean?" I asked.

"He died of a rare form of small intestinal cancer," Henry said. "Basically, his organs ate themselves until he starved to death."

"Geez," I mumbled.

"My guess is, he came in contact with some bacteria, or infection, in the Otherworlds that caused it. As Jumpers, we have a certain protection against hazardous materials we come across because of Giftshop. But that only works if you pass through Giftshop regularly. If you don't, well . . . you're liable to be exposed to some pretty nasty things."

I swallowed, suddenly conscious of all the plants and strange atmospheres I'd been in contact with in the last few months. It didn't occur to me that just *breathing* in the Otherworlds was dangerous.

Roger cleared his throat. "So we know that Laura was after the book."

"It seems so," Bea said. "She probably thought she was researching the origins of the legend. Not the legend itself."

"So . . . who is Legion?" Roger asked.

Bea and Henry looked at each other again.

"Apparently, they were also after the book," Bea whispered.

"But who are they?" I asked.

There was a long stretch of silence.

"There are some groups," Henry said finally, "that see the Otherworlds as nothing more than a means for power. They're nothing more than a weapon to them. They want control. Domination. They will stop at nothing to get it."

"So . . ." I said, "Legion is one of these groups?"

Both Bea and Henry nodded.

"Why are they called Legion?"

"They took it from the Bible, ironically," Bea said. "It originates from the book of Mark, in which a host of demons inhabit a man. When asked its name, the demon replied, 'Our name is Legion, for we are many.'"

Those words. Those words hurt to listen to. Bea hadn't shouted them, but they bounced around my skull. Like the phrase was the preceding sentence of a sharp, resounding bang.

Roger rubbed his eyes. "Look, this isn't anything new. We've had problems with similar groups for almost two hundred years. Most of the time, they're pissed off ex-Jumpers looking to stir up trouble. Why is Legion any different from them?"

"They've been around a lot longer," Henry said. "Before the Shift, before Jumpers even existed, they were here. They've been quietly manipulating world events for thousands of years, under different names and titles. Somehow, after all this time, they've survived. Since the Shift, they've targeted Jumpers to get what they want. Nothing is beneath them. Torture, subversion, murder, that's all small potatoes to them."

"What is their goal, exactly?" I asked. "If they've been working underground for all this time, what are they trying to accomplish?"

Bea propped herself up against a pile of pillows. "That's the problem; we don't know. They must have some long-term plan, but no one knows what it is. Their actions are never random, but they don't seem to correlate, either. Everything they do has a purpose. Or, did."

"Did?"

Henry cleared his throat. "They were—well, we *thought* they were wiped out. There was a big resurgence back in the early nineties of an unnamed terrorist organization. They used the Los Angeles Riots as a cover to attack one of our storage facilities there. They got away with a few crates and documents, but nothing else. We assumed their mission—whatever it was—was a failure."

He glanced at Bea and returned his eyes to the floor. "My team was part of the cleanup crew. It was a mess. Bodies everywhere, some ours, some theirs, and piles of innocent civilians. We covered it up later to the public as a gas leak. After the dust settled, we searched for the organization responsible, but they had disappeared without a trace. The search continued for years after, but we found nothing."

"Wait, so you never caught them?" I asked. "Then how do you know it was Legion?"

Henry leaned against the wall. "A few weeks after Los Angeles, some higher-ups received identical brown paper packages, delivered directly to their doorsteps. Inside them were decomposing human heads with notes stapled to them. They later identified the heads as missing Jumpers from the storage facility in LA."

It fell quiet.

"Well, I mean"—Roger coughed—"just because it happened soon after the riots doesn't *necessarily* mean it was the same group."

"They stamped the notes with the phrase 'Our name is Legion, for we are many' in thirty-five different languages. Including Braille and ancient Greek."

Roger shifted awkwardly. "Or . . . maybe it did."

"So they've been completely dormant since then?" I asked.

"Nearly," said Henry. "There've been a few isolated incidents, but there hasn't been another large-scale attack since Los Angeles. Most of us thought they were splinter groups. I thought they'd broken up for good. We were wrong."

"And now . . . they're going after the book," Bea said. "Something must've triggered it, otherwise why wait almost twenty-five years in the shadows? It has to be for something big. Something that they've been planning."

The reality of the situation seeped into the room. I tried to swallow, but my mouth was too dry to manage it. A small *pat-pat* sound over our heads signaled the beginning of rain. It did little to thaw the frozen air of dread.

Roger cleared his throat, seeming hesitant to speak up. "What does Legion have to do with my dad?"

The heavy atmosphere increased. A sudden spike of sadness snaked its way through my stomach. I gripped the edge of my seat until it passed.

Henry stared at the floor. "I'm sorry, but it's not my place to tell you that."

Roger stood. "What's that supposed to mean?"

"It's just not my place to tell you. I'm sorry."

Roger bristled. "I'm not a child. Whatever it is, I can handle it. So—"

"Rog." Bea grabbed the side of his sleeve and shook her head. "Listen to him, please. He knows what he's talking about this time."

"This time?" Henry muttered.

Roger's expression softened at Bea's voice. "But I—"

"It's been a long day," Henry said, "and I think it's going to be a long night. Bea needs to rest. We can pick this back up in the morning, figure out a plan then. Also, I don't want you two to go back to Stars Crossing. You're safer here until we figure things out. Roger, stay at your dad's house. Lily can bunk with Irene's team tonight in Sarah's place; I'll send her a message that you'll be coming. All right?"

I glanced at Roger, who seemed confused and frustrated. We nodded.

Henry took a deep breath and turned back toward Bea. "Get some sleep. Try to, at least."

Bea nodded grimly. Roger and I followed Henry out of the medical hut into the dripping forest.

ELEVEN

Sarah's Corner

Henry zipped his coat against the drizzle and pulled up his hood. "Rog, could you show Lily where Sarah's place is? I'm going to round a few people up to keep watch on the perimeter. Just as an extra precaution."

Roger shoved his hands in his pockets. "Sure. You have any idea where my dad went?"

Henry sighed. "No clue. Hopefully, he's up at your place. Otherwise, he just needs some time to cool off."

"You don't think he'd do anything . . . stupid, do you?"

Henry lifted his shoulders. "Honestly? I wouldn't be surprised at anything that hot-headed fool would get himself into. You might find this familiar, but he has a hard time following orders."

Roger's face flushed. "Yeah . . . familiar."

Henry cracked a smile. "Goodnight, you two. We'll talk in the morning."

We watched him walk away into the rain. The darkness of the quiet forest seemed deeper than usual. Drawing our hoods, we headed toward the main village in silence. It was devoid of life except for us, some cooing owls, and the rustling of pine boughs over our heads.

"You doing okay?" Roger asked.

I couldn't see his face, but I didn't need to; the anxiety in his voice spoke volumes.

"I guess. I can't believe that just happened. Poor Bea." I shook my head. "She looked so scared. I just saw her yesterday, and that could've been the last time I ever saw her alive. And if she didn't escape, we never would've had any warning. It's just so . . . unbelievable."

"You saw her yesterday? When?"

"When I was in Giftshop the first time. Margot and I were talking in the study, and she came through. It must've been . . . God, it must've been right before she got the letter from Laura. Right before she got taken."

"Margot was there?"

I cleared my throat. "Yeah. She, uh, she came to find me after you confronted her about training. You didn't need to do that, by the way. I'm not made of glass. I can take a few bumps and bruises."

"Lily, she beat the crap out of you."

"Well, I—that doesn't mean you have to be involved."

"What was I supposed to do? Just stand back and let you get beaten to a pulp?"

"I'm just saying that you don't have to protect me from everything. If I can't learn to defend myself, then that's my fault. Not Margot's."

"Why are you covering for her? You don't even like her."

"Last I checked, I still have the right to change my mind," I snapped.

Things grew quiet.

Something inside me sank. I didn't mean to say it so harshly. It was just so frustrating when he treated me like I couldn't survive without him. I knew he had good intentions, but it didn't make his protective nature any less stifling.

He rubbed his eyes. "Look, let's not talk about this right now. I think we've got enough things to worry about."

We kept walking.

Passing a shed stacked to the brim with wood, Roger headed for a spaced-out grove of cedars. I'd never been on this side of the outpost before. There was only one large treehouse and a few smaller shacks on the ground. The treehouse was out of the ordinary for the outpost, as it was big instead of compact.

Also, it looked like a pirate ship.

The curved wooden hull stared down at us, complete with captain's quarters, crisscrossed rope netting, and long timber masts. Orange-and-yellow lights illuminated the old bubbly windows. Blob shapes of people milled about inside.

"Whoa," I mumbled as we came to a stop. "What is this place?"

"This is Sarah's Corner," he said. "Sarah Simon and her husband Cornelius built it in 1921. They had three sons who enlisted in the army when World War I began. None of them made it back to the States alive."

"That's terrible."

He gestured up at the pirate ship treehouse. "Their boys had a thing for *Swiss Family Robinson*, so Sarah and Cornelius made it as a memorial for them. Over the years, it became a kind of community halfway house."

I craned my neck to see the tops of the masts. An old crow's nest sat on top, a Metatron's Cube flag flapping in the wind. "Wow. It's definitely big enough."

We stood in silence.

Roger took a step back. "I'd better go see if my dad is at the house. See if he can explain any of this. And, you know, make sure he doesn't do something stupid."

I nodded. "Yeah, I guess so. I hope . . . whatever is going on with him, you'll find out soon."

He nodded silently, his eyes flicking back and forth as he stared at the ground.

I nudged his arm. "Hey."

Roger looked up and swallowed. "I'm fine. Just . . ." He returned his eyes to the ground. "Things feel so wrong."

"What do you mean?"

"I feel like everything just got turned upside down, you know? Life was just starting to get back to normal after The Bound, and now . . . Laura is dead. Bea almost died. Everything feels like it's closing in from all sides. I'm—"

His voice faltered. I reached forward and tugged the sleeve of his jacket. He pulled me into a hug. I wrapped my arms around his shoulders and buried my face in his shirt.

"I know," I said. "I'm scared too."

We stood in the rain. Neither one of us seemed to want to let go of the other. Despite everything that had happened, despite my frustrations, being close to him felt so safe. Standing together in the rain created a small bubble of protection from the rest of the world. Maybe if we stood there long enough, the impending danger would pass us by.

Roger finally released me and stepped away. The bubble popped, and I was cold again. "I should go. We both need to get some sleep."

Nodding, I took a step toward the suspended ship. "'Night, Roger."

"Goodnight, Lily."

His footsteps faded away behind me as I strode to the bronze ladder beneath the sturdy wooden railing. Grabbing hold of the slick cold metal, I heaved myself on board and came face-to-face with a large silver button.

Glancing around, I pushed it. A small metal ball dropped from the button and rolled along a track in the wall I hadn't noticed before. It zigzagged down the doorframe until it disappeared behind the wood. A moment later, a series of clanging bells vibrated the boards beneath my feet.

I braced myself against the railing and waited until the shaking stopped. Silence followed shuffling noises and mumbled conversation. The door flung inward. I squinted at the bright yellow light blazing in my face.

"Hey, Chelsea, there *is* someone out here!"

"Well, of *course* there—you just heard the bell! Why do you never listen to me?"

"Because most of the time, you give more information than any human being needs to hear."

"Well, I—!"

"Knock it off, you two," came a familiar voice. My eyes adjusted, and the tall, lean form of Irene stared back at me, her white-blonde hair pulled back into her regular tight braid. She stuck out a hand. "Hello, Lily, glad to see you're well."

Shaking her hand, I blinked a few times against the bright lights. "Thanks, it's good to see you too. Did Henry . . . ?"

She held up her Chatterbox. "Henry sent a message telling me you were coming. Come in, we're just about to have dinner."

She turned to head inside, and I closed the door behind me. A small rolling noise in the doorframe signaled the doorbell mechanism being reset.

"So *you're* the Psychic Wonder Child, eh?"

I jumped back against the door as a raspy voice hissed behind me. I turned around, and the convex end of a long, drooping spyglass hovered in front of my face. The enlarged brown eye inside it twitched before retracting into the hands of a strange-looking man. He sported a long gray beard, an old letterman's jacket, a makeshift eyepatch, and a hat made from some kind of furry animal.

"S-sorry?" I stuttered.

"You're the one who got us out of that pickle in October." He raised the spyglass against his dark eyepatch. Despite it, I could still see the twitching brown eye beneath the glass. "You have a few too many voices inside there, eh? Must get a little noisy sometimes, I'll wager?"

I swallowed. "Uh . . ."

A red-haired, bespectacled man in his twenties pulled on the tail hanging from the bearded man's hat. "Ease off, Snuff. You're gonna give her a heart attack. But yeah"—he squinted at me—"how does that work? Do you just tune into stuff like a radio or what?"

"Oh, for the love of God, you two," came an exasperated voice behind them. It belonged to a petite girl with short blue hair who punched both men in the arm with gusto. They retreated, rubbing their shoulders and mumbling to themselves.

The blue-haired girl smirked and leaned in as if to tell me a secret. "Don't mind them. They've spent too much time away from Earth. Gone a little off the deep end, if you know what I mean."

"Easy for you to say," called another voice from a nearby table. A younger man with a dark complexion and long black hair sat sideways in a cushioned armchair. He had his nose buried in a book, not bothering to look up. "You've skipped out on—what was it now—*three* assignments in the last two months? What do you even *do* when we're gone? Got a secret boyfriend?"

The blue-haired girl flushed. "You're such a—"

"Okay, we're ending this here." Irene stepped forward and rubbed her eyes. "Lily, I'd like you to meet my team. What's left of it, anyway." She gestured to the red-haired man. "This is Jack Longmoor, from Cincinnati, Ohio."

Jack smiled and waved enthusiastically. "Pleasure to meetcha."

"Chelsea Gombarro from Wichita, Kansas."

The blue-haired girl glared sideways at the guy sitting at the table before smiling. "Hiya."

"Nigel Fitzwallace from . . . well, take your pick."

The man with the beard and the eyepatch pulled off his fur hat and swept into a dramatic bow. "Please, call me Snuff."

"And this is Artemus Delgado from Colorado."

The guy reading the book stood and joined the rest of the group, giving a single wave. "Evening."

"Everyone, this is Lily Masters, whom I'm sure you all have probably heard of by now. Be nice to her, and don't ask her to read your mind."

Jack's face fell. "Aw."

Irene waved me forward. "C'mon, let's eat. I'm starving."

The group shuffled across the room as I surveyed the extensive area. The walls tucked into each other in an octagon shape. Hammocks filled the spaces that weren't occupied by tables and chairs, creating little nooks and niches around the room. In the middle of it all was the trunk of a thick pine tree jutted up from beneath the house. It was the base for a spiral staircase leading to the second floor.

I followed a few paces behind the group, listening to the bickering between Jack, Artemus, and Chelsea, with interjections from Snuff.

"So, are you saying that *I'm* the one who got us lost in that Connector?" Artemus raised an eyebrow. "Are you kidding me? You were the one with the map!"

"Just because I had the map doesn't mean I'm solely responsible for every single turn we make," Chelsea huffed.

"Um, yes it does," Jack said. "Otherwise it defeats the purpose of having someone titled *navigator*. You know, with a *map*."

Artemus and Snuff stifled laughs behind their hands as we took our seats at a low-set round dinner table. Seven woven mats and cushions sat on the surrounding floor. Bowls and plates full of food were already on the table, places set for all seven seats.

Chelsea plopped next to Snuff and Irene. "Well, I, for one, think that navigating is a group effort."

Jack and Snuff shared a look. Irene rolled her eyes and smiled covertly at her team. It seemed like this was a regular discussion, and she knew better than to get involved.

"Okay, if that's how you're going to play it." Artemus sat next to me and set *The Mysterious Island* by Jules Verne on the table. "I think we should establish some baseline facts."

"And I believe it would help if you held the map right side up next time, my dear," Snuff added.

Jack and Artemus burst out laughing. Chelsea turned red, letting her blue hair fall into her face.

"All right, that's enough. The food's getting cold," Irene said. Jack and Artemus composed themselves.

"Whose turn is it, anyway?" Chelsea asked, reaching to grab Snuff's and Irene's hands.

"I think it's Artie's. Jack said it last time."

"What? No way! Jack hasn't said it for, like, decades!"

Jack stuck his nose in the air. "That is false, and I won't stand for such slander."

Irene sighed in exasperation. "Fine, I'll say it."

The group joined hands and bowed their heads. Artemus reached out a hand to me. I took it reluctantly. To my right was an empty seat, with Jack on the other side. He rested his palm on the empty place and lowered his head. I watched the small team before closing my eyes. Why were there only five of them? Usually a team of Jumpers consisted of seven people.

Irene cleared her throat, and the entire table became still. "To whatever higher power is listening right now, and for anything that it's worth, we're thankful to make it to this table alive today. We're glad that we can be here, in this moment, for as long as this moment lasts."

She paused and inhaled. "We are thinking of those who are no longer with us, and hope that wherever they are, it's somewhere better than here. And we have reserved all rights to slap them when we see them again for being general idiots. We say all these things to whoever may be listening, and end this nondenominational grace with an amen, or something."

"Amen, or something," echoed the group.

A flash of a thousand memories swept across my eyes. Memories that I'd tried so hard to forget over the last few weeks. Countless dinners just like this one. Countless Gates explored and mapped. Countless days spent together. Laughing, crying, sharing the last food ration or the last drops of water in an inhospitable Otherworld . . . I had lived it before. I had lived and laughed with the people sitting around this very table before. Or rather, Leo had.

Because this had been Leo's team.

And I was the one who killed him.

Twelve

<u>Vague and Unhelpful</u>

"Lily?"

I blinked as the memories faded. Artemus held a ceramic bowl toward me with a spoon stuck in a mound of mashed potatoes. The food on the table had looked good a moment ago. Now the thought of eating anything made me queasy.

"S-sorry, what?" I asked. My throat was dry.

Artemus tilted his head. "I just asked if you wanted some mashed potatoes. You all right?"

I swallowed again and looked back down at the table. "Yeah, I'm f-fine, I just, um . . ." I stood. "I'm sorry, but I'm not really feeling well. I think . . . I think I need to lie down."

The team shared strange looks across the table, and Irene rose. "Sure, I'll show you where you'll be sleeping." She cast a glance at her team and narrowed her eyes. "There better be food on this table when I get back, so help me God."

The remaining occupants at the table raised their hands in defense. I followed Irene to the spiral staircase and tried to swallow away the guilt. It was hard to breathe.

"You all right, Lily?" Irene asked. "Day catching up with you?"

She watched me with such innocent concern. Was it possible that she didn't know how Leo died? Few people knew the full story of how we closed the Tear. Many assumed that he had fallen over the side by accident, and I wasn't about to correct them. But did Leo's old team know that I was the one that dropped him? Did Irene?

I cleared my throat. "I, uh . . . yeah, I guess it is. Sorry, I just . . . I just don't feel well."

"We'll probably be up for a while," she said, "so if you get worse, let me know. We'll get you checked out by a medic."

She started up the stairs. My face flushed with shame. I didn't deserve to be treated with kindness from these people. I opened my mouth to say something, to tell her what happened, but closed it. It was just for a night. I was just staying here for a night. After that I would never have to look any of them in the eye ever again. I would never have to be reminded of the other life still inside my head.

I followed Irene to the second floor. Dark rafters above me were home to a few dozen hammocks slung in neat rows around the octagonal room. Mats, cots, pads, and stacks of pillows sat on the floor. A few of the beds looked well established and had things cluttered about them, while others were neatly made with taut precision. Some people were already asleep on the far side of the room.

Irene shuffled to a cluster of sleeping pads. "Here, you can take this one. Extra blankets are in that trunk over there."

"Thanks, Irene."

"Hope you feel better." She paused at the top of the stairs. "Try not to let what happened tonight get you down. I'm sure whatever happened, we can figure it out in the morning."

Oh, you mean the group of murderers who now have information on the whereabouts of the most powerful book in the world to summon monsters to destroy the planet?

That was extremely comforting.

I faked a smile. "I'm sure you're right. G'night, Irene."

She nodded and headed downstairs.

Dropping the smile, I took a seat on the sleeping pad and put my head in my hands. Taking some deep breaths, I listened to the muffled chatter of Irene, Snuff, Artemus, Jack, and Chelsea. They were fighting again, but this time there were pauses between outbursts. I attributed that to the food.

I shut my eyes tight. There were so many questions swirling around my brain. Legion, the Book of Bones, the events of the night, Roger, Cliff, and now, the resurgence of suffocating guilt. My head pounded. It was hard to breathe.

I needed to get my thoughts together.

I needed to talk to Jerry.

Swallowing the panic that had somewhat dulled over the past few weeks, I felt around the confined darkness until I touched the slimy wall. It was impossibly stretchy, impenetrable, and unyielding. I knew better than to push against it. I closed my eyes against the darkness and stepped away from my body. The twinge of pain in the back of my head was familiar. I blinked until my eyes adjusted to the harsh light.

The orange clouds and indistinct murmurs of the Collective were the same as always. The pod suspended by thousands of tangled threads hung in stasis. In a few minutes, black viscous liquid would fill it, which was the signal for me to wake up in the physical world. Drowning in cold sludge proved a jarring way to awaken, but luckily, I'd gotten better at staying distant in my incorporeal form.

"Welcome back, Miss Masters."

I turned. A man with white hair, matching mustache, square glasses, and a worn tweed jacket nodded at me. He sat behind a large wooden desk covered by open books and strange knickknacks. A squishy red armchair sat across from him, surrounded by towering bookcases. Everything bobbed slightly in the air.

Drifting to the armchair, I took a seat. "Hi, Jerry."

He leafed through a few pages of a worn, spiral-bound manuscript. I never knew why, but he never seemed to devote his full attention to me when I visited. It didn't bother me, because he never had a problem keeping up with the conversation. Most of the time, he was leading it.

"It's been quite some time since we spoke last." He flipped over a plain wooden hourglass, beginning the steady trickle of sand from one level to the next. "What's on your mind, my dear?"

I heaved a sigh and slumped against the chair. "I don't know where to *begin*. There's been so much that's happened." I shook my head. "My parents, defensive training, Margot, Bea, the *Ossabrium*, Legion, Roger, Leo, and just . . . everything. I don't know how to explain everything to myself, let alone you. And after tonight . . . I don't know how any of it is going to turn out. There's too much."

Jerry glanced up from his reading. "Do you remember when you first came here, Miss Masters?"

I blinked. "Um, yeah."

"Do you remember how overwhelmed you felt? How confused, how helpless you were when you first Discovered?"

"Well . . . yes."

"And do you remember how everything seemed lost beyond repair?"

"Yes."

"Why is this situation any different?"

I shifted in my seat. "Because . . . this time we're up against something we can't explain. People have already died. Things feel like they're going to get bad. Really bad. And—"

"Forgive me if I'm wrong—which I'm not—but I believe you're making my point for me."

I looked down at my translucent hands. Taking a deep breath, I looked around at the swirling clouds. The voices that were so consuming when I first came here were now faint whispers. The pounding in my head whenever I listened to the Collective was little by little ebbing away. I was getting better. Slowly, sure, but I was improving.

"What do you know about a book called the *Ossabrium*?" I asked.

Jerry glanced up at me over the rim of his glasses. "Need I remind you that I am merely a construct of your subconscious and the Collective? Asking me questions is no more helpful than asking yourself."

I smiled a little. "I don't think that's completely true. When we first met, you explained things to me that I would have no way of knowing. Most of the time, you give more questions than answers."

"Maybe you're smarter than you think you are."

"Maybe you're more alive than you think you are."

We stared at each other. Jerry closed his fragile manuscript and reached for a new book. "There are some things in your world"—he cracked open the cover and licked his fingers to turn the page—"that have been around since before the beginning of time. This includes what you would call good forces and evil forces and everything that falls in between. They have shifted and changed over time, as most things do, but some . . . some things become corrupted."

"Corrupted?"

"Changed, metamorphosed, transfigured," he supplied. "Things that—while could have been created with the best of intentions—are now nothing more than instruments of destruction. The Book of Bones is one of those objects. Its very existence infects those around it."

"What do you mean? Who created it?"

He shot me a look.

"Right." I sighed. "If I want a specific answer, 'listen for it.' But what do you mean, created with the best of intentions? What else was it used for? What does it do?"

Jerry stared at the edge of the desk before putting his book down. "Miss Masters, do you have any idea what beings exist outside of your realm?"

"Well . . . besides The Bound and some creatures I've seen in the Otherworlds, I—"

"No," he said. "Those beings exist in your plane of reality. Do you know of what lives *outside* it?"

"Outside my . . . reality?"

"Things that use creatures like The Bound as foot servants. Ancient beings that influence your world. Places that defy meaning, hidden away in plain sight. They house things that have been whispering to humanity through the cracks in their minds longer than life itself."

My stomach had a strange sinking sensation.

Jerry gave me a level stare. "Something . . ."

"Old," I finished.

The voices of the Collective hushed. The clouds darkened as if a shadow had passed above us.

"That . . . that voice I heard before at the outpost," I said. "I remember now. It . . . it said . . ." I trailed off and looked at my hands.

"Yes, Miss Masters?"

I looked up. "It said it had answers to my questions. It said it knew my mind. It told me to find it."

"Do you wish to?"

"What? No! I'm not stupid enough to follow a voice in my head!"

"Again, correct me if I'm wrong—which I'm not—but I believe you're doing that very thing right now."

I sank lower in my chair and sighed. I hated it when he was right.

"There are creatures, and people, for that matter," he said, "who may have answers to the questions you seek. What are those answers worth to you? Are they really that important?"

I squirmed in my seat. I *did* have a lot of questions, if not about the events happening around me, about mysteries inside myself. Why could I hear the Collective, and why did it surface only a month and a half ago? Why did I have these abilities? What was I supposed to do with them? Where was it all taking me?

Whoever spoke to me at the sparring ring obviously knew something. Otherwise, why reach out to me? Maybe whoever, or whatever, it was had some answers. Maybe they could help me figure out who I was. What could be harmed by that?

Besides, the thought of giving up an opportunity for answers scared me more than the unknown.

"Tell me, how are things between you and Roger?" Jerry asked. "You listed him as a catalyst of your anxiety."

I leaned on the armchair. "He's not really, I just . . . I dunno. Things have been weird in the last few days, I guess."

"Why is that?"

"We just . . . I started combat training with Margot, and that's thrown everything out of balance."

"And?" he prompted.

I huffed a breath through my nose. "He just . . . It's frustrating when he treats me like I can't survive without him. It's like he feels responsible for keeping me alive, even after we closed the Tear. Maybe that's the only reason he sticks around. I guess that worries me."

"Why?"

"I don't want to feel like that. I don't want him to feel like that, either."

"Consider his view of things," he said. "He's grown up knowing the effect of loss in his own family. Perhaps he's afraid of adding you to the list."

I tilted my head. "What do you know about Roger's mom? Cliff never talks about her, and no one else wants to mention the fact that she existed. What happened to her?"

Jerry glanced over at the hourglass that was now almost empty. "I believe we have discussed enough matters for now, Miss Masters."

"Wait, but there's so much that—"

"And as always, your questions know no end. Unfortunately for you, and fortunately for me, time exists in your world, so we'll have to reschedule this chat for later."

Frowning, I slumped back against my armchair.

Jerry closed his book and leaned on crossed elbows. "When you wake, tread carefully. Dark times are coming, Miss Masters. As bad as things seem now, rest assured they can always get worse. Which brings us to my last piece of advice."

"Which is?"

"Don't die."

Thirteen

Accident

"Miss? Excuse me, miss?"

The pounding in my head began as soon as I was awake. My eyes didn't want to open, but something prodded my shoulder.

"Miss?"

Squinting at the bright light, I blinked at the figure leaning over me. She wore a strange ensemble of a loose white button-down shirt, a gray vest, slacks, and hiking boots. Dark curls were piled atop her thin face. Clear green eyes peered at me with concern.

"Are you all right?" she asked. "You were tossing in your sleep."

I sat up and cleared my throat. As always, after visiting Jerry, I felt like I hadn't slept at all. The large octagonal room was lighter than it had been when I went to sleep, the many bunk beds and hammocks vacant.

"I'm fine, thanks," I said. "Just . . . had some weird dreams."

She flashed a sympathetic smile. "I understand. Some demons only show themselves in the night." She held out a hand to me to help me up. I took it. "What's your name, miss? I don't believe we've met before."

"Lily. What's yours?"

"Adeline, but you may call me Addy. Everyone in this time seems to be much less formal than I am accustomed to." She shrugged and smirked. "I can't say I mind terribly, however."

"This time? What're you—oh!" I realized. "You're one of the people taken by The Bound, right? You came through with that other guy. What was his name? Nicholas?"

Her eyes brightened. "You've met Nick?"

"Briefly," I said. "We had a very . . . interesting introduction."

She smiled and gave a light musical laugh. "Don't judge him too harshly. He is adapting to the situation quite well under the circumstances." She nodded over her shoulder. "A young man is inquiring about you at the front door, which is why I woke you."

Nodding, I rubbed my neck and tried my best to clear my head. Roger must've come for me. We had to figure out a plan to fix . . . well, everything.

I tugged on my shoes and jacket. "Thanks for waking me up. I have to go, but it was nice meeting you."

Adeline smiled warmly. "The pleasure was mine. Good luck, Lily, and try not to get stuck on the events of last night. I am sure that whatever it was, it will resolve itself soon."

I swallowed and faked a smile. "Yeah, sure. Till again, Addy."

I hurried down the spiral staircase to the lower floor. Irene's team was nowhere to be seen, and I breathed a sigh of relief.

When I opened the door, Roger wasn't the one standing behind it. Carl smiled and gave an awkward wave.

I glanced around, but he was the only one there. "Um, hi, Carl."

"Hullo," he said, fixing his glasses. "Rog asked me to come get you. He's with the others on the west side of town."

"Oh, okay." I nodded and looked around again. "Um, where's that?"

He gestured for me to follow. "C'mon, I'll show you."

I followed him down the ladder and back onto the forest floor. The morning was gray and cold, but it hadn't started raining yet. Given the pattern of the last few weeks, I wasn't holding out hope for that trend to continue.

"You sleep all right?" Carl asked, stepping on a trail I'd never taken before. "Irene said you weren't feeling well."

I looked down. "I'm fine. Just tired. How are you doing after last night?"

He shrugged. "Fine, just another day at the outpost. Always crazy shit happening."

"How long have you lived here?"

"Pretty much my whole life. They send you to public schools out of state when you're a kid, so you get a somewhat normal education. Besides that, this is home."

"Is that where you met Roger? At school?"

Carl let out a laugh. "Not exactly."

He took a right on the trail. The vague outline of the main village was barely visible through the trees and fog. "We met in training when I was about seven. I got stuck on a rope course one day, and absolutely refused to continue. Rog tried to talk me down, but I wasn't budging. So he climbed up there with me, got stuck too, and we had to wait for the adults to get the ladder. When I asked him why he got stuck too, he just shrugged and said, 'Now you don't have to be stuck alone.'"

I smiled. "Aw."

"After that, we made a pact to watch each other's backs through thick and thin. I guess it stuck all these years. Which is good, because—"

He broke off. A few yards ahead, a figure stooped over a large supply box. Margot pulled out two heavy clunking sacks and heaved them over her shoulder. She wobbled at the weight before regaining her balance.

Carl seemed to lose any ability to speak or move.

I waved a hand in front of his face. "Uh, Carl?"

His face flushed pink. "What? I was just looking at the new supply boxes, that's all. I wasn't even looking at her."

"I never said you were."

His face darkened to a deeper shade of red.

Margot turned when she heard voices and spotted me. Dropping the heavy sacks with a *chunk*, she strode over.

"Hey, flower girl," she said, crossing her arms. "You're late. I was waiting around for you forever. We're practicing with proper weapons today. I'm calling the mace."

I swallowed. Suddenly, planning to stop a group of ruthless murderers seemed less terrible than it did a minute ago.

"Uh, sorry, Margot," I said. "But I have to skip training today."

"What? Why? And where is everybody?" her eyes swept around the woods and then back to me. "Why do you look like shit?"

I ignored that comment. "Didn't you hear what happened last night?"

"What're you talking about?"

Carl and I shared a look.

"They're waiting for you, Lily," he mumbled.

"Wait, what happened last night?" Margot asked.

My eyes flicked to the sacks on the ground.

"Hey, Carl," I said. "Why don't you help Margot to the sparring ring? You can explain while I get to the others."

Carl's eyes widened. "Well, I mean . . . you don't know where to go."

"I'm sure I can find it," I assured him and glanced over at Margot. "Okay?"

She shrugged. "Fine. I was dreading having to carry these across town, anyway."

I turned to Carl and raised an eyebrow.

He moved his mouth a few times before any sound came out. He pointed down the trail. "Um, just head that way until you get to a blue painted woodshed. They're in the supply cabin near Rog's house. Do you know where that is?"

I nodded. I'd never been inside, but Roger had pointed it out to me before.

"Rog may still be at his house if you wanted to check there first," he added. "He was still getting ready when I left."

Margot dragged a large sack over to Carl and handed it to him. "All right, *andiamo*. You can fill me in on the way."

He lifted the sack onto his shoulders with surprising ease. I started on the trail and glanced behind me.

"Your name's Carl, right?" Margot asked. "I think you live across from my host house. In that big redwood cluster?"

He fumbled with the bag. "Y-yeah. Yeah, that's me. Um, how are you liking town so far?"

I smiled and turned away as their conversation went out of earshot. I hoped for Carl's sake his puppy dog eyes weren't as noticeable to Margot as they were to me.

Walking through the quiet village, I looked for the blue woodshed Carl had mentioned. Before I could find that, I spotted Roger's house high above me. I glanced at the still town, stopping myself before I called up the ladder. By the lack of sound, people were still sleeping. I didn't need to add "rudeness" to my list of grievances with the Northwestern community.

Sighing, I grabbed the smooth rungs of the old ladder and climbed. Unlike other homes closer to the ground, Roger's house was set high in the branches of a sturdy Douglas fir. The time-consuming climb was one reason it had stayed empty during Cliff's absence.

I pulled myself onto the weather-worn deck surrounding the small hut.

"Rog, you up here?" I called.

Hearing nothing, I knocked on the closed door. Nothing. The door squeaked as I eased it open.

"Roger?"

A small kitchenette sat in front of the door. Its chunky, messily carved frame betrayed that it had been made by hand. Similarly built shelves and bookcases lined the small room, two cots pushed against opposite walls. The right bed looked unused, while a conglomeration of photos, paper stubs, and children's drawings surrounded the left cot. A nightstand sat against the wall between them.

Roger must already be with the others. I was hoping to have a minute in private to apologize for snapping at him last night, but it would have to wait until later. Turning back to the ladder, I paused. Something flashed in the corner of my eye.

Looking around at the deserted village, I stepped inside the dark house. Walking to the nightstand, I blinked as my eyes adjusted. The glint came again. It was a ring. The faint light from the open door danced in rainbow waves inside the small round diamond. It sat quietly on an overturned Polaroid photo, reflections warbling in the black plastic backing.

I reached to turn over the picture. My fingers brushed up against the delicate gold band. Ruffling static consumed my head. I slumped forward as everything faded to a large, fuzzy black circle.

Sunlight filtered through the dirty windshield as the cramped car sped down the freeway. Four people rode without conversation. The buzz of the poorly tuned radio filled the silence.

The man and the woman in the backseat sat close together. The woman leaned her head on the man's chest as their grasped hands tapped along to the beat of the music.

"How many dead, Ed?" asked the man in the passenger's seat.

The driver shrugged, accelerating to go around a semi. Police cars barred entry to most exits. "I dunno yet. From the sound of it, more than they wanted to tell me. Most civilians have evacuated from the surrounding area, but there's a few of the attackers left. They're not going down easy."

"Any clue how long we'll be?" asked the man in the back. "We gotta get back to Rog before tonight. I don't think Rhonda'll like us being out for an all-nighter again."

"Your guess is as good as mine, Cliff," Ed said, "but don't worry, we'll keep Amy out here and let you get back."

"I like that idea," said the woman, nuzzling against the man's shoulder. "We'll let you be the one who has to stay up all night with Rog this time. See how you like it."

The car chuckled collectively, and the man in the backseat gave a playful scowl. "You didn't need to come today, you know. You were more than welcome to stay home. Alone, and bored, with our screaming one-year-old."

The woman smiled and twisted up to give a lasting kiss.

The man in the passenger seat groaned loudly. "Ugh. I would've thought that being married would make you two less insufferable. Get a room."

"Shut up, Harold," they retorted in unison.

After taking an unblocked exit, the car rolled to a stop in a dirty back street alley littered with trash. The crew shuffled out of the car and sidled against the wall as a group of people waving assault rifles ran by. The din of helicopters and wailing sirens followed distant shouts and gunfire. Flames rose from a nearby building and screams fluctuated in and out of range. The air smelled of burned plastic and smoke.

Ed checked the edge of the alley. "Okay, everyone on alert. Henry's team is inside already. We need to make sure nobody slips through the cracks. Cliff and I will clear the sewer."

"Aw, what?" Cliff complained. "Why doesn't Harold take the sewer?"

"Because Harold passed me the ketchup yesterday when you were too busy eating pie," Ed said dryly. "Harold, try to get in contact with Henry's team first. Let them know we're here, then do a perimeter check. Amy, you can take the north exit. Stay out of sight. This is recon only."

Amy rolled her eyes. "Ed, c'mon, it'll be faster if I just—"

Ed gave her a level stare. "You will not engage with these people, do you understand? I don't know who they are, or what they want, but they obviously don't have a problem killing people that get in their way. Just keep a low profile."

Harold and Cliff nodded. Amy heaved a begrudging sigh.

"Let's move," Ed said, breaking away and crossing to lift a grimy metal grate.

"Hey," Cliff said, pulling the woman into a tight embrace. "Be safe out there. Call if you need me?"

She snickered. "You wish."

There was a screeching of metal. Ed stepped onto the top rung of the ladder leading to the sewer. "Cliff, let's go."

Amy pulled away and pushed him toward the grate. "See you later, loser."

She jogged down the alley, leaving the man staring longingly after her.

"Harold's right," Ed said, smirking. "You two really are insufferable."

Cliff sighed with a small smile. "That's okay with me."

Ed descended the ladder. "All right, lover boy, get down here."

Cliff gave another, much different, sigh.

At the end of the alleyway, the woman crouched behind a large water drum. She ducked deeper into the shadows as a helicopter passed overhead. The flames from the next building were dying down, but a new pyre had been set ablaze next to it. She kicked some trash while tapping the edge of the leather bracers buckled to her forearms. Her blue eyes darted around the alley as she shifted her weight from foot to foot.

Screams echoed behind the door to the building. Three quick bangs preceded the metal hinges screeching open. The woman jumped out of sight.

A bald man with waxy skin and a branded scalp stepped into the sunlight, his clothes and face splattered with blood. The gun clenched in his fist was still smoking. He strode toward the adjoining warehouse across the alley, unscrewing the silencer from his weapon. The black circle tattoo on the back of his neck was barely visible above his collar.

The woman watched him go, hesitating. Shaking her head, she tailed him to the warehouse door, boosting herself through a broken window and creeping along a rusty metal beam above him. The man stopped and raised his wrist to fiddle with a watch-like device. Taking a few deep breaths, the woman crouched, holding out her arms and forming two large pink-colored shields. They hovered over the backs of her leather bracers.

The man's head tilted as she dropped, but he didn't move fast enough. A shield slammed into his back. He stumbled, shifting to block her foot, swinging into his knee. He grabbed her leg and wrenched it to the side. The woman yelled through gritted teeth as she hit the ground. Rolling, she blocked another few hits before raising a pink shield.

It didn't stop the bullet.

The shot echoed violently through the warehouse. Her arms clutched her stomach, a scream silenced by shock and pain. The man waited as she tried to stand, failing and falling to her knees. She looked down at her hands. Red. Blood spread across her shirt.

"You lot will never learn, will you?" the man said, reloading a full magazine into his gun with a snap.

The woman wheezed a few labored breaths. Rose-colored light flickered around the bracers feebly, but the shields did not appear. Blinking a few times, she tipped forward.

The man grabbed her shoulder, stopping her from hitting the ground. He wiped some blood leaking from his nose and smiled. "You're not half bad, you know. We could use someone like you. Do you want a chance to make a difference? A real difference?"

He leaned down and looked into her eyes. They struggled to focus. "Join our Master. He will protect you. He will provide for you. Follow Him, and we can make this world a better place for those who know who to put their faith in. Only the strong will survive the rise."

Her eyes focused on his. She spat in his face.

Wiping away the spittle with the back of his hand, he shrugged. Cocking the gun, he pointed it at the woman. Her eyes widened.

"Shame," he said. "What a waste."

The woman looked down at the ring glinting on her finger and clenched her fists. She closed her eyes.

A figure barreled through the door on the other side of the warehouse. Spotting the woman on the ground, he sprinted toward her.

"Amy!" he screamed.

BANG.

I stumbled away from the nightstand. The ring tipped onto the floor, rolling to a stop at the door as my knees gave out. Tears streamed down my face. My heart pounded so hard it hurt.

"It's rude to snoop through someone's house," came a voice to my left.

I scrambled to my feet. Cliff stood in the doorway, staring at me. The pain in his eyes was hard to look at. He knew. He knew what I saw. I backed against the wall.

"I-I wasn't—I was looking for Rog," I stammered. "It . . . it was an accident—I'm s-so—"

Cliff's gaze dropped to the ground, his arms hanging limp at his sides.

"Get out," he whispered.

I tripped running out the door, failing to hold back a sob that didn't belong to me.

Fourteen

Something New

I sat down hard behind the blue painted woodshed and covered my mouth with my hands.

Trying to stop shaking was useless. I rocked back and forth on the wet ground until my head stopped spinning. A drop of water splattered against my face. Others followed it. Staggered *drip-drips* filled the forest. Thankfully, they carried no warnings of static.

The memory of the cemetery when The Bound tried to recruit me played itself over and over. The simple gravestone and the words *Amelia J. Owens, Beloved Wife and Mother* engraved onto it. Roger had told me she'd died in some kind of accident, but that was a lie, and he didn't even know. It seemed so *wrong* that I now knew more about his own mother than he did. I now understood Henry and Bea's reluctance to tell him last night.

I couldn't get Cliff's scream out of my head.

Glancing through the rain, I spotted the cabin Carl had mentioned and stood on shaky legs. Through the cabin windows, Henry, Bea, Irene and her team, and a few others milled around. Roger shuffled into view and leaned over a table, pointing at something. I'd never noticed it before, but it was so *unnerving* how much he looked like Cliff. Now I recognized features of his mom too. They had the same nose. Their eyes crinkled the same way when they smiled.

I wiped my face. The pain from the memory stabbed through me like an icicle, but curling into a ball behind the woodshed wouldn't help anything. Walking up to the door, I took a few deep breaths and pushed it open.

No one noticed I entered, all engrossed in discussing the papers littering the table. Laura's plentiful research notes had been printed out and piled into messy stacks.

"They're not numerically based, are they?" Irene asked, holding a few sheets in her hands.

Jack shook his head. "I wouldn't think so. Unless she used three separate ciphers for each note she took. Meaning she'd have to put them from letters to numbers, then back to letters again. I mean"—he shrugged and sat down on a stool—"it's not completely out of the question. But knowing Laura, it's not likely."

"I agree," Henry said. "I think we were on the right track with quick coders rather than detailed encryptions. Something she could remember while taking notes."

The group continued their discussion. Roger crossed his arms, leaning against the wall. He seemed tired. It didn't look like he got much sleep last night, either. I couldn't get my feet to move toward him.

He looked over at the door and spotted me. Glancing back at the table, he shuffled behind Chelsea.

"Hey," he said, "I was wondering where you were. Didn't Carl come to get you?"

"Ye—" My voice was gone. I cleared my throat. It hurt. "Yeah, he did. I just took a wrong turn on the way over here."

He tilted his head. "You all right? Irene said you went to bed early last night."

I looked into his brown eyes and couldn't speak. They were so full of kindness and trust. I wanted to tell him. I wanted to tell him everything I just saw. The words wouldn't come.

I faked a smile instead. "I'm fine."

He frowned. "You sure? You look pale. Are you getting a fever?"

He reached up to feel my forehead. My eyes locked onto the leather bracers on his forearms. The same bracers his mother wore when she was murdered. My stomach lurched. I jolted away, knocking a nearby coatrack into the wall.

The clamor caused the group to turn around.

"Morning, Lily," Henry said, turning back to the table. "Glad you could stop by."

"S-sorry," I mumbled.

They went back to discussing possible codes. I felt Roger's eyes on the side of my face. Guilt twisted my insides. I wished the floor would swallow me whole.

"Right, so we're fairly certain that these notes are all the same encryption method?" Artemus clarified. "They don't look like a mix to me."

"Nor to me," Snuff agreed.

"It almost looks like we could use a Vigenère cipher," Chelsea said, "but we'd need a keyword or phrase to make that work."

"Nah, that'd be too simple," Artemus said. "A fifth grader with a notepad could break that. But looking at the number of repeating letters, it looks like it could be a polyalphabetic substitution cipher, maybe just in reverse. Then again, we'd need a keyword to make that work, too."

"How long does it have to be?" Henry asked.

Artemus shrugged. "It depends. Anything over three letters could fit. The length just makes it more difficult to decode. Here . . ."

He flipped through a nearby book and started explaining something about numbers and keywords. Static ruffled past my ears. A sharp pain stabbed through my skull. I swayed on my feet and tried to catch the words floating past me, but I couldn't. The pain was too intense. My vision pulsed red and black. Something caught me as I fell over, but every sensation was numb. Distant. Disjointed.

An unfamiliar voice broke through the pain, one I'd never heard before. Unlike the voice at the sparring ring, this one was human. It came from inside my head. Deep inside. It seemed almost a part of me. Something different.

Something new.

"*Lighthouse,*" it whispered. "*The keyword is 'lighthouse.' Come find me, Lily. We were meant to find each other. I have the answers. He has the answers.*"

I coughed. My mouth tasted metallic. The pounding in my head lessened.

"Is she all right?"

"I dunno, she just passed out."

"She's shaking. Does she have a fever?"

"I think she's accessing the Collective. What do you think, Bea?"

"Maybe, but—oh, she's waking up."

My eyes fluttered open. Everything was fuzzy. "Lighthouse," I slurred. "The keyword is 'lighthouse.'"

I tried to move, but something held me still. Blinking, I saw Roger's blurry face. We had crumpled onto the ground; the group huddled around us. I coughed and sat up. Roger held a hand against my back to steady me.

"What did you say, Lily?" Henry asked.

My head throbbed. "I-I think the keyword is 'lighthouse.' That's what you're looking for, right?"

"Did you just access the Collective?" Bea asked. "You rarely pass out like that."

I shrugged. Something warm dripped down my face. I reached up a hand to my nose and my fingers came away streaked with blood.

"Jesus, Lily, you're bleeding," Roger said.

I shifted to my knees. "I'm all right, I just —"

I winced again as my head flashed with pain. Blood dripped to the floor as static haunted my ears.

"*Find . . . me . . .*"

I shut my eyes tight.

"Hey," Artemus said, "it worked. The keyword worked. She's right."

"Roger, take her to the medical building," Henry said. "We'll get working on the codes, see what we can glean from them."

Roger nodded and helped me stand, grabbing a few napkins that Snuff passed to him. He pushed them into my hands and steered me out the door, keeping a hand firmly under my arm.

We walked through the rain in silence, shuffling into the small cabin where Bea had slept last night. From the sharp smell of disinfectant, someone had already cleaned it.

Roger flipped on the overhead light and walked me to the table. "Here, sit down a minute."

Cupping the handful of napkins under my nose, I lowered myself onto the bed and closed my eyes against the pain in my head. The blaring lights above made it sharper.

"Could you turn the lights off?" I asked. "It hurts."

The light beyond my eyelids shut off immediately. I heard some crinkling of paper and cracked open my eyes.

Roger peered at me through the dim light. He seemed to want to say something but stopped himself and handed me some new tissues. "Pinch your nose and lean over. It should stop in a few minutes."

I nodded and did as I was told. My head hurt less now that the lights were off, but I was still shaking.

"What's going on?" he asked. "You haven't passed out like this since you Discovered."

I shrugged and looked away. "I don't know."

"You do, I know you do. I'm not an idiot, Lily. I know something's up." He shook his head. "You look like you're getting sick. Why do you keep blowing it off?"

"Well, maybe I am getting sick," I mumbled. "Maybe that's all this is."

I leaned forward and breathed through my mouth. Roger rubbed his eyes and sat down on a few overturned plastic crates, staring at the ground. Guilt spread through my entire body, and I tried to focus on how much my head hurt.

"Have you eaten today?" he asked.

"No."

"When's the last time you ate?"

"I dunno, yesterday sometime? I can't really remember," I said. Everything past last night's events seemed fuzzy. The closest thing I could remember was pudding with Margot in New York. That seemed like ages ago now.

Roger rummaged through some plastic bins in the cabinet and pulled out a protein bar. "Here. It's not much, but at least it's something."

I took it and set it aside while keeping the napkins against my nose. The thought of eating anything made me want to vomit.

"You really need to eat something," he insisted.

"I don't think I can right now."

A few minutes later, I pulled the napkins away. My nose wasn't bleeding anymore, at least. I took the face wipe Roger handed me to clean myself up.

I stood slowly. "Thanks. We should get back to the others."

"Hang on, you need to sit for another few minutes so it doesn't start bleeding again."

I shook my head. "No, I'm fine, we can just—"

"Lily, please." He sighed. "Do me a favor and don't argue right now. Okay? Just not right now."

I sat back down again and tried to keep my hands from shaking. Usually, after accessing the Collective, the shaking went away after a few minutes. Now it only seemed to be getting worse.

Roger dug out a blanket underneath the exam table and wrapped it around my shoulders. Sitting on the table, he tried to look at me. I let my hair fall in front of my face.

"Listen," he said, "I know that things have been . . . tense. For everyone. But if something's going on, you need to talk to me."

I glanced at him.

"What happened back there?" he asked. "I know you heard something. Was it something bad?"

Shutting my eyes, I hunched further into the blanket.

Roger put a hand on my wrist and squeezed gently. "Lil."

I opened my eyes and tried to fight the tears swimming around my vision. Through them, I could see the kindness in his gaze. The honest concern. It was almost too much, and the guilt gnawing at my insides stabbed again. How could I tell him about anything? How could I explain that I'd just watched his mother die, and I heard voices that weren't the Collective? How could I explain the horrible need to find out what those voices had to say? I didn't even know where to begin.

The silver light from the small window was gentler than the harsh fluorescent bulb above us. Roger sat close, his hand on my wrist warm and familiar. I hadn't noticed how cold I'd gotten, even with the blanket wrapped around me. I blinked away the tears as the pounding in my head dulled.

"You can tell me, whatever it is," he said. "What's going on?"

I swallowed. "I—"

The door to the medical building squeaked open, and Henry, Bea, and Cliff walked in. Cliff and I made eye contact for a moment before I looked away.

"Are you feeling better?" Henry asked me.

"Yeah," I mumbled.

Roger stood. "What's up? I thought the plan was to meet back when you guys were done decoding."

Bea held up a stack of papers. "We are. Turns out Artemus from Irene's team is a whiz with codes. We had enough information to start searching around for ourselves. These aren't all of them. They're still working on the rest. But, well"—she glanced sideways—"things just got slightly more complicated."

"*More* complicated?" Roger's jaw dropped. "How could things get any *more* complicated?"

Henry held up a paper with a detailed floor map of a very large, very complex series of buildings.

"Well, for starters," he said, "Legion is going to rob the Vatican. Tomorrow."

Fifteen

A Brief History of Bad Luck

"They're going to *what*?"

Bea eased herself into a nearby chair. She tugged at the bandages encasing her head and sighed. "From what we've pieced together, I'm afraid so."

"But . . . but *why*?" I asked. "What do they have to gain from that? What could be in the Vatican that . . ." I trailed off. My eyes widened. "The book is there, isn't it?"

Solemnly, Henry and Bea nodded.

"How is that even possible?" Roger asked. "How could something that . . . notorious wind up in a museum after thousands of years? How did they get it?"

"Now that"—Bea sighed—"is a very long story. Laura did a lot of digging."

"As far as we could tell from her research notes," Henry said, "the book wound up in a bookshop in Cairo. How long it was there, we don't know. Some curio collector named Alfonse Strauss bought it in the early nineties along with a few other artifacts."

"Did he know what it was?" I asked.

"I doubt it." Henry rubbed the back of his neck. "He must've gotten quite the surprise when his entire collection mysteriously caught fire in the middle of the night. The book was counted as destroyed with the rest of Strauss's inventory. Three weeks later, Strauss was found dead in his home with three bullets stuck in his chest." He inhaled slowly. "This happened a few months before the events of Los Angeles."

Cliff, who had been standing silently against the back wall, glanced up at me. We held eye contact before his eyes shifted over to Roger, observing his son's face. His gaze traveled back to the floor.

"Wait, so did Legion go after Strauss?" Roger asked. "Is that who killed him?"

"Most likely," Henry said. "They must've caught wind that he had it, and got there a little too late. The book was gone when they got there, so they cleaned up their trail."

"So, where did it go? The book, I mean," I asked. "Obviously it didn't burn."

"That's where Laura hit a dead end too." Henry sighed. "For almost a decade, there was no evidence that it survived the fire. Until it showed up again."

"Where?"

"Boston, 1996. Two students were found dead outside their apartment after attending a rare book exhibition," Henry said. "Rumor has it that an unprocessed book was taken from storage. The two allegedly stole the book and planned to sell it for tuition money. The next morning, they were found steps from their apartment, where they both died of simultaneous pulmonary embolisms. They were nineteen."

"After that, the sightings became more frequent, and even more bizarre," Bea said, shaking her head. "In 2003, a group of fishermen off the coast of Chile recovered a life raft, carrying three passengers and a single unopened metal box. The box contained a strange book. The passengers were dead, all mummified where they sat.

"In 2008 a military rescue team went unresponsive after conducting a search operation at a research base in Antarctica. Six months later, they were found with the inhabitants of the base. Their cause of death was spontaneous combustion. The book was recovered from the base and taken to Europe. I believe the Catholic church acquired the *Ossabrium* not long after."

I put a hand to my head. "Okay wait, is someone doing these horrible things to people? Is this Legion?"

"It's the book," came a quiet voice from the back. Cliff had finally spoken, his gaze fixed to the floor. "The book is responsible for all those things. People who've tried to read it end up dead. Even just coming into contact with it can kill you. It's powerful. It's evil. It's why Legion wants it. I'm sure they believe they can harness the power to take over the world, and they believe they can summon . . . something to do it for them."

Something clicked in my memory. "They said Him . . ."

"What was that, Lily?" Bea asked.

A flash of pain flared in my head again, but I ignored it. "They . . . I remember them saying the word *Him*, but like they were talking about a specific person. It's not just any random monster they're trying to summon, they're trying to bring someone back. Or . . . something."

"How do you know this?" Roger asked.

"I—um, Jerry mentioned it last time I saw him," I mumbled. "He, uh, also mentioned something odd about the *Ossabrium*."

"Like what?"

"He said there were things in this world that have become corrupted over time," I said. "And that the *Ossabrium* might've once been something that was created with good intentions. I'm not sure what that means, but that's what he said."

Henry nodded slowly. "Anything else?"

I shrugged. "Just confusing riddles, like always. He said there were creatures outside this realm that are . . . more real than we think. That some things have been here for a long time, hidden. Not just creatures, but places, too. Places that have been buried, locked away in plain sight. Things that are just . . ." I glanced at Roger. "Old."

"Laura mentioned something like that in her notes. A place buried or hidden," Bea said, shuffling through some papers. "She must've been more interested in Lovecraftian lore than we thought, because she cites more of his works than any other research source. Yes, here it is." She held up a paper and glanced at the corresponding decoded notes. "Lovecraft called his fictional take on the hidden realms 'R'lyeh,' which is a kind of lost prison said to hold the Great Old Ones."

"Great Old Ones?"

"Also called Elder Gods. They were fictional deities who once controlled Earth and the cosmos but dropped into hibernation. Imagine them like a pantheon of gods to an extent, like Greek and Roman theology," Henry said. "They were powerful, with devout followings of demons, dark creatures, and—"

"You mean . . . like the monsters in the Book of Bones?" Roger said.

We became quiet.

"Oh my God," Bea muttered. "That's what they're trying to summon. They're trying to wake one of them up."

"Wait, but they're just fiction," I said. "Sure, Lovecraft had some background in the Otherworlds, but that doesn't mean that these creatures actually exist."

"Lily has a point," Roger agreed. "Not all of his work was based in fact. A lot of it was just imagination, right? Besides, how would he even know about beings like that? Who told him?"

My insides wriggled silently as Jerry's words echoed back to me.

"*Things that use creatures like The Bound as foot servants. Ancient beings that influence your world . . . things that have been whispering to humanity through the cracks in their minds longer than life itself.*"

"But the pieces fit," Henry said. "It would make sense why they used the term *Him* and why they've been after the book for years, maybe centuries. And it explains why . . ." He broke off and closed his eyes. "Oh God. It explains the attack in LA."

"What do you—" Bea gasped. "Wait, the Tillinghast Papers? *That's* what they were after?"

"It must've been," he said. "Everything else stolen was just random specimens. No one thought much of the Tillinghast Papers going missing, because no one knew what they were for. I guess . . . I guess we do now. Or at least, what they correlate to."

"What were the Tillinghast Papers?" I asked.

"Journals recovered from a shipwreck in Greece in the late eighties," Bea said. Her hands shook as she leaned against the cabinet. "They were strange. They mentioned some mechanical device, possibly related to the Otherworlds. We put it in one of our facilities for safekeeping. I almost forgot they existed."

"Me too," Henry agreed. "Which was probably how Legion wanted it to be. It was something so insignificant that no one really paid it any mind. We were more concerned about cleaning up the destruction they left behind."

"So apparently they had something to do with . . . all of this," Roger said.

"Apparently," Henry mumbled.

"And . . ." I began, "whatever was written in the Tillinghast Papers gave Legion some kind of information about the *Ossabrium*?"

"It had to," Bea said. "Otherwise, why risk so much to go after it?"

"Do we have copies of these papers?" Roger asked. "I mean, c'mon, we document everything. We have to have something."

"It's possible," Henry said, "but they were recovered back in the eighties. A lot of stuff was hand filed. Any copies are sure to be buried pretty deep."

"But if they . . ." I shook my head. "I don't understand. If they already had some kind of information about the book, why didn't they go after it then? Why have they been dormant all this time?"

"I don't think they've been dormant." Henry shook his head. "From the sound of it, they've been waiting. I think they've been planning on this for years, just biding their time until the right opportunity."

"But *what* was the opportunity?" Roger leaned against the table. "What happened that suddenly made them mobile again?"

The room fell quiet again, as no one could think of an answer.

"What do we do now?" I asked. "They're going to rob the Vatican. Tomorrow. What are we supposed to do about that?"

"Well, we can't let them get the book by any means," Cliff said, uncrossing his arms. "You heard Laura. No matter what happens next, we can't allow them to summon whatever demon they worship."

"Which begs another question," Henry said. "Which Elder Being are they trying to wake up?"

"Wait, they're supposed to be gods or something, right? How many could there be?" I asked in disbelief.

"Mentioned in the mythos? Over a hundred and fifty."

Roger's jaw dropped. "*A hundred and fifty? Are you kidding me?*"

Henry chuckled darkly. "I wish. If it's any consolation, most of them are probably fiction. But I'm willing to bet that some are real."

"That's not any consolation at all!" Roger sat back down on the exam table and leaned on his knees. "We are so screwed."

"The important thing is that we know where they're going to be," Cliff said. "We go to Rome. We stop them before this escalates further. We weed them out of their hiding spot and end them once and for all."

"How do we do that?" I asked.

"We get the book before they do."

"So . . . we steal it before they can?" Roger blew a breath through his teeth. "I dunno. That sounds risky. Maybe a little too risky. The Vatican Archives aren't a joke. They've got some of the most advanced security on Earth. Even with our connections, we could risk exposure."

"So we do it when security is lower," Cliff said. "We do it tomorrow. We do it when they were planning to, tomorrow night."

"But . . . we don't even know what Legion's plans are," I said. "Shouldn't we try to figure out what they wanted with the Tillinghast Papers? That might give us an idea of what their goal is. And who, or *what*, they're trying to wake up."

Cliff glanced at me. "None of that will matter if we stop them tomorrow."

"I think Lily has a point," Bea said, seeming hesitant to speak up. "What if we're missing something?"

Cliff shook his head. "I don't think wasting more time trying to make sense of these people will help anything. We can figure out everything else after we secure the *Ossabrium* and track them down."

"Maybe. But what if we don't?" Henry said. "What if they get the book before us? What if they can't be stopped after that?"

"We will stop them. There isn't any other option."

"Cliff, you're not making sense," Bea said. "You can't control every variable. And come on, the Vatican? That place is full of civilians. If something goes wrong, something that we can't control, bystanders could get hurt. You know these people, they don't care about who gets in their way, and they don't care about consequences. Innocent lives could—"

"I know!" Cliff snapped. He took a few breaths and lowered his voice. "I know. But I don't see what other options we have. At least none that we have time for." He strode to the door. "I'm going to call the higher-ups, let them know the situation in full, and request backup. Henry, I need you to get a few teams together for tomorrow. Start with volunteers, then we'll move on to assignments; keep this on the down-low. I don't want anyone involved in this unless they have to be."

Henry took a few steps toward the door. "Cliff, I don't think we're thinking this through enough—"

Cliff turned his back on the room. "That's an order, Henry."

He shut the door behind him.

Henry let out a frustrated sigh. "This is not good."

"No shit," Roger mumbled, staring at the door. "*What* is going on with him?"

"Actually, *I* was referring to the hordes of hibernating dark gods that could be awakened by tomorrow night. But you have a point; having an emotionally unstable region leader isn't great either."

"How do you know they're going to strike tomorrow?" I asked.

"Laura detailed possible security procedures in her notes," Bea said. "It seems like she was even thinking of getting the book herself, though I'm not sure how serious she was. She must've heard chatter that something was going down tomorrow. Legion is a safe bet."

"Tomorrow, security will be more spread out for an event," Henry said. "Some kind of collector's gala or banquet. Lots of people. Lots of distractions."

Bea rubbed her eyes and swayed on her feet. "I need to get in touch with my contacts in Rome. Maybe I can call in some favors and—"

Henry put a hand on her arm and steered her toward the door. "You need to get some rest. At least for a few hours. C'mon."

Bea seemed like she wanted to argue but noticed how shaky she had become. She followed willingly, fidgeting with the bandages over her face.

Henry glanced back at Roger. His expression turned to pity as he looked at me. "You two should get ready; I think there's going to be some rough waters ahead. And, Lily, I'm sorry, but we're going to need all the intel we can get."

I forced a smile and again ignored the throbbing behind my eyes. "I was counting on it."

Henry returned the smile and waved as they exited the medical building.

I slumped forward onto my knees, closing my eyes. I just wanted the pain to go away, but it wouldn't. Static floated past my ears, and the back of my eyelids pulsed red.

"Papers . . . You need to find out about the papers."

I pressed my palms into my forehead.

"Find . . . me . . ."

"Shut *up*," I whispered.

"Lil?"

155

Swallowing away the bitterness in my mouth, I opened my eyes. "I . . . I think we should find out about the Tillinghast Papers. While everyone else gets ready. It seems as good a place as any to start digging."

Roger peered at me, his eyebrows knitting together again. "Lily, you don't look good."

I rolled my eyes. "Thanks. That's what every girl wants to hear."

"I'm serious."

"Clearly."

He sighed. So did I.

"See? I'm fine," I said and shrugged off the blanket. I stood slowly, wobbling on my feet. "We have work to do."

Roger stood and grabbed the protein bar that I'd left on the table, unwrapping it and handing it to me. "If we're going to be moving around, you need to eat this. You can't be passing out again."

I reached out to take the bar, sighing internally; the thought of eating anything right now sent waves of nausea through my stomach. But I knew he wasn't going to budge, and I was too tired to argue with him. Swallowing, I nibbled on the corner and flinched. My vision turned green.

I stuck the bar in my pocket. "I'll . . . eat it on the way. You mentioned that there may be copies of the papers somewhere. Do you know where we could start looking?"

He put his hands on his hips, chewing on the side of his cheek. "Well, lucky for us, *I* just so happen to have an in with the archives guy."

I smirked. "And lucky for us, *I* just so happen to know where he is right now. *And* who he's trying very hard to impress."

Sixteen

Created

Roger and I stood a fair distance away from the sparring ring, watching the strangely endearing interaction between Margot and a very nervous Carl.

"Wow." Roger crossed his arms and chuckled. "You weren't kidding. I haven't seen him like that since that news reporter in Chicago. Poor girl was so confused."

I smiled as Carl handed Margot a piece of protective padding from a sack. He stuttered and stumbled over his words, but Margot listened intently.

"Should we head over there?" I asked.

Roger waved a hand. "Give it a minute. He's on a roll."

"We're kind of on a time crunch, Rog."

"C'mon, he's my best friend. I have to help out when I can."

We continued to wait in silence.

"He told me about how you two became friends, by the way," I said with a smile. "You were a tiny superhero for him. Who, you know, also got stuck."

Roger laughed. "He probably made it sound more heroic than it actually was. He's got a knack for that."

"How did he take it?" I asked. "When you . . . left? Did you tell him?"

Roger shuffled his feet and looked at the ground. "I didn't tell anyone I was leaving. As far as everyone here knew, I was dead. When I showed up at his house one day, he did something that I never thought anyone could."

"What?"

Carl spotted us and gave a goofy wave. Roger waved back. "He forgave me."

Margot jumped the fence of the sparring ring in one quick movement. "Hey, flower girl! Carl just caught me up on what's been happening. Why does all the interesting stuff happen when I'm gone? It's just not fair."

"Uh." I looked to the side. "I guess *interesting* is one word for it."

"So what's the deal?" she said, surveying me and Roger. "You here to continue training now? Or is your boyfriend here to yell at me again?"

Roger's eyes narrowed. "We're actually on our way to borrow him"—he jerked his thumb at Carl—"to help us with a little situation."

She raised an eyebrow. "Situation?"

"A . . ." I thought for a moment. "Research situation."

"What about?" Carl asked, joining the group. "You looking for someone?"

"More like something." Roger waved him to follow. "C'mon, we'll explain on the way."

"Wait, hold up," Margot said. "I'm coming too."

Roger crossed his arms. "No way. This is sensitive information. We can't involve outsiders right now. Especially outsiders who show up as things turn bad."

"What is that supposed to mean?"

"I'm just saying ever since you came around, weird stuff's been happening, and people have died."

"Are you really blaming me for this?"

He turned. "No, but we don't need more problems than we already have. And at this point, you're considered one."

Margot bristled. She shook it off and raised her chin. "You sure you want to do that? Leave a good opportunity on the outside?"

"What're you talking about?"

She picked at her fingernails. "You guys only have clearance to view records for the Northwestern community, but I—being so well traveled and wise—have access to not only the East Coast community but a few others as well."

"How?" I asked.

She smirked. "I've been around."

"Uh . . . I . . . um, she has a point," Carl muttered to Roger. He fixed his glasses. "That would widely increase our search range."

Roger exhaled sharply. "Okay, fine. But what we're going to tell you needs to stay under wraps. We don't want to start a panic. C'mon, I'll explain to both of you on the way. Are all the computers still at your house?"

"Er, no, I'll show you. But what are you talking about? What panic?"

Roger, Carl, and Margot walked in front of me while Roger explained most of what we'd just discussed with Bea, Henry, and Cliff. Their light-hearted smiles vanished.

I shuffled behind them and tried unsuccessfully to block the shifting static from my head. There weren't any specific words, but an incessant noise—like a refrigerator trapped inside a shipping container. The electrical hum echoed back and forth, gaining intensity with each passing minute.

"So, let me get this straight." Carl rubbed his eyes. "You want me to find a copy of some random journals recovered from a shipwreck at a time when *printers* were considered advanced technology? Do you *want* me to have an aneurysm?"

"I know it's a long shot," Roger admitted. "But right now, it's the only thing we've got to work from."

"This day sure took a turn for the weird," Margot remarked. "So, what, are we just biding time until tomorrow? What exactly is the plan to stop . . . I'm sorry, what was their name again?"

"*For . . . we . . . are . . . many . . .*"

I rubbed my head and closed my eyes. I just wanted to make the sound stop. I just wanted to make the pain stop.

Why wouldn't it stop?

"Legion. And as for the plan . . . we're going to try to get the book before they do. We're going after it tomorrow like they are."

"Why wait?" Carl asked. "Why not just get the book before they do? I'm sure we could get a team together before tomorrow."

"Well, for one, security is going to be stretched thin tomorrow. Some kind of gala, Bea said. And I think . . . I think my dad is more concerned about losing their trail. I think he wants to stop them before they go into hiding again."

"So we're risking our lives just so we can try to apprehend some of these crazies?" Margot rolled her eyes. "Gee. What a great leader."

"Hey, um, here we are," Carl said loudly as Roger's eyes flashed. "The archive room where I spend most of my waking life. Exciting."

I looked for another tree house or cabin but only saw a chunk of cracked concrete set in the ground. A round metal grate sat on top of it.

"Wait." Roger looked back at the village. "They *finally* built an actual archive room? It's not in your house anymore?"

"Yeah, I know. I guess the scare with the fire last summer got it through their heads. I have my own space now." Carl swelled with pride. "And now everything runs on its own power supply, so no more surges wiping out a whole day's work. Thank *God*."

"Didn't this used to be the old fallout shelter?"

"Still is." Carl lifted the grate with a grunt and made a wide, sweeping gesture. "Enter, weary travelers, to my humble place of work."

Roger laughed and punched him in the arm, mounting the ladder and descending out of sight. Margot went next, deftly hopping down the rungs as Carl nodded for me to follow.

The cold ladder was longer than I thought, but eventually, my feet hit solid ground. The soft sounds of our breathing echoed in the almost pitch-black space. The air tasted stale. A moment later, pink and magenta tones washed over us as Margot and Roger took out their weapons for light.

"Hang on," Carl mumbled. He tugged a few times on a rusty metal switch, which eventually screeched in protest and flipped.

Weak white lights above our heads illuminated, accompanied by the low hum somewhere up ahead. The tunnel reminded me strongly of the one Henry, Tinker, Pete, and I had used when we were running from The Bound.

"Wow." Roger approved. "They really cleaned this place up. Is it better than being cooped up in your house?"

"Yeah, unless the main tunnel floods. You know that mountain to the northeast? By the river?"

"Yeah."

"There's something funky with the soil around there. It's way too wet, even in the summer. But all things considered, it could be a lot worse down here. C'mon." He flipped a few smaller switches and waved for us to follow. "I just disarmed the security system. We need to go before it reactivates."

We shuffled single file down the hall, making a few turns before winding up in front of a rusty metal door. Carl heaved it open and led us into another dark room.

Carl flipped a few more switches. A dozen screens illuminated the cramped room, bathing us in bright blue light. The setup reminded me of the surveillance station in the Forest of Luminescence, but bigger and more complex. Lines of letters and numbers flashed across the screens too fast to read before going dark. Finally, a Metatron's Cube displayed across them, followed by a blinking input cursor on the biggest screen.

Carl cracked his knuckles and input a series of long codes. The old keyboard clattered as he typed.

"Okay," he said, settling into the chair. "What am I looking for?"

"Any record or copy of something called the Tillinghast Papers," Roger said and spelled the name out letter by letter as Carl typed it in.

"Any record?" Carl asked. "That might bring up a lot of results."

"Here's hoping," I mumbled. "The more you can find, the less I need to listen for. And I'm not sure how reliable that's going to be right now."

"Gotcha."

He scrolled down through some minuscule text before shaking his head. "I'm just getting a bunch of stuff on golf courses and Massachusetts fruit stands. You got any other keywords or dates I could use?"

Static assaulted my head, and I swayed as the pain peaked.

"*May 1985, Section 3, A. S, 27.*"

"May 1985, Section 3, A.S, 27," I repeated, leaning against a filing cabinet. "Try that."

I closed my eyes as loud clicking noises filled the room,

"Wow, that did it," said Carl's voice. "This doesn't look like golf courses or fruit stands to me. Um . . ."

Roger inhaled a quick breath. Margot let out a low whistle. I opened my eyes, squinting at the light.

A pair of red, wild eyes stared down at us, surrounded by thick scratches of black ink. The illustration was too detailed to be made by imagination; each popped blood vessel and distorted reflection seemed as though it could pulse at any moment. Below the eyes were scribbled letters of another unfamiliar language. Inkblots splattered the shakily drawn words. The image was crooked and washed out, confirming my suspicions that the page was scanned.

"What do you think it says?" Roger wondered.

Margot leaned closer to the computers and squinted. "'Knowledge by works alone rivals the powers of kings and devils' . . . or something like that. I don't think it translates directly into English."

We all looked at her.

"How could you possibly know that?" I asked.

She shrugged. "It's Italian. But, like, really old Italian."

"You know Italian?" Roger asked.

Margot shrugged again. "I spent some time with the Southern European community."

"When?"

"I dunno, a year or two ago. They were short staffed, and my team leader in New York was looking for a way to get rid of me. Are there any more pictures of this thing?" she asked Carl. "This looks like a title page."

Carl snapped out of staring at her and typed in a few more commands. "Uh, I might be able to organize these by input date instead of . . . Just give me a sec."

We waited in silence again, and I closed my eyes. It helped lessen the pain, but the drawing of the wild red eyes was burned into my vision. It filled me with dread. The knot in my stomach writhed and flopped.

"Okay, here," Carl said. I opened my eyes again. The new images were similar scans, filled with more jumbled phrases and drawings of some mechanical design. It almost looked like blueprints for something. Something complicated.

"Any idea what these say?" Roger asked.

Margot stared at the screen. She swallowed once and shook her head. "The scan is too blurry. I . . . I can't read it. Sorry."

Carl scrolled to another set of pages, a diagram of a human being strapped into a chair attached to a large circular table. The figure in the diagram seemed to be screaming in pain. More words below were numbered, creating a list that continued onto the next slide.

Carl continued scrolling through the scanned images. Most of them were blurry and hard to read. Some pages were completely scribbled out in black ink, the word *REDACTED* stamped across them.

"What *is* all this?" I whispered. "They almost look like blueprints to . . . make something. Like a device. Or a machine."

"But what would be so important that would make them risk an attack on a well-guarded Jumper facility?" Carl asked. "I thought they were after the book."

"They are," I agreed. "But maybe whatever device this was helped them get it?"

"Wait a minute." Roger leaned forward and pointed at a disturbingly accurate drawing of a skinned human being. "I recognize that one. It was in Laura's research notes, at least a copy of it."

"What does that mean?" Carl asked.

"Maybe she came to the same conclusion that we did," Margot said. "Maybe she found out about the Tillinghast Papers when she was searching for the *Ossabrium*, which led her to discover these 'Legion' people were connected. I mean, for whatever reason, these papers are affiliated with the book, so maybe she came across them in her research. Here—"

She leaned over the keyboard, clicking on a series of confusing links and entering a password into a small box. A new series of information came up, but this time it was all in a different language. "I just logged you into the Southern European database. Try searching here for things. I can translate."

Carl hesitated. "Um, Margot, you really aren't supposed to look at other community's private records. It's against protocol. We could get in a lot of trouble for this."

"Look, if this book is really as dangerous as you say it is, then we don't have time for protocol." She crossed her arms and chewed the bottom of her lip. "And they haven't changed the password since I was there. So really, it's their own damn fault."

We all raised our eyebrows at her. More than a little bitterness was laced into that statement. It made me wonder yet again what got her transferred out of the Northwestern community.

"Besides," she huffed, "isn't this why you let me come along in the first place?"

None of us argued. Carl cleared his throat and clicked through a sea of new file icons.

"That one," Margot said, pointing. "That looks like them."

The file pulled up was the same scans as before, but these images contained notes off to the side that someone had made post-scan. This file seemed to have more pictures in it than the last one, too.

Margot leaned forward on the table and began scanning the screens. We waited for her to lean back and turn around. "I can't find anything groundbreaking, but there are a few letters that keep repeating."

"Like keywords?" Roger asked.

She shook her head. "No, like an acronym. 'AMB' appears several times. They seem to be connected with these notes. Maybe another Jumper researcher?"

Roger furrowed his brow. "'AMB' . . . Why do I feel like I've seen that sequence of letters before? Recently, too."

"Maybe you saw it while looking through Laura's notes?" Carl suggested. "That was the most recent thing you read, right?"

"Yeah . . ." Roger mumbled. "Maybe."

"What else did you find?" I asked.

Margot turned her gaze to me, and something behind her eyes shifted to sadness. In an instant it was gone, replaced by her usual haughty glance. "Whoever wrote these notes must've known something was up about these papers, because they left a warning at the end."

"What does it say?"

Her eyes flicked up to the screens. "'Whatever this machine has created, God help us all.'"

Seventeen

Preparations

Carl grabbed my hand and pulled me up the last few rungs of the ladder. Roger and Margot waited on the surface, assisting Carl as he heaved the metal grate back into place.

"Hey, Lily!"

We turned.

Irene jogged toward us. "There you are. I've been looking everywhere for you."

I looked at the ground. "Sorry."

"There's a big group gathered in the main village; Cliff wants to talk about, y'know"—her eyes flicked to Margot and Carl—"tomorrow. Anyway, he asked me to come find you in case you heard anything we should know."

"Thanks, Irene," Roger said. "We'll be right over."

Irene shuffled her feet. "Um, actually, Rog, Cliff said you should probably sit this one out. Specifically, you."

"What?"

She held her hands up in defense. "His words, not mine. I told him you wouldn't like it."

"Damn right I don't like it." He shook his head. "Sorry, tough for him, but I'm going."

Irene smirked. "That's also what I told him. C'mon, we should get going." She nodded to Carl and Margot. "Do they know what's going on?"

"They know enough."

The five of us started on the trail to the main village. Within minutes, the tightly packed trees opened into the large clearing dotted with firepits. Despite the gathering of a few dozen people, none of the fire circles were lit.

Cliff stood at the front of the group, recapping some basic information that we had learned in the last few hours. Among the gathering, I saw the rest of Irene's team, a few faces I recognized from the Northwestern community, and more that I'd never seen before.

We stood at the back near Chelsea and Artemus, who turned and gave bracing smiles as we approached. A few others turned, including Adeline and Nicholas, who were close by. Adeline spotted me and gave a conspiratorial wink while Nicholas smiled politely, his eyes flicking between Adeline and me.

". . . we have reason to believe this group will strike tomorrow night," Cliff said. "I'm asking for volunteers to help stop them from doing so. I'll be honest, this could be extremely dangerous. Most of what we know about these people is pure speculation."

"I'll say," a voice near the front said. "You haven't told us anything about who we're up against. What's that all about? You afraid we're going to run for the hills or something?"

Cliff looked down at his feet. "Some of you here remember the events of the Los Angeles Riots back in '92. The group who orchestrated that attack and the current threat are one and the same."

Some gasps and other hushed reactions swept through the crowd. Many faces who before had shown confidence now displayed fear.

"They go by the name of Legion, though we're not sure how many of them exist. But we know there's enough of them to pose a genuine threat. I'm not saying this to dissuade you from coming, because we need all the help we can get. But I am telling you this to prepare you: these people *will not hesitate* to kill you if you get in their way. Whatever your choice may be, remember your families, and the responsibility you have to them before anything else."

He looked around for a moment and then cleared his throat. "Anyone who's staying here with backup resources, go with Bea; she'll brief you on standby positions. Everyone who's coming on the strike force, come with me. If there's not enough volunteers, I'll move on to assignments. Questions?"

He waited for a long moment and surveyed the crowd that had gone still. There were a few whispered arguments between teams. A petite woman in front of us clung to the sleeve of a stocky man, her face filled with pleading. He shrugged her off and shook his head, embarrassed by her reaction.

Slowly, people split into groups. More than half the group shuffled toward Cliff, and the rest sheepishly stood with Bea. The small woman had chosen the standby team, while her companion ignored her and stood with the strike force.

Roger, Margot, and I shuffled toward Cliff, but Carl stayed put. He gave a wry smile. "Sorry, I'm not allowed on sensitive assignments like this. Hazard of being the archives guy. I'll meet up with you later."

Roger shot him a look. "One day, we'll sneak you onto a fun mission."

Carl snorted. "Yeah, one day. Be safe out there, I mean it. And uh . . ." He looked around and lowered his voice. "Try not to let the end of the world happen anytime soon, 'kay?"

"Aw, c'mon, where's the fun in that?" Margot said with a wink.

Carl blushed a deep red and hurried away.

Joining the rest of the strike force, we shuffled up behind the group and awaited instructions. Cliff's eye flitted around and ended up on Roger. He refocused and cleared his throat. "All right, everyone head to Giftshop. We meet in the viewing bay in ten minutes. Dismissed."

The group produced Teleporters, and one by one people disappeared into Giftshop. Margot, Roger, and I waited for the crowd to clear. Roger strode forward to his father.

Cliff took one look at his son and held up a finger. "No."

Roger gave a short, harsh laugh. "C'mon, you can't—"

"Absolutely not," Cliff said. "You aren't coming."

"Oh, so we're back to treating me like a kid again? There's no reason I shouldn't come. You said it yourself; we need all the help we can get."

"Yeah, and I've got enough volunteers already without you. We don't have time for this, so stop arguing." Cliff dug a Teleporter from his coat pocket. "Lily, Margot, get to Giftshop. Don't make me ask twice."

Roger pinched the bridge of his nose. "Are you serious? Lily can go, but I have to stay behind? Dad, you aren't thinking clearly right now. If you were in a better state of mind, you'd see that."

"My state of mind is just fine," Cliff snapped. "And you're not the one who gets to make that decision."

"You realize you're sending a recruit on an assignment that seasoned Jumpers opted out of, right? She's barely started combat training!"

"No, I'm sending someone who can hear warnings that other people can't. She's a valuable asset and might give us an upper hand."

"Asset?" Roger said, his voice rising. "Are you—she's a person, not a tool! You *know* she's still new to this!"

"Roger—"

"You're going to get her killed!"

"Roger, that's enough."

"At least let me come along for—"

"*You will not engage with these people, do you understand?*" Cliff shouted.

The phrase bounced around my skull. For a moment, I could've sworn I stood in an alley filled with the smell of burned plastic and gun smoke. Everything went fuzzy. I blinked. Margot grabbed my arm before I fell over. I coughed a few times. My mouth tasted salty.

"You all right?" Margot asked.

I nodded, not trusting myself to give a confident answer.

"This is exactly what I mean." Roger lowered his voice. "You can't let her go alone like this. You know you can't, and you know I won't let you."

Cliff sighed and turned away. He rubbed his bloodshot eyes. "All right. *All right.* But I want a third person for insurance. Margot, stay with them both. Don't let them out of your sight."

". . . Yes, sir."

"And I want *all* of you on the sidelines. We're going to do this quick and clean, and try to avoid conflict altogether if we can. There's going to be a lot of civilians around, and I don't think I can—"

His eyes turned to his son. A hint of the unbearable grief I'd seen a few hours ago flashed across his face. "I mean it, Rog. If something happens, don't try to fight. Just run in the other direction. Please."

After a moment of pause, Roger nodded. "... All right."

"Then get to Giftshop. I've got to give an all clear to Henry and Bea."

Cliff hurried out of sight. I sniffed back the blood dripping from my nose.

Margot released my arm and grabbed her Teleporter. "You heard the man. Let's go."

She opened a portal, and the three of us shuffled into Giftshop's Guest Book room. A few people hovered around the Guest Book itself, waiting for their turn to sign it. We got in line and dug around our pockets for pens.

After signing out, Roger led the way to the viewing bay, where the majority of the strike force had gathered. Despite the many people, a sudden draft brought the smell of peppermint and wild oranges past my face. It felt tentative, like Giftshop was wary of approaching me.

I stumbled to a nearby table and half fell, half sat in a sturdy wooden chair. I leaned on the tabletop and panted a few breaths. Roger and Margot followed but stayed standing.

"You look really pale, flower girl," Margot said. She turned to Roger. "Has she eaten anything recently?"

"I'm right here," I said. "You could just ask me."

"I don't think so," Roger said. "I know she had dinner the night before last, but I don't know about anything after."

Margot put a hand under her chin. "We had some pudding, but that was when she was with me in New York."

"Again." I waved. "Still right here."

"I tried to get her to eat something before we came here," Roger said, "but she wouldn't."

"Does this happen often?"

He glanced at me, looking more concerned than before. "Not anymore."

Margot frowned. "Do you feel nauseous, Lily?"

"How should I know?" I said loftily. "Maybe you should ask someone else."

"Lily."

"Sorry." I rubbed my eyes. "Yeah, I have been for a while now."

"Does it come in waves?"

"Yeah. Headaches too. Bad ones."

Margot nodded, pursing her lips. "You're not pregnant, right?"

I sat up. "What? No, I'm not pregnant!"

She shrugged. "I just figured since you two, you know—"

"Margot, for the last time, *we are not a couple.*"

"Well, *excuse me,* but you *have* been living together. It's not out of the question."

"It's not like we—I mean, we haven't had . . . we're not—"

"All right, attention, everyone," a loud voice called. Cliff walked to the front of the room. Everyone paused their conversations and swiveled toward him.

"Some contacts in Rome have generously supplied us with more information on the event at the Vatican tomorrow evening," Cliff said. "It's a celebration of the *Museo Gregoriano Etrusco* and its recent additions to their collection of Etruscan artifacts. The gala is a black-tie affair, so that means anyone on the ground team needs to blend."

Various groans swept around the room.

"I'll be splitting you into two separate teams: the ground team, which will move about inside the gala, and the recon team, which will locate the book. Ground team will provide assistance if needed."

"So, we *are* going after the book, then?" a voice in the crowd asked.

"Yes, that's the plan." Cliff nodded. "We should have a better chance of doing it quietly during the gala."

"Isn't that why Legion is attempting the same thing?"

"Yes, and this will not only be an opportunity to apprehend them but also an insurance that we get the book before they do. They have no reason to know we're coming, so we should have an advantage."

"Do we have any idea where their base of operations is? Or how many of them are involved?"

Cliff sighed. "Given that we only found out who they were last night, there hasn't been a lot of time to do much investigating. Bea's working on that now with the standby team, so if anyone would rather do research, you're welcome to join them."

No one moved.

"Right." He cleared his throat. "I'll be coming around with assignments. Once you have them, meet up with your team and head out. We've got a lot of work to do." He pointed to both sides of the room. "Ground team over there, and recon team over there."

Cliff moved about, explaining assignments, and I continued in vain to ignore the pounding in my head. Why was this headache only getting worse? Why wasn't the pain letting up at all? There had to be something to make it stop. I didn't care what it was, I just wanted silence in my head. I just wanted to think without pain.

People milled about to their new team leaders, and eventually, Cliff made his way over to us. I noticed we were the last group he had approached.

"You three will be part of the ground team. Take no risks. Get out when you can. Okay?"

The three of us nodded, and I got up from my chair as Margot and Roger joined the ground team.

"Lily, can I talk to you for a minute?" Cliff asked.

I swallowed. He didn't look upset, so I nodded. He led me through the room and into the hallway blocked by a heavy purple curtain. I couldn't bring myself to look him in the eye.

"Listen," he said, "I know things have been hard for everyone since the events of October, and I know things have been moving fast for you. This is a crucial time for all of us, and it's important that we execute this mission with caution. You understand?"

"Yes," I mumbled.

"And that can't happen if people aren't being honest with their teammates."

I looked at the floor.

"Lily, you need to tell me what's going on. If not because I'm your region leader, then because I'm worried about you, and so is everyone else. Roger especially. He's worried you're pushing yourself too hard. But I don't think that's all, is it?"

I glanced up. He was trying to make eye contact. I avoided it.

"I know you saw something this morning," he said. "Something about . . . something about Los Angeles, right? You were talking in some kind of dream state when I found you."

My eyes welled with tears.

"Lily, please."

I inhaled a shaky breath and looked up. "You never told him, did you? You never told Roger what happened."

His expression broke down, seeming to age a hundred years in an instant. "How could I? It would've just put him in danger. You didn't know him when he was younger, but he . . . let's just say he had a lot of fight in him for the wrong reasons. If I told him who was responsible, he would've gotten himself killed going after them, and I—" His voice broke before he cleared it. "I couldn't let that happen. I still can't."

"That's why you didn't want him to come," I said. "You were afraid he'd find out and go behind your back to get revenge."

He nodded slowly.

"You don't know that's what he'll do."

"I do know." He flashed a sad smile. "Because he's my son. And I'd do the same thing if I could. You . . . you haven't told him, then?"

Shaking my head, I swallowed. "I couldn't. It's not my place to tell him, it's yours. It's something you should've done years before now."

"And I will tell him. After all of this is over and these people are gone for good. I swear it." He straightened and folded his arms. "Lily, is there . . . anything else you wanted to talk about?"

"*He only wants to use you.*"

"Huh?"

"Is there anything else that you want to tell me?"

"*Don't trust him.*"

I looked at the ground again, closing my eyes hard. "Cliff, I . . ."

"*You know he'll never understand. He'll ruin your chance at finding answers.*"

"I . . . I've been feeling like—"

"*I'm the only one who can help you. They can do nothing.*"

"I . . ."

"*They are n o t h i n g.*"

Cliff tapped the side of my arm. "Hey, you still with me?"

"Hm?" I shook my head and faked a smile. "Don't worry about it. It was nothing."

He looked wary. "You're sure?"

"*Nothing.*"

"Yeah, it was nothing."

Someone called Cliff's name from the viewing bay, and he sighed, opening the door. "All right, it's go time. Stay safe tomorrow, and please"—he glanced at Roger across the room—"keep him safe too."

He left through the heavy purple curtain. I followed, wiping some blood from my nose as I surveyed the room of Jumpers.

"*Hey, Psychic Wonder Child. I'm talking to you.*"

I jumped and looked down. Catacombs sat at my feet, his tail swishing behind him.

I breathed a sigh of relief that the voice in my head was something familiar this time. "Hey, Catacombs."

"*Geez, Spacey McSpace Cadet over here. I was trying to get your attention forever.*"

"Sorry, I'm a little distracted today. What're you doing here?"

"*Came to check out all the commotion. Things are a-happenin' without me.*"

"No kidding. What do you think of all this?"

He leapt from his position on the floor to a stack of books and watched the crowd with me. "*Looks pretty intense. I haven't seen this level of mo-bilization in years. Sorry you had to get paired with the crazy girl. Tough draw.*"

I furrowed my brow. "Are you talking about Margot? What do you mean, crazy?"

He cocked his head. "*You don't know? She got transferred from the North-western community after an incident a few years ago.*"

"Well, yeah, I knew about that. What was the incident?"

"*She kidnapped a guy and tortured him for information. Well, until some of her teammates intervened. I hear he didn't survive long enough to get his memory wiped.*"

EIGHTEEN

Something Borrowed

To add insult to injury, Irene was head of the ground team.

Now not only did I have to avoid telling Roger that Legion murdered his mom, pretend not to be terrified of Margot, and try not to lose my mind to the Collective, but I had to do it all while suffocating from guilt every time I looked Irene's team in the eye.

Piece of cake.

"All right, everyone," Irene called. "As ground team, our job is to move about the gala undetected until the recon team can locate the book. We will handle any hitches that go off with the recon team, and then, if necessary, the standby team will get involved. There's going to be lots of people from different backgrounds at this party. That gives us an excellent opportunity to blend. I have invitations for all of you." She waved a manila folder in the air. "Courtesy of our contacts in Rome. Since this event is black tie, dress accordingly. I'm talking to you, Snuff."

Snuff swept off his animal-skin hat and bowed. "Whatever thou desires, milady."

The group chuckled, and Irene cracked a smile. "I'll be briefing you when we head out. We'll meet here at five tomorrow morning to meet our connection to Rome. Questions?"

"What kind of security will be at this thing?" Margot asked.

"Standard fare for high-end gatherings, maybe more. We'll have a storage kit on the inside, just in case. Have emergency packs ready to go. Anything else?"

A few more people asked questions, and I closed my eyes. I just needed a moment. I just needed some time to get everything straight in my jumbled head. Thoughts and warbled sounds passed through my brain. The constant consuming static swallowed me whole.

Why wouldn't it stop?

Some pressure on my hand made me jump. I opened my eyes.

"Lil?" Roger asked. "Can you hear me?"

Clearing my throat, I nodded and glanced around the room. Everyone else had gone except for Irene's team, Margot, and Roger. Chelsea, Jack, Artemus, and Snuff peered at me with furrowed brows.

"S-sorry, what's up?" I asked, blinking. "I must've dozed off."

Roger released my hand. "We were just about to get ready. The recon team has already left. Now it's our turn to wait until tomorrow morning."

"I can't believe I have to stuff myself into one of those awful monkey suits," Jack lamented. "I can't even remember the last time I had to wear one."

"You think *you* have it bad?" Chelsea raised an eyebrow. "Try wearing foot torture for hours at a time! I'm bringing sneakers in my purse if I can swing it."

"It's definitely been a while since we've had to infiltrate a black-tie event," Irene admitted, smirking. "You remember the last time you wore a tux, Rog?"

Roger groaned. "Oh, do *not* bring that up again. I don't even know where that thing went after the watermelon incident."

"A blessing in disguise." Irene chuckled. She turned to me and cocked her head. "Lily, do you have anything formal to wear?"

I frowned. "I have the dress I wore to Terry and Susan's funeral, but you're talking about fancy-fancy, right?"

"Right. You'll stand out if you look too casual." She scrutinized me, planting a hand under her chin. "I don't think I have anything that would fit you. I'm taller, and formals are notoriously long as it is."

"I probably have something for you," Margot said.

I blinked. "Wha—really?"

She rolled her eyes. "Don't look so surprised. We case a lot of black-tie events in the Eastern community. I'll find something."

"What about you, Rog?" Jack asked. "You need to borrow a tux? I've got a spare."

Roger rolled his eyes. "I s'pose so."

Chelsea clapped her hands and squealed. "Okay, I know this is a crisis situation, but this is becoming too fun. I love dressing people up. Lily, can I do your hair tomorrow?"

I sighed.

This was going to be more painful than I originally thought.

"Well, what do you think?"

I turned around in front of the mirror again and swallowed. "You're sure it looks all right? It's a bit . . . tight."

"That is kind of the point."

Sighing, I adjusted the satin ribbons across my back and tugged on the straps of the lilac gown. Margot had brought over three options to the house in Stars Crossing: a black dress that barely constituted as a shirt, a sickly yellow monstrosity, and this one. It was a good thing most of my training bruises were gone thanks to Giftshop; otherwise this ensemble would've had to include a lot of makeup.

Trying on formal dresses while simultaneously testing out various weapons was odd. I felt like we were in a heist movie.

I tried to adjust the bodice so it was less formfitting. I'd lost a little weight since becoming a Jumper, but I still was uncomfortable with wearing something so fitted and so . . . exposed.

"Well, I guess this is it, then." I ran a hand over my stomach in an attempt to make it flatter. "Thanks for letting me borrow this, by the way."

Margot zipped closed a pouch on her backpack. "No problem. Just make sure I get it back someday."

Margot had opted for a wine-red backless dress that emphasized her fit figure. Watching her try on dresses and giggle while picking out accessories and shoes, I couldn't get over how *normal* she seemed. I never would've guessed she had the capacity to torture someone to death. I still wasn't sure if I believed what Catacombs said, but there definitely was something in her colorless eyes that made me think twice.

She popped a few glass cartridges into a smooth rounded sphere and tossed it in her backpack. "Well, that about does it. I'm going to get back to the outpost. I guess I'll see you tomorrow at Giftshop." She shrugged on her pack and shot me a look. "Do yourself a favor and relax. Look in the mirror, flower girl. You look damn good."

I nodded with a small laugh. She smiled and opened a portal to the outpost, disappearing with a *zap.*

Reaching behind me, I searched for the zipper. I found the tab, but it wouldn't move when I pulled it. Moving all my hair to one side, I tried again and sighed. It was stuck.

"Hey, Lil, you here?" Roger's voice came from the stairwell.

"Up in the loft," I called.

The wooden stairs creaked as he climbed the ladder. "Hey, what did you want to do for —"

He stopped short when he reached the top and stared at me. My insides sank; I knew I should've just gone for the yellow dress, even though it was baggy. This one showed too many curves where there shouldn't be curves.

I cleared my throat. "Does it . . . does it really look that bad?"

He seemed to realize he was staring and snapped out of it. "N-no, that's not why I was—I, um, you look . . ." He swallowed. "I was actually going to say you look . . . nice."

I tried the tab again, but it was still stuck fast. "Could you undo me?"

"W-what?"

"The zipper. I think it's stuck."

"Oh, um, yeah. Of course."

I held my hair to the side and turned so he could reach the zipper. "This might take a minute."

"Thanks."

He tugged gently, working the fabric back and forth.

"Are you all set for tomorrow?" I asked.

"I think so. Just have to get my pack together. You?"

"Same. It feels so weird to just be waiting for tomorrow. Like we're just biding our time while the world burns, and we're not doing anything about it."

"We are doing something about it," he pointed out, "just not until the right moment."

"Does that make it strategy or procrastination?"

". . . I'm not sure."

He moved his fingers through some ribbons to get leverage. He brushed against my back, and I hoped the goosebumps it gave me didn't show.

"Are you nervous?" I asked.

He exhaled. "Honestly? Yeah, I am. There are a lot of things I wish we were more prepared to handle." He tugged the zipper. "But worrying about it won't change anything."

I shifted in the dress to give him some room to work. "I hope that it'll be over by tomorrow. Though I don't know what'll happen after that. My parents are still selling the house and are still blissfully unaware of . . . everything."

He gave a soft laugh. "I think if we're still alive tomorrow, we'll be grateful to deal with *that* set of problems."

I laughed too. It stopped halfway out of my throat as tears stung my eyes. The thought of losing anyone tomorrow hadn't really sunk in until now. Who could be dead by tomorrow night? What if it was me? What if it was Roger? I couldn't even think about that possibility.

"Hey." Roger put a hand on my shoulder. "It's going to be okay, Lil. We'll get through this."

I let out a rushed breath. Unfortunately, I also let some tears out too, and the pounding in my skull worsened. "I-I don't think I can lose anyone else,

Rog. There's too many people who've died already. Good people. Not just from the last few days, but . . . Ed, Terry, Susan, Leo, everyone who didn't make it after The Bound. Now Laura. I don't think I can handle any more death. Maybe I'm not . . . maybe I'm not cut out for this kind of life."

Roger continued to work on the zipper and gained another inch. "I don't think any of us are, really. We can pretend that it becomes normal after a while, but it doesn't. We see the ugly side of the world more than most. The sacrifice that it takes just to keep things normal for everyone else. I guess the only consolation is that we get a chance to make it better when others can't. We get to do something about it. Losing friends and family is hard as hell, sure, but I think doing nothing would be worse."

He pulled one last time, and the zipper came down smoothly. I hugged the dress to my chest to keep it on.

Roger stepped back. "Should've given you some warning, sorry."

I secured the dress and turned. "It's okay. Thank you. What did you come up to ask me?"

"Hm? Oh." He refocused. "Um, I was just asking you what you wanted to do for dinner. We still have some leftovers in the fridge."

Ugh. Food. As if I needed another reason to be nauseous right now. "Um, let me get changed first, okay? I've also still got to pack, so . . ."

He folded his arms. "Is this a tactic to make me forget you haven't eaten in almost forty-eight hours?"

"No, but I'm standing here in an unzipped dress and, therefore, have the right to ask you to leave."

He raised his hands and descended the ladder. "I concede."

Roger shoved a plate unceremoniously into my hands as I entered the kitchen.

"There," he said. "Rice. Something nice and calm that won't upset your stomach. We can add some chicken too, if you want."

The smell of warm rice wafted to me. I shied away from it. Why was everything making me so queasy?

"Rog, I really don't think I can do it right now."

"Please, just try?" he pleaded. "It doesn't have to be a lot, just a spoonful or two."

I was about to argue but noticed Roger's face. He was worried. Really worried. And he was right. I knew I should eat it, and I knew I should be hungry, but I just . . . wasn't.

Sighing, I sat down and picked up a spoonful of fluffy white rice. Mustering my willpower, I stuck the spoon in my mouth and tried my hardest to swallow. I couldn't do it. The muscles in my throat refused to work. My eyes watered. I pushed away from the table and hurried to the bathroom, where I coughed out the rice and rinsed out my mouth.

I returned to the kitchen, where Roger stood holding a small glass of water, looking even more worried than before.

"Sorry," I mumbled. "I tried. I really did."

I took the glass of water and sipped it, ignoring for the thousandth time the pain spreading behind my eyes.

"I'm the only one who can help you."

Roger felt my forehead with the back of his hand. The pain lessened for a moment, returning worse than ever. "You don't feel like you're getting a fever—"

"*He can't help you. No one can help you.*"

"I know," I said. "I know."

"Maybe it's nerves for tomorrow—"

"*Your only chance is to find me.*"

I closed my eyes. "M-maybe you're right."

"Come get me if you get worse in the middle of the night, okay?"

"*Find me tomorrow. I'll be waiting.*"

"I will." I swallowed and opened my eyes. "I will."

Nineteen

<u>Stone, Blood, and Fire</u>

I didn't sleep at all.

When I finally found the courage to go to bed, the static in my head was too loud to sleep through. For hours I lay with my hands clamped over my ears and my eyes shut tight, but I couldn't block out the noise inside me. Two hours before we had to leave, I gave up and got ready. I paced, repacked my emergency backpack with extra clothes and my long-range bracer, and paced some more. I left Margot's dress neatly tucked inside a plastic bag; the gala didn't start till later, and I figured walking through Rome wearing a formal gown would raise some eyebrows.

At four thirty, I headed downstairs and stood in the kitchen. It was dark outside, and my reflection from the windows stared back at me. I looked awful. My eyes and cheeks seemed sunken. My skin color was a chalky shade of green.

Filling a glass from the sink, I tried to take a few sips. The water tasted like gasoline. I managed another sip before spitting it out.

"There's only one way to make this all stop."

"I know."

"I can help you."

"I know."

"Find me, Lily. I will answer all your questions."

"I will."

"Because what else can you do?"

"Because what else can I do?"

"Who are you talking to?"

I started and turned. Roger had emerged from his room and was in the middle of setting down his backpack. He watched me warily and glanced around the kitchen, searching for someone else. I hated the way he looked at me, like this time, I had finally lost it and gone completely insane.

I cleared my throat, shaking my head. "No one. I wasn't talking to anyone. Are you—" I coughed and pretended to rinse the glass when I could feel blood trickling out of my nose. "Are you ready to go?"

"Yeah, I should be. I'm guessing we're waiting to get changed so we don't attract attention."

I nodded and sniffed, bending down to put the cup in the dishwasher. "That's what I thought too. I'm just bringing my stuff along with me."

Blinking away some spots when I stood up, I turned. "When do you think the gala will start?"

Roger buried his head in the cabinet and searched for a granola bar. "Not sure. I think Irene is going to brief us when we get to Giftshop. How are you—" He turned, and his eyes widened. "God, did you sleep at all last night?"

"Yeah," I lied. "I slept fine."

"Really."

"Yes, really."

He rubbed his eyes. "Fine, whatever. Are you ready to go?"

I took out my Teleporter. "Yeah. You got everything?"

"I just need to grab my suit."

He shuffled off to his room, and I leaned against the counter.

"He's getting tired of you."

I just needed to breathe.

"He thinks you're weak."

Just in.

"A burden."

And . . . and out.

Roger returned with a similar plastic bag to mine and shrugged on his backpack. "All right, let's go."

I grabbed my stuff, opening a portal to Giftshop. We stepped through to the Guest Book room and took turns signing out. I noticed that Irene's team was already here, along with more names I didn't recognize. Looping swirls of ink decorated the lines above mine, so intricate that I couldn't decipher the name it belonged to.

We pushed aside the heavy purple curtain separating the hallway from the viewing bay. A large group milled around, sifting through their emergency packs while others stood around chatting. Irene hunched over a cluster of tables, looking over a few schematics and blueprints. A tan, good-looking man with dark hair and deep-set eyes stood with her, a scowl prominent on his face.

"There you two are," Margot said, spotting us. "I was getting worried you overslept . . ." She raised an eyebrow at me. "Though I can see that wasn't a problem for you."

I rolled my eyes. "I'm getting a little tired of everyone telling me how terrible I look."

"Then try looking less terrible."

"Lily!" called a voice across the room. "I did not know you would be joining us on this escapade."

I turned. Adeline strode forward with a wide smile on her face, an elegant, messy bun bobbing in rhythm with her steps. Nicholas was in tow behind her, inclining his head in a polite nod. Instead of his regular scuffed-up suit, he had donned plain modern clothing. It looked . . . weird.

"Hi, Addy. Hi, Nicholas. You guys are coming on this thing too?"

"Indeed," Nicholas said. "Bea thought we would be suited for this event, as my specialty is ancient history. I must say, it feels good to get out and accomplish something. Not to be a bore, but it has been rather ghastly sitting around all this time."

"Hogwash," Adeline said. "You've always enjoyed the peace and quiet."

"Perhaps," he allowed. "But for this extended amount of time? I think not."

"Trust me, pal." Margot nodded sagely. "I know where you're comin' from."

"Do you know anyone else here?" Adeline asked. "I'm afraid yours is the only familiar face to me."

I glanced around. The only people I recognized immediately were Irene and her team, and of course, Adeline, Nicholas, Margot, and Roger. There were a few people I'd seen around the community, but I'd never spoken with them. The stocky man who'd had the argument with the woman yesterday at the outpost was here. He was deep in conversation with a red-haired woman, a large scar spanning the back of her neck.

Irene shuffled some papers into neat stacks and blew one quick whistle through her teeth. "All right, this should be everyone. Listen up. This is Marco." She gestured to the man on her left. "He's our inside contact while we're in Rome, specifically getting us into the gala. The name of the game is to blend. If people talk to you, talk back. Mingle. Pretend that you're supposed to be there, and no one will think otherwise."

Marco cleared his throat. "If anyone questions you, just say you're a patron or donor of the Etruscan exhibit. There are hundreds of pieces donated to the Musei Vaticani, and no one knows the name of every donor on demand. Any questions?"

The room was silent.

"It is my understanding that this is a very sensitive operation," he continued. "Tread carefully, make no rash decisions, and above all, keep our oaths in mind. Protect the people of Earth, the people of Rome, and watch each other's backs."

Marco stepped back and held out a Teleporter, opening a portal. The room shuffled into a neat line immediately. As we headed into the portal, I caught the faintest whiff of peppermint, cinnamon, and hot chocolate.

The group shuffled forward until we blinked and squinted as the sunlight streamed into our faces. Sounds of people and cars hummed nearby, accented by the smell of cigarette smoke and freshly baked bread. The narrow alley looked straight out of a travel magazine. Ivy crept up the cracked walls, the buildings painted an earthy red color. Windows studded with black iron bars surrounded colorful wooden doors. It was all so enchanting that, for a moment, I forgot how horrible I felt.

"I've always wanted to go to Rome," I whispered. "This is really cool. I didn't know it would look so . . . picturesque."

Roger chuckled once behind me. "Just don't get yourself checked for a passport."

Our group came to a standstill as Marco knocked on a door with peeling paint. It opened, and a petite old woman with leathery skin stepped out. She dried her hands on her worn apron and surveyed the group.

Marco and the woman conversed in Italian for a moment, and the woman raised an eyebrow, shaking her head. "Sembrano più pallidi di quanto ricordi."

Margot giggled. "Ma almeno non siamo fantasmi," she called and shrugged. "Ancora."

The woman laughed, waving her hand for us to come inside. We entered single file, and I turned to Margot. "What did she say?"

She smirked. "She said we seemed paler than she remembered."

My eyes watered, but I refrained from blinking. "Is this really necessary?"

Chelsea dabbed at my face one more time before leaning back. "If you want to blend in, you have to look the part. No one's going to a formal gala with chalk smeared on their face. Well, except maybe Artie."

"Hey!" Artemus shot her a dirty look from across the room. "That was one time!"

Chelsea uncapped a tube of lipstick. "Now hold still . . . just one finishing touch."

I sighed and did as she asked. The entire ground team had spent the last hour getting ready for the gala, and it was an interesting whirlwind of commotion. Some got ready in a matter of minutes, while others seemed like they didn't know where to start. I was one of those people.

Our host, Marietta, watched quietly from the back of her modest home, answering questions as translated by Marco. She seemed wary of us, with a general dislike for Americans. Margot, however, scored big points being able to converse in her native tongue.

"We leave in ten minutes," Irene called. "Get yourselves together."

Jack tugged on the collar of his shirt, his hands wrapped around an untidy black ribbon. "Does anyone know how to tie a bow tie? I think . . . I've just made a noose."

Chelsea rolled her eyes and rose to help him unstrangle himself. She undid the knot as he leaned down close to her. "I swear this is the hundredth time I've had to do this. When will you ever learn?"

He shrugged and shot me a covert smile. "I guess I'll always need you around to help me."

Adeline tugged on the sleeves of her long-sleeved lace dress, her face blushing a soft pink. "I must say, dress customs have certainly changed in the last two hundred years. I did not know fashion was allowed to be so . . ." She cleared her throat. "Scandalous."

"Even for your tastes?" Nicholas called across the room, where he helped a line of men with their bow ties. He looked much more himself in formal wear. "You were the one always intent on 'stepping away from convention,' dear Adeline."

She made a face. "Even for my tastes, dear Nicholas."

The stocky man from earlier hopped over a few backpacks and nodded behind me. "Sorry, but could you hand me that suit coat?"

I stood and reached for a black coat hanging precariously from a wire hanger. "This one?"

He nodded and took it. "Thank you . . . Sorry, I don't think we've been introduced, but I've seen you around." He stuck out a hand. "I'm Eli."

I took his hand. "Lily."

"You're new, aren't you?"

I faked a smile. "How can you tell?"

He gave a toothy grin. "My wife and I just transferred from the West Coast community a few months ago. We're expecting, and it was *supposed* to be quieter up here."

"Congratulations," I said. "When's she due?"

"June, but we have a feeling it might be earlier."

I smiled. "My brother and his wife are having a baby, and she's due in May. I still can't believe it."

"Well, maybe when they're older, we'll have to arrange a playdate." He laughed. "I think Gina would like someone besides me to chat with."

I looked around. "Is she here?"

"Nah, of course not. Too potentially dangerous. She's with the standby team. We, uh, had a bit of a disagreement about it, though. She seems to think I don't know how to handle myself, and—" He turned his head when someone called his name. He shot me an apologetic smile. "Sorry, gotta go. Nice talking with you."

"You too."

I waited until he turned away before I closed my eyes. It was so loud in here, so stuffy. Too many people. Too many voices. My head hurt so badly. I just wanted everything to be quiet for a moment. Just for a moment.

"Get your packs to Marco and let's head out," Irene called. "We'll be shuttling people over in separate cars so we don't all arrive together."

I just needed a moment.

Someone poked my arm. "You ready, flower girl?"

I jumped and almost fell over.

Margot raised an eyebrow. "Little jumpy?"

"I'm f-fine," I stuttered.

"Whatever." She shrugged. "I guess we're ready. Where's your boyfriend?"

I ignored that. "I don't know, haven't seen—"

Someone who looked like Roger walked in from the next room. I blinked. It was Roger. His hair, usually messy and unkempt, had been combed and styled, revealing a small triangle-shaped scar above his left eye. The borrowed tux even seemed to fit him well. Really well. He dropped his backpack with the others and scanned the room, quietly paying attention to everyone around him.

"Wow," I said. "I've never seen him look so . . . um, he looks good."

"Yeah, he cleans up well." Margot agreed and picked up her backpack. "C'mon, let's drop these off."

We dropped our packs and shuffled across the room to meet him.

"Hey," he said. "You get everything together?"

I tried to talk, but my throat had gone dry. I cleared it. "Yeah, I think so."

He shuffled his feet. "You, um, look really nice."

"Thanks, um, you . . . you too."

There was a drawn-out stretch of silence until Irene called for the first car to leave. We were at the front, so Roger followed two other people out the door.

"Take a breath, Lily," Margot whispered. "You're going to pass out again."

"Shut *up*," I hissed.

Another picturesque cobblestone lane greeted us past the doorframe. The air was cooler outside than I expected, the sun just about to set in the icy-blue sky. Cars drove past infrequently, but the annoying hum was just as loud as it had been inside the house. Maybe the car would be quieter?

We piled unceremoniously into the car and squished all five of us into the cushy seats. Along with Margot and Roger, Adeline and Nicholas rode with us as well.

"What a marvelous invention, this carriage," Nicholas said. "It's so *compact*."

"And no horse to drive it, either." Adeline nodded.

"Uh, are you guys going to be okay?" Margot asked. "I mean, blending in is kind of important. That'll be hard if you don't even know what a cell phone looks like."

"Beatrice was kind enough to prepare us for such things as that," Nicholas said with a hint of offense. "Worry not. We will appear as normal as can be. We will 'be cool,' as you say."

"Oh dear," Adeline murmured.

I tried to look out the window as we drove on, but I was sandwiched in the middle of Margot and Roger and couldn't see much. It was still unbearably noisy. Why wasn't anyone else bothered by it?

"Do you think we could turn the radio down?" I asked.

Everyone exchanged glances.

"Um, Lily, the radio isn't on," Roger said.

I hunched in my seat. "Oh."

Eventually, we slowed to a stop at an enormous stone wall. Marco turned to the backseat and handed us each an envelope. "Here are your invitations. I'll let you out here. Follow the wall. You'll see the entrance to the gala outside of San Pietro. Hurry, it's already started, and the recon team is in position."

Roger helped me out of the car as I tried not to trip over my dress. Just the slight movement of exiting the car made my head spin. Blackness encroached around my vision, and Roger caught me by the shoulders. Luckily, no one was walking past as I stumbled into him.

"Sorry," I mumbled.

Marco sped away, leaving our strange assembly standing together on the curb. The wall Marco told us to follow was huge, old, and shaded by many twisted pine trees. We set a fast pace on the cracked sidewalk and, after a few minutes, spotted large stone columns and a long line of people. The sun had set behind the towering buildings. Multicolored sconce lights illuminated the ancient marble columns from below.

"Everyone ready?" Roger said.

We nodded. For the first time—probably ever—Margot looked nervous.

Security guards manned the barricade between the columns, funneling into a security gate at the end. We stood in line with other formally dressed people, all smiling and conversing with each other. I was relieved to see we weren't the only ones who spoke English, but we weren't in the majority.

It took longer than I would've liked, but we made it to the end of the line. Except for Margot, who got pulled aside because of a safety pin in her dress, we were ushered through the security gate without incident.

A lady with a plastered-on smile took our invitations. "Enjoy your evening and thank you for your contributions."

We nodded back politely and walked past her into the courtyard. Adeline and Nicholas took each other's arms and walked gracefully forward, as did a lot of other couples. Roger offered his arm to me, and I took it. I felt his leather bracers under his coat and jolted away before I could stop myself. He noticed. I tried to ignore how hurt he looked, or how he dropped his arm immediately when we passed the columns.

My breath caught as the full sight of the courtyard opened. It was enormous. The rushing of the ornate fountains splashed and sputtered, but the sounds of laughter and the nearby string quartet drowned it out. The cobblestones beneath my feet reflected pools of light cast on every column in the perfectly symmetrical courtyard. At the head of it all stood

St. Peter's Basilica, shining like an enormous marble-jeweled beacon from another time.

"Oh . . ." I breathed. "This is incredible."

"Haven't been here in a while," Margot remarked. "It looks so different when there's not a thousand people with cameras all over the place." She sighed. "Man, I miss gelato."

"I suppose we'll just mingle, then," Nicholas said. "Care to join me, Adeline?"

Addy tipped her head forward and curtsied. "Of course."

They glided across the courtyard, arm in arm.

"Maybe Bea knew what she was doing, having them come along," Margot said. "They look more natural here than the rest of us."

"Agreed," Roger said.

We walked toward the fountain area, where many groups milled around a table full of champagne glasses and hors d'oeuvres.

Margot inclined her head to the left. "Our storage kit is behind that pillar in the workbox. See it?"

Roger squinted and nodded. "See it."

"Storage kit?" I asked.

"A multidimensional space that's contained in an ordinary secondary object," Margot said.

"Like a coat room that holds more than coats," Roger supplied.

I nodded, even though I had no idea what they were talking about. The quartet ended its fast-paced song and slowed to a more waltz-like beat.

A tall, attractive man with olive-toned skin approached Margot and held out a hand. "Vuoi ballare?"

Margot smiled and inclined her head. "Beninteso," she said, and took his hand, giving us a look as she left.

"And then there were two," I said. "I wonder how the recon team is doing. I hate not hearing anything from them."

"Let's just hope that we don't hear anything," Roger said. "*Nothing* in these situations is usually a good thing. I hope they get the book and get out before anyone realizes what's—" He broke off as a man walked past with a tray laden with champagne glasses.

Roger stared after him and swallowed.

"You okay?" I asked.

He nodded, staring at the ground. "Yeah, it's just . . . um, there's a lot of alcohol here. I uh . . ." He laughed a little, rubbing the side of his fist against the hem of his sleeve. "It . . . never really gets any easier, I guess."

Looking around, I spotted a less crowded spot far away from the drink table. I nodded to it. "Let's move over there. I think we can see the courtyard better. You know, for surveillance's sake."

Roger nodded, and we weaved through the crowd. "Thank you."

We stood in silence and watched the party. I noticed other members of the ground team throughout the crowd, though they acted like they'd never met before. Chelsea and Jack stayed together, as did Irene and Artemus, but Eli, Snuff, and many other team members wandered the courtyard by themselves.

The consuming hum crept back to full volume as I ran out of things to distract me. I clamped my hands to my sides to stop myself from covering my ears. The hum turned to crackling and then back to a hum again. Were my eardrums about to burst? It sure felt like it.

In an instant, everything went quiet. I could think clearly again. The pounding in my head lessened to an almost tolerable level. Someone walked by me, just long enough to glimpse the back of their head before they disappeared into the crowd. It was a man with short honey-blonde hair, head tilted slightly to the side. As soon as they passed out of sight, the pain and the noise returned in full.

Who was that?

The band ended another lively song. The music turned into a beautiful, slow melody.

Roger took a deep breath and held out a hand to me. "Would you like to dance?"

I blinked. "Um, I don't really know how to dance. I think I'd be terrible."

"That's okay, I'm not great at it either." He shrugged. "We can be terrible together."

I looked up. His brown eyes stared at me like they were searching for something familiar they had forgotten.

I took his hand. "All right."

He led me a few steps to where other couples were dancing and put a hand on the small of my back. I reached up to his shoulder, and we shuffled back and forth. The pain behind my eyes ebbed away. It got easier to think.

"See?" he said. "Not so terrible."

I laughed. "I guess not." I looked around and spotted Adeline and Nicholas dancing as well, but they seemed much more proficient than we were. "It definitely helps us blend. You know, for surveillance's sake."

Roger blew a chuckle through his nose. "For surveillance's sake."

We held eye contact until we realized we were staring at each other. I wasn't sure which one of us was doing it, but we seemed to be inching together. For a moment, I felt the same as I did on the roof a few nights ago: warm, safe, and at peace. It seemed like a lifetime ago we were watching the stars together, worrying about training and how we were going to continue forward. Now those worries seemed like a luxury.

"It's so beautiful here," I said. "I still can't believe I'm in Rome. Like actually *Rome*."

His eyes crinkled as he smiled. "I know. It's pretty cool."

"What's your favorite place you've been to?" I asked. "On Earth, I mean."

Roger thought for a moment. "Notre Dame, Paris."

"Really?"

"Yeah. There's something about it that's just . . . I dunno. You step inside, and everything's different. Even when it's crowded with tons of people, there's just . . . something *there*. Something that makes you feel not so alone in the universe."

"I guess. Like Giftshop?"

"Kind of, but . . . bigger. Maybe after all this is over, we could go. You know, together. Spend some time around the city, get a baguette or two. I could show you what I mean."

"I'd . . . I'd like that."

We shuffled in a circle and listened to the music, inching closer together. Everything seemed so normal. I had to remind myself why we were here. The recon team could get the book any second. We could be called into action any minute now. But . . . maybe it was okay to forget for a little while.

He cleared his throat. "Hey, um, I've been wanting to ask you something."

I looked up. "Yeah?"

We inched closer.

"We've been . . . we've known each other for a while now. Long enough to know that things between us are real. And . . ." He trailed off again like he'd forgotten what he was going to say. I found myself leaning upward.

"Yeah?"

Roger leaned down. "And I . . . I think . . . I think I—"

Stabbing pain tore through my skull, shattering everything inside. The high-pitched hum on the edge of my hearing dragged itself to the front of my mind. Did I just get shot? Was my head still whole? It didn't feel like it.

My legs buckled, and Roger caught me by my elbows. *"Lily!"*

The noise. The noise was all that mattered. What was happening? Why was it getting higher?

The muscles in my legs shook as I stood. "I-I don't—"

I stopped. Someone was staring at me across the crowd. The man with honey-blonde hair, head tilted to the side. He wasn't much older than I was. We met each other's gaze, and his bright golden eyes bored into me. His lips curled into a slow smile. His mouth moved.

"You found me."

I was shaking. "Rog—"

The man raised both his hands to the sky and closed his eyes. Others in the crowd did the same.

"By stone, blood, and fire . . ."

"Rog, something's about to happen—"

"And for all who came before us . . ."

"We need to stop it—"

"We invoke the power of the One, the Only . . ."

"Or . . . or we need to—"

"Amen."

The man lowered his arms and smiled before twisting the watch on his wrist and disappearing with a flash of light.

Similar flashes echoed through the crowd. There was a moment of silence before the entire courtyard exploded.

Twenty

While the World Burns

Something dragged me to the ground before the wall of heat hit me.

Everything went gray as my head smacked onto the cobblestones. The rest of my body followed what seemed like minutes later. I couldn't breathe. I couldn't see. My hearing had become a muffled flatline noise.

Was I dead?

I heard the screams first, then the crackling of fire. The rest of my senses flooded back like a dam bursting. Wails of sirens. Agonized shrieks. Someone called my name.

"... Lily ... !"

More screams.

"... Lily, please ... !"

Something shook my shoulder.

". . . You have to get up . . . !"

Get up? Did I still have legs?

"Lily, please!"

A shaking in my chest made me gasp. My mouth tasted like dirt and blood. My eyes snapped open, but I couldn't see much because of the smoke.

Something grabbed my arm hard and tugged. "Come on! Lily, please, we have to move!"

"Roger, get out of here!"

"No! I'm not leaving her!"

"Are you kidding? You can't carry her right now!"

"But I can't—"

"I'll take her. We'll meet you at the south radius line in five minutes. Go!"

Another tug came, and I shifted to my knees. "What's . . . what's happening?" I slurred. "Where am . . . where am I?"

I looked up to see Margot's blood-streaked face through the smoke. She pulled me again. "Get up, Lily. We need to move! Now!"

She pulled me to my feet and supported me until I started walking on my own. Chunks of fractured marble and shards of stone littered the courtyard. The smoke was so thick I could hardly walk without running into something. My foot hit something soft, and I let out a noise when I realized what I tripped over.

Bodies. Pieces of people. Everywhere. The falling dust coated the puddles of blood leaking from them.

I stumbled with every step, but Margot pulled me forward over bodies and hot stone. I fell to my knees and almost landed on another body. I gasped in horror as I recognized Eli on the ground, eyes wide and still. The back of his head was gone.

Everything turned wet as Margot tugged me through the remains of the spewing fountain. The water cleared away some of the smoke, but not enough. People ran, crawled, limped, and stumbled past us, but I could barely focus on them through the numb daze.

Finally, blackened marble columns loomed from the darkness. Margot led me to a large metal workbox behind the pillar.

"Margot Johnson and Lily Masters." She coughed. "Emergency, code 0-2-2-8!"

There was a sucking sound behind the lid and Margot pried it open. To my amazement, both of our emergency packs sat waiting for us.

She grabbed her backpack and shoved mine into my arms before slamming the lid. She turned to hop over a barricade. I stumbled behind her until she came to a stop and ripped open her backpack. "Get changed. They'll be looking for people dressed up."

I nodded, and we pulled on our clothes back to back. I tried to zip up my backpack, but my hands shook, and something was getting in my eye. My hand came away covered with blood as I wiped my face. I wasn't sure if it was mine.

"Where's Roger?" I asked.

"Hopefully, he went on ahead. The ground team needs to scatter before they . . . before we get cornered." She zipped up her backpack and mine, now in regular clothes. "Come on, run!"

We hopped another barricade and sprinted down the street full of people gaping at the smoke rising from the Vatican. No one paid us any mind as we ran past, covered in dirt and blood. The dust from the explosion had spread across most of the nearby streets.

Finally, gasping for air, we stopped in a side alley, and I fell to my knees. Blackness swam around my vision, but the adrenaline in my veins kept me conscious.

Someone shouted from the end of the alley, and we tensed. Roger sprinted down the street, bleeding from a wound on his shoulder but still standing. He was also dressed in normal clothes.

"You guys hurt?" he gasped.

"Still alive," Margot panted.

I was still shaking. "Eli. I saw Eli on the ground, and he was . . . he was . . ."

"I know." His voice broke. "I saw him too. And Jenny, and what was left of Carlisle, and . . ." He closed his eyes and swung his good shoulder to punch a stack of wooden crates. "God *dammit!* How did we not see this coming? We should've *known* this would be a trap!"

"How?" Margot said. "How could we have known they would take it this far? How could I . . . How could we have known?"

Roger leaned on his knees, grabbing his shoulder with gritted teeth. He seemed pale. He lost his balance and sank to the ground.

"That looks bad," Margot said. "Let me see."

He reluctantly leaned back. She peeled away his soaked shirt and grimaced. "It's deep, but I think it missed the artery. Lily, go stand guard at the end of the alley to make sure no one's following us. He's going to bleed to death if I don't patch this up."

I stood, wobbling on my feet. ". . . Okay."

She took off her backpack and pulled out a suture kit and two bandage rolls. She held one roll to Roger. "Here, bite down on this." She glanced at me, still frozen in place. "C'mon, we don't have a lot of time. Go."

Roger nodded at me and stuffed the roll in his mouth while she pulled away his shirt. I ran to the end of the street before I saw the rest. Roger's muffled grunts of pain started as I turned the corner. I slid down the wall. The street had emptied. Maybe they were all watching Rome burn together.

I put a hand to my mouth and watched the smoke billow into the dark sky. Did that really just happen? Did I really just watch that take place? Minutes ago Roger and I were dancing in the lamplight. Now . . .

"Lily?" Margot called. Her voice faltered. "I-I'm done. We . . . we have to move."

I stood up and wiped some more blood away from my eyes. My head pounded, and I wondered if that made it bleed more.

I rounded the corner, and my stomach jolted. Roger lay sprawled on the ground, shoulder bandaged with gauze, but unconscious.

"Rog?" I called as I ran down the alley. "Margot? Where are you?"

Before I reached him, a pair of hands yanked me backward. A sickly-sweet-smelling rag was clamped over my face before I could scream.

"Sorry, flower girl," someone whispered. "Nothing personal."

I tried not to inhale, but the rag had already made my head spin. I struggled for a few more moments before the darkness around my vision compounded with the dizziness, and everything went black.

The world shook.

I couldn't bring myself to open my eyes. Bright spots of light followed flashes of darkness. Both the light and the dark hurt to look at.

The steady hum of movement rocked me back and forth, interrupted occasionally by a bump or jostle. Voices jumbled together. Were they speaking a different language, or was my hearing just warped? I tried to swallow, but my mouth was closed around something rough.

Suddenly, the movement stopped. Slamming noises preceded the brightness that split open my head. I whimpered as my eyes opened a crack.

Hands pulled me from the black van. They dropped me a few inches from the ground, and my head screamed in pain. I smelled water, concrete, and something salty. They dropped another unconscious person next to me. He didn't stir. His chocolate-brown eyes were closed.

"R-gh . . ." I choked. Tears streamed sideways down my face. "R-ghar . . ."

The people pulled out more bodies from inside the van and looked back at me. They muttered some words and covered my face with a rag again.

I tried not to breathe in. After a few seconds, I sobbed for air, and everything went dark again.

Bouncing. I was bouncing now.

This time was much more jarring than the car, and I felt nauseous immediately. Cool spray hit my face. The view above me was a sharp cerulean blue with wisps of white. Dark triangle shapes moved across it in a V formation. Where was I?

I tried to move my hands or feet, but both were bound tight.

"How is she still awake? This is the second time she's woken up."

"I dunno. Just give her some of the heavier stuff."

"You sure? He said he wanted her lucid when she got in."

"Just— Oh, hang on, she's going again."

I tried to fight it, but it was too hard to push away the tendrils of sleep that came for me. I could sleep, just for a bit.

Just a . . . little . . .

"*I'm so proud of you, Lily.*"

Just . . . a bit. I could sleep for a bit.

"*You found me. You found us.*"

I tried to swallow, but something was around my mouth again.

"*And more importantly, you let me find you.*"

Why did everything hurt so much?

"*Now it's time to wake up.*"

Why were my hands stuck?

"*Wake up, Lily.*"

"Wake up, Lily."

My entire body jerked, and my head smacked against the wall. I already felt blood dripping from my nose.

"There you are."

I choked on the gag and looked up. The man with short honey-colored hair knelt alarmingly close to me. His eyes . . . There was something wrong with them. Something *moved* within his bright golden irises. Something flickered and twitched like a parasite. He stared at my face with unyielding focus. My stomach twisted into knots.

There wasn't any way to describe his gaze other than insane.

"Welcome home, Lily," he said with a wide smile. "I can't tell you how *great* it is to meet you in person."

I tried to scoot away, but my hands were tied to something behind me.

"You know you don't need words to talk to me, right?" He stroked my hair with clammy hands. "Go on, try reaching me. I'm wide open. It should be easy."

I tried my best to hide against the wall.

He waited expectantly for a few seconds before his face turned red. He slammed a fist into the wall. "You won't even try?" he yelled.

My head peaked in pain, and my vision went green.

"Take it easy. She doesn't even know who you are yet," came another voice behind him. It seemed vaguely familiar. "You're going to kill her if you're not careful."

The golden-eyed guy's expression returned to calm in a split second, and he gave a warm smile. "Okay, then maybe we start slow? Okay." He reached up for my face again, fingers hovering over the gag. "I'm going to take this off now, so no screaming, hm'k?"

I nodded and waited for him to undo the knot tangled in my hair. He got impatient and ripped it out, making my eyes water.

I coughed and swallowed. My throat felt rubbery and dry. "Wh-where am I? What happened? Who are you?"

"You see?" the voice said. "She's just confused. She'll come 'round."

"Yeah, you're probably right," the golden-eyed guy agreed. "You know how cranky I get when things take too long."

He stepped back from me, and I looked around the room. It was a cold, wet, briny-smelling space lit by flickering square yellow bulbs. An overwhelming smell of rotting meat permeated the air, but the salt smell masked it occasionally. Constant drips of water leaked down the chipped stone walls and puddled onto the slick floor.

Two shapes lay nearby. Roger and Cliff sat gagged and slumped against the opposite wall. Each had a small metal patch on his neck. Blood trickled from them.

"Rog, Cliff . . ." I whispered, "A-are they—"

"A big pain in the ass? Why yes, as a matter of fact they are." The golden-eyed guy sauntered over to Roger. He pulled a small knife from his pocket and traced the edge of Roger's jaw with the blade. "Maybe we should save some time, get rid of them now. What do you think?"

"No!" I cried. "Please, just leave them alone. Please!"

"I wasn't talking to you."

He tilted his head like he was listening for something. Some static ruffled past my ears and blended with the sounds of dripping water.

S...p...a...r...e...

N...e...e...d...e...d...

"All right." He stood. "I'll save it for later."

I froze. "What did you just say?"

"They said to spare him, so I will. For now, anyway."

My mouth tasted bitter. "How do you—"

"But I'm getting ahead of myself." He turned his attention back to me. "Actually, I'm just getting ahead of everyone else. We have a problem with that, don't we, Lily?"

He gazed down at me and grinned, his irises twitching. "My name is Allister Friedrichs, and I can hear the Collective, just like you."

TWENTY ONE

<u>Fooled</u>

I tried to avoid his gaze, but he just kept staring.

"What did you say?"

"I'm sorry, I didn't realize I stuttered."

The pain in my head peaked again, and I shut my eyes. His voice echoed in my mind so violently it made my head spin.

"S-stop." I choked. "How are you . . . How can I hear—"

"You know, it's funny," Allister said. "I've been preparing for this moment my whole life, and you're not nearly as talented as they said you'd be. I can't *believe* you were the one to force them back to the Outskirts." He tipped his head back and laughed. "I guess there really is such a thing as beginner's luck."

"Them?" I said. "What're you . . ." The words died in my throat. I swallowed. "The Bound. You've . . . you've spoken with them, haven't you?"

"Spoken with them?" the man behind Allister said. He stepped forward into view, and I held back a gasp. It was him. The man from Los Angeles with the black tattoo. He looked older than I'd seen in the memory, but the lack of sympathy behind his cold eyes remained the same.

"I'd go a little further than that," he said. "I'd call it more of a . . . cooperative working relationship, wouldn't you, Allister?"

"You know, Declan, I just might," Allister agreed. He glanced at me and shrugged with another smile. "Let's just say they give me a little extra help when I need it. Extra intel. Extra power."

"You're getting tricked. You know that, right?" I said. "Whatever they've told you is a lie. They don't care about you. They only want to return to Earth in their physical form so they can—"

"So they can feed on the soul of every human on the planet?" Declan said. "Is that what you were going to say?"

I stayed silent. I didn't like their knowing smiles.

"You're right." Allister knelt next to me again. "They would if they had the chance, but that would constitute a breach in their contract."

"Contract?"

"A deal. A deal made before the beginning of everything," Declan said. "A deal with Him and, therefore, a deal with us. The Bound, as you call them, are just servants. Their power may have seemed great to you in October, but it's just a *pittance* compared to what lies in store."

"How do you know about October?" I asked.

Allister chuckled and leaned close to my ear. I moved away as far as I could, but he followed. "Because we were the ones who planned it," he whispered.

I froze.

"I've known about you for years, you know," he said, leaning back, "Well, not specifically *you*, but who you're supposed to be. I've only known your name since June. Unfortunately, you weren't ready yet. So I dug a little deeper and got some help from my friends. What better way to nudge you on the path of a Discovery than to drop you next to a hole in the fabric of space? It may take a little time, but eventually, the magnetic fluctuations affect your brain. Your chemistry. It opens your mind enough to hear what others can't." His hands tightened into fists, and the veins stood out on his arms. "Or, at least, it does for people like *you*."

"Wait, that's . . . that's why I only Discovered a month and a half ago?" I stuttered. "Because I was close enough to the Gate?"

"Partly. Otherwise, I doubt you would've Discovered at all." He shrugged. "Your mind seems weak. Too weak to take the step on its own. So I pushed you. Cars are *so* easy to tamper with these days."

My mouth tasted bitter. "What?"

"It was easy to weaken the brakes on your great-aunt and uncle's car," he said, scratching his ear. "It was even easier to target The Bound on your friend. When they were dead, and he was Linked, everything fell into place."

I tried to fight back the burning in my eyes and the anger bubbling underneath my skin. I struggled against the bindings again. "You monsters!"

"After that, it was just a matter of time until you were open enough to reach you," Allister said. "People like us have ways of communicating with each other. We're just"—he pushed some hair away from my face, and I flinched—"connected that way. Destiny, I call it. It was easy to burrow into your mind and plant a few seeds. It was easy to encourage those doubts. It was easy to make you sick." He clucked his tongue. "Like I said, you're weaker than I thought."

"So . . . everything in October . . . The Bound, Leo, everything . . . that was just to get me to Discover?" I said.

They smiled.

I clenched my hands behind my back. "People died! Good people! Innocent people! And what about The Bound? If we didn't stop them, the entire world could've ended!"

Allister shrugged. "Call it a gamble that paid off. Besides, breaking the Link gave you that one final push you *so* desperately needed. You felt it, didn't you? It strengthened your connection to the Collective. It strengthened your connection to me."

My stomach tightened, and I closed my eyes as the events of the last few months made horrible sense.

Declan smiled. "We may have our faults, but planning ahead is a specialty."

Roger jolted as his breathing became shallow. His eyes opened slowly. He blinked at the ground and coughed.

"Well, well, well, look who's awake," Declan said, striding over. He grabbed Roger's arms tied together at the wrists and jerked them up.

Roger screamed through the gag as Declan hoisted him to a large metal hook in the wall. His arms bent at an awkward angle as he half stood, half crouched. Blood dripped from his still-bandaged shoulder. I watched his head loll to the side as he almost passed out, breathing ragged gasps through the gag. I pulled against the restraints, but they wouldn't budge.

Cliff stirred at the scream. Declan attached him to an identical hook next to his son. His head hung against his chest, displaying a swollen bloody bump on the back of his scalp.

"Let's have a party, huh?" Allister said cheerfully, yanking the gags away from their mouths. "We got a lot of catching up to do. And . . ." He tilted his head again and listened. I couldn't hear anything, but he nodded. "Yeah . . . you and sleepy over here got some history, right, Declan?"

He shrugged. "Don't remember."

Roger spotted me on the floor. He coughed and blinked until his eyes focused. "You all right, Lil?"

I gave a humorless laugh. Did I look like I was all right? "Not really."

"Where are we?"

"No idea."

He hung his head. "Fantastic."

"Venice," Cliff wheezed. He looked up, his right eye swollen almost completely shut. "We're in Venice. I woke up when they threw us on the boat. By my calculations, we're on one of the outer islands."

"Very good," Allister commended. "Specifically, you're *under* Venice in one of its best-kept secrets."

"An entire underwork system spanning a good part of the city," Declan said, dusting off his hands. "Built during the Crusades, later expanded by merchants and smugglers, now used by us." He pointed up at the ceiling. "There's over thirty feet of stone and seawater above us right now, only two entrances, and enough interference for your little Teleporters to be absolutely useless."

"No one knows you're here"—Allister chuckled with glee—"so no one's coming to rescue you. And before you get any ideas, no one's ever escaped, either."

"Hate to break it to you," Roger said, "but someone has escaped. Just in the last few days."

"Oh, you mean your lady friend—what was her name, Beatrice?" Declan laughed. "We let her go. How else were we supposed to tip you off about the book and the gala?"

"You wanted us to know?" I asked.

"Of course." He shrugged. "To get you into the open. Easy pickings from there. You even got the book for us. Guess I can thank you for that, right?"

Cliff stared at Declan as he spoke, recognition burned into his face. His bound hands clenched into fists.

The large metal door on the other side of the room swung open. A man armed with an assault rifle entered and nodded to Declan. The guard said something in Italian, and Declan nodded back, waving a hand forward.

I stiffened as Margot walked into the room. Her colorless eyes swept over the three of us tied up.

"I came to collect," she said. "I held up my end of the deal."

A sharp sting flashed through my entire body. I stared at her in disbelief. She looked down at me for a moment before returning her eyes to Allister.

"I knew it." Roger struggled against the hook. "I *knew* there was something off about you. Traitor!"

Margot inclined her head in his direction, her stoic expression flinching. "Then you should've taken care of me when you had the chance." She turned back to Allister. "So?"

"You'll get it, don't worry," he said. "As soon as I'm done with her."

"You said when I brought her here, that was it."

"No, I said you'd get your information once I was done. And let's not forget you also saddled me with an extra *problem* you were supposed to take care of." He nodded at Roger and clicked his tongue. "Sloppy. You can wait."

She breathed out through her nose and turned to go.

"Why?" I whispered. "Why did you do this?"

She paused in the doorway but didn't turn around. "Because they had something I needed. Sorry, flower girl, but you were my golden ticket."

Margot walked past the armed guard, and he closed the door behind her.

Allister clasped his hands together. "Right, let's have some fun. I think you need to ascend to everyone else's level, don't you, Lily?"

I struggled and squirmed as he jerked me to my feet by my shoulders and wrenched my arms higher up my back. He hooked me to a bolt in the wall just above rib level, making me stoop to keep my shoulders in socket. My legs wobbled.

"Why don't we try this again?" He leaned in close to my face, our foreheads almost touching. "You know who I am now, and what we can do. Just reach out. I'm wide open. You can join us. We could do great things together. We have the answers. *He* has the answers."

"Lily, don't listen to him!" Cliff called. "Whatever he says—"

Declan elbowed him in the stomach and returned the gag to his mouth.

I shook my head. "What are you talking about?"

He pulled his fingers through my hair. "Talk to me like I've been talking to you. Go on, use the gift that was just *given* to you. We'll be closer than ever. We'll be a part of each other."

"Talk to me, Lily. It's easy."

I stood as straight as I could. Now that I knew exactly who he was, the voice inside my head felt different. He wasn't powerful or all-knowing but a petulant child whining for a toy. I wasn't playing his game.

"No," I said.

"Try."

"No."

"Do it."

I closed my eyes. The pain was back. "I won't."

"Now."

So much pain. "N-no."

"Do it. Do it. Do it. Do it. Do it. Do it. Do it. Do it. Do it. Do it. Do it. Do it. Do it. Do it. Do it. Do it—"

"*Get out of my head!*" I yelled.

Silence.

The echo of the small room told me I had shouted, but it was the stinging behind my eyes that told me I'd done what he asked. Like a floodgate had opened, a door that had been previously bolted shut was now unlocked. I felt it.

I opened my eyes to see Allister smiling. "There you go."

He was still close, so I slammed my head into his nose.

He stumbled back, recovered, and backhanded me across the face. My head snapped to the side with a crack. White spots sprinkled my vision. He pulled back and readied to hit me again.

"Hey!" Roger yelled.

Roger's pink shields flickered and dislodged him off the hook. He slammed into Allister with his hands still tied, only to be pulled off seconds later by Declan. He threw Roger to the ground and kicked him again, and again, and again.

"Stop!" I cried. "Please, just stop!"

Declan dragged him back to the wall. Roger struggled against him and tried to jerk away when Declan tugged the leather bracers off his arms.

Declan wrenched him back up onto the wall and held the bracers in his hands. He smiled at Cliff. "Wait a minute, I *do* remember you now. Los Angeles, right? In '92. You were with that girl."

Cliff fought against the gag.

"That's right. She put up quite a fight, didn't she?" He laughed. "What was her name? Amy?"

Roger's eyes widened. Cliff pulled so hard against his bindings that blood trickled down his wrists.

"She would've made quite the addition to our family." Declan nodded wistfully. "I almost felt bad putting a bullet in her head."

Cliff sagged against the wall.

"W-what?" Roger whispered. "You . . . you told me she died in an accident. You said—"

"What, is this like a father-and-son duo going on here?" Declan said, nodding at Roger. "Congratulations; you added another problem to the world. You self-righteous bastards disgust me."

Roger stared at his father. "You didn't tell me?"

"Neither did she," Allister said, wiping some more blood from his nose. "She's known for, what, a few days now? Saw the whole thing from a residual memory in the Collective."

Roger turned his attention to me. Hurt and betrayal seeped into his eyes. I could hardly bear to look at him.

"You . . . you knew too?" he said.

"I-I didn't want—" My voice broke. "I wasn't trying to—"

"And to top things off," Allister continued, "*she* was the one who wanted to find *me*. We've been talking to her for almost a week, but she didn't tell you anything, did she? Practically led you into the trap for us."

Roger's eyes widened. "Lily—"

"I didn't know!" I sobbed. "I swear!"

"All right, enough," Declan said. "I'm getting bored with this little reunion. Allister, I'll tell your father you'll be with him shortly."

Declan left the room with a nod and closed the heavy iron door with a *cur-chunk*.

Allister turned to Roger. "Oh, and by the way"—he reeled back and slammed a fist into Roger's jaw—"that *hurt*."

Roger's head bounced back into the wall. He spat onto the ground and glared at him, shaking off the daze. "You'll pay for this, you understand me? All of this."

A few more guards armed with rifles walked into the room. Allister leaned close to Roger. "And just exactly what are you going to do, hm? Kill me? Torture me? I don't think you have it in you as much as you think you do."

The guards grabbed Roger and Cliff off the wall and pointed them toward the door. Roger twisted to look back when he noticed they hadn't taken me too.

Allister put a hand on the back of Roger's neck. "I want you to remember this feeling. This feeling you're having right now of being alone, scared, and helpless. Having the knowledge that I can do *whatever* I want to you, to him, or to her." He nodded back at me and grinned. "And you can't do a *damn* thing about it."

Roger paled, his eyes flicking to me.

Allister patted his shoulder. "Remember this feeling."

He nodded at the guards, and they jerked Roger and Cliff through the door. Roger looked back at me one last time, eyes wide.

"Lily!"

"Roger!"

Allister turned his attention to me. I shrank against the wall.

"All right, let's get started. We have work to do."

Twenty Two

<u>The One</u>

Allister jerked my arms from the hook on the wall and pushed me forward.

I stumbled onto the floor, scraping my cheek against the rough ground. The world wobbled at the sudden movement, like my brain couldn't keep up with it. My ears rang. Darkness crept from the edges of my vision.

"Oh, no you don't."

Something pulled me to my knees. A shaky breath pushed warm air into my ear. "Don't go passing out on me now. We haven't even started yet."

The darkness ebbed, and I blinked. Allister stood behind me, his clammy hands clamped onto my shoulders. He pulled me to my feet, my legs shaking too much to support me. I fell again.

He clucked his tongue. "Can't even walk? Too bad. Guess we'll have to take a shortcut."

There was a small clicking noise behind me. The air compressed to a crushing level. Flashes of light blocked my vision, and I couldn't breathe. When the pressure let up, I doubled over, Allister still holding my hands behind my back.

We weren't in the small room anymore. A rusty metal door—the kind you see on submarines—blocked our path. It sat at the end of an impossibly long, domed stone tunnel. A horrible feeling of displacement lingered in my body. Nothing felt connected, not even my skin. For a moment, I feared I'd fall into pieces, leaking to the floor as everything disconnected. The feeling passed within seconds.

"W-what was that?" I gasped.

He held out a chunky black device on his wrist. It was larger than a watch, the face a conglomeration of numbers, wires, and small buttons. "Short-range matter transporter. We got the design from an ex-Jumper 'bout ten years ago. You get used to it."

He released me to turn the crank on the heavy metal door. I considered running for it but discounted the thought. Where would I run to? There was no way out of here.

The realization sank deeper into my stomach as the door screeched open to another hallway. Allister tugged me again as we walked side by side. Every few steps, he would pull me closer, letting out small noises of pleasure. We passed other people in the hall, mostly armed guards and sentries, and other locked rooms. It was hard to ignore the screams coming from behind them.

I tried not to think about what he was going to do to me. Or what they were doing to Roger and Cliff and whoever else got captured. I knew Allister wouldn't kill me yet because he clearly needed me for something, but that didn't mean he wouldn't torture me. Could I withstand torture? Probably not.

Finally, the hallway ended, and he cranked open another door. I squint-ed against the fluorescent lights. The room was large, most of the space taken up by old computer machinery and stuffed bookcases. Strange paint-ed symbols and numbers covered the walls. Smears of chalk dusted an old blackboard in the corner. A large glass window took up the entire wall opposite me, the glass riveted into the iron frame. The room beyond it was dark.

"This is her, then?"

I turned my head. A small man shuffled toward us, his hands clasped behind his back. A scraggly gray beard covered most of his face, tired blue eyes hidden beneath his bushy eyebrows.

Allister shoved me. "Yes. Lily Masters, this is my father."

He inclined his head. "Reginald Friedrichs. Pleased to make your ac-quaintance."

"Are we supposed to shake hands now?" I asked dryly.

Reginald's mouth twitched, his attention turning to his son. "How is she?"

"Weak," Allister said. "Can barely talk to me at close range, no shielding whatsoever. Four turns on the Table, at least."

"Four?" Reginald raised his eyebrows. "We'll start with one and see how she does. You're going to kill her if you're not careful."

Allister rolled his eyes. "So everyone keeps telling me."

"Table?" I asked. "What are you talking about?"

"Get her set up," Allister said. "I need to start with the book. Can you handle her?"

His father nodded, gaze flicking to me. "Yes, I think so. I won't begin until you get back."

"Good." He relinquished his hold on me and pushed me forward. I stumbled to my knees. "I won't be long."

I glared at him as he closed the door behind him. Reginald grabbed under my arm, and I thrashed.

"Now, now," he chided as he hoisted me up. "That is beneath you." He produced a knife, and my eyes widened. He smiled and cut the cords binding me. "There. Better?"

I rubbed my wrists. Thick red burn marks circled them like permanent bracelets. I eyed the door.

"You can try to run for it," he invited, "but I think that would be rather unwise, don't you?"

I swallowed.

"Come." He waved. "Allister will be back soon and will do this far less kindly than I will. You don't have many options, so I suggest you pick the less painful one."

I stepped back. "What are you going to do to me?"

"At the moment? Patch up that gash on your head and attach a few electrodes." He shuffled to a nearby desk covered in papers and sat with a huff. "I will do nothing to harm you; you have my word."

After a moment of deliberation, I moved my wobbly legs to the desk and sat. Reginald opened a large black bag and pulled out some basic medical supplies. I glanced at the papers on the desk and jolted. Wild ink eyes stared up at me.

"The Tillinghast Papers," I whispered.

He pushed back my hair and dabbed at my forehead with a cotton ball. "So you know what those are? Good. Allister wanted you to find them."

"I know what they are but not what they're for," I said.

Reginald unwrapped a cotton swab tinted orange with disinfectant. "You'll find out soon enough." He paused, eyes flicking down. "I am . . . sorry about this."

"What?"

"All of this. What you've been pushed into. What you're about to experience. I'm sorry. You didn't choose this path."

"You're . . . apologizing?" I asked in disbelief. "Is this some kind of trick?"

He chuckled. "No. Just the thoughts of a regretful old man, I suppose. Things have . . . things have changed. Legion has changed. We used to seek answers. Freedom. Balance. Now it seems the ends justify horrible means."

"Freedom?" I laughed. "Is that what murdering innocent civilians means to you?"

Reginald's eyes flashed. "We're not the barbarians that Jumpers make us out to be. Legion uses the discoveries of the Otherworlds for progress, while Jumpers keep those gifts locked away. Hypocrites. They preach camaraderie and peace, but with their power, they help no one but themselves."

"That's not true," I said. "Jumpers' priority has *always* been the people of Earth. They die for it. They give everything for it."

"You think so?" Reginald raised an eyebrow. "Do you have any idea how many resources, how many secrets they've hoarded over the years?"

"What do you mean?"

"Alien specimens. Biological weapons. Cures for countless diseases. Clean energy sources. There are things in the Otherworlds that would change the world, yet they hide them. Control them. They watch this planet die from the inside out, and they do nothing to stop it."

"And you think you're any better?" I shook my head. "How many people have you slaughtered in the last twenty-four hours?"

His face fell. Staring at the ground for a moment, he dug around in his bag and pulled out a bandage. "We aren't any better. Not anymore. What happened in Rome . . . They crossed a line I never thought they would. It's become madness, their search for the book."

I rubbed my aching wrists to distract from the pain of the freshly sanitized wound on my head. "So, why do you still follow them? Why not leave?"

Reginald inhaled a slow breath and taped up my forehead. "I have done many things—horrible things—in my lifetime. It's too late for me. I have nowhere else to go. Besides, Allister is here. I couldn't leave if I wanted to."

"Why not?"

He glanced at the door and lowered his voice. "He knows my mind. *All* our minds. I've survived this long because I haven't given him any reason to distrust me. I've given him no reason to *look* for my doubts. If he did . . . I wouldn't last long."

"It's not too late," I said. "You could help us. We could escape together. We could keep you safe until—"

"Until . . . what? Until they inevitably wake Him up?" He shook his head. "I know what the outcome will be, and I prefer to stay on the winning side. It's only a matter of time."

He cleaned up the wrappers and crossed the room to retrieve another bag. Reaching inside, he pulled out a bundle of electrodes. Swabbing more areas on my head with disinfectant, he attached one electrode at a time.

"Reginald . . . who is 'He'?" I asked. "Who are they trying to wake up?"

He looked around and inhaled a shaky breath. "The Master. The One, the Only. We can't speak His name. No one can speak His name."

"But what is He? What did Allister mean about a deal and contracts?"

Reginald thought for a moment, sticking an electrode under my chin. "There was a time, eons ago, we're told, that magnificent creatures reigned supreme over Earth: the Ones. They weren't from our world. They came to this realm on cosmic dreams and desires, finding power here, creating true freedom. The pitiful human presence on the planet was mere cattle to them. For thousands of years, they ruled. Until one day, an old enemy came searching, other creatures of pure light, pure energy. It's said their power came from the stars."

"Who were they?"

"We don't know. Their name was lost to time. There was a great war, and the Ones and their servants were sealed away in hibernation, scattered across the universe. Before they slumbered, the Ones made contracts, pacts, and deals to one day return and take vengeance on those who defeated them. If not for all of them, then for their Master."

"Is . . . is that what He is then?" I asked. "One of the . . . the Ones?"

He gave me a level stare. "He is the *Master*. The Whispering God."

The door screeched open, and Allister strode into the room. His twitching pupils swept over me and glared at his father. "You're not done yet?"

Reginald cleared his throat and placed the last electrodes against my temples. "She's ready. Start the Table."

Reginald helped me stand and kept a hand on my arm while Allister unlocked the door near the pane of dark glass. Reginald tightened his grip.

The door opened, and Allister flipped on a light. I threw myself away from the room when I saw what was inside.

It was the machine. The device from the Tillinghast Papers.

The large round table sat bolted to the floor, a single chair welded to it. The leather straps attached to the chair were stretched and stained with dark blotches. Silver gears, golden springs, copper cables, sparkling jewels, and bronze coils intertwined impossibly under a sheet of crystal-clear glass.

"It's funny," Allister said as he helped his father drag me into the room. "You take it for granted, being able to hear the Collective. You don't think twice about your gift, do you? How many people have died for it? How many have been broken for it?"

Reginald released me and stood at a control panel on the other side of the glass. Allister dug his fingers into my skin with a smile. I twisted my tired limbs until I grew too exhausted to fight anymore. He threw me into the chair, tightening the straps against my wrists and legs. Nail marks and gouges covered the armrests.

"Wh-what is this thing?" I stuttered.

Reginald kept his head down and fiddled with the control panel.

Allister leaned on the back of the chair. "You want to know why your mind is so weak, Lily? You haven't had to fight for it before. You're too *sane*." He strapped my hands to the table. My sweaty palms had no choice but to rest on the smooth glass. "And we can't continue forward if you die on me right from the get-go, see? The only way to make something stronger is to break it first."

I swallowed as the Table vibrated in pulsing waves.

"Because if you thought me breaching your mind was enough pain to make you crack"—he chuckled, slamming a fist on the back of the chair—"then you know *nothing*."

My entire body shook. Static shuffled around my head as my vision went black.

A small boy sat strapped to the Table, his little hands quivering on the surface. Tearstains streaked his face, his golden eyes bloodshot and swollen.

"Please, let me out!" he sobbed. "I can't do it anymore. I'm scared!"

A younger Reginald and Declan conferred over a few sheets of paper before Declan exited the room to view from behind the window. Reginald put a hand on a large switch and turned his pained expression to the boy at the Table.

"Daddy, please!"

Reginald closed his eyes and pulled the switch down.

"You should go, Allister."

"No, I want to watch this."

I jolted as the brief memory faded. Reginald stood against the wall, his hand on the same large metal switch.

His haunted eyes watched me. He shut them as he tugged his arm down.

Twenty Three

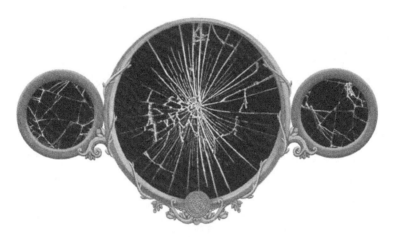

The Spinning Table

I screamed.

My brain was gone, melted into a puddle between my ears. Razor blades slashed the inside of my skull. Acid bubbled behind my eyes. My arms and legs strained against the straps, and for a moment I thought I'd break them. They held, keeping my hands welded to the top of the Table. The coils and gears spun in a whirlwind of gold, copper, silver, and gemstones. It dragged my vision to it. The chair fell away beneath me, the room dissolved, and the ceiling vaporized as I slipped into the center of the Table.

Images flashed around me as I fell. I clamped my eyes closed, but it didn't stem the flow of scenes pouring into my head—

—*mountains of bones splintered into jagged spears, corpses impaled upon them. Thrashing seas of shifting black cubes. Rivers of green bubbling tar.*

Stark flat deserts, with no distinction of land and sky. Living stones twisted and cracked, wailing in agony as chunks fell away. Space without space. Meaning without meaning. Great mounds of swirling multicolored sludge bubbled grotesquely in noxious tar pits. Enormous creatures dragged their feet through oceans, mangling reefs and seabeds beyond recognition with a single step—

I slammed into something hard. Bones shattered, crumbling into shards inside me. Somehow, I was still able to move. I dragged my broken body across the smooth black marble floor, gasping for air. No matter how much the pain peaked or how much I screamed, I didn't pass out. I couldn't pass out. I didn't have the option for relief.

Finally, after crawling forward for hours, I looked behind me. I had barely moved. The trail of blood I left behind was unchanged. Shadows flashed from the corner of my vision. Hisses and growls followed me with every inch, but I couldn't see what they belonged to. The clacking of footsteps and hooves surrounded me. The room stretched and warped, but still I crawled. A few more hours passed, and I looked behind me again. Nothing. Not even a few feet of progress.

The room groaned. I barely had time to scream before I was falling again.

The wind rushed around me. I twisted and rolled as I hurtled through the air, dropping into something hard and clanging. A box. A metal box. I didn't have time to orient myself before the lid slammed shut and locked.

I banged on the cold metal sides, begging to be let out. Strange sounds and mumbles echoed from outside my confines. Growls. Hissing. Shrieks. I attempted to move my vision outward, to escape in my incorporeal form, but it was useless. I was trapped.

Days passed. Weeks. Months. Hunger and thirst gnawed at me, but I couldn't die. The endless suffering stretched into monotonous passes of time, broken up by occasional claustrophobic outbursts. Just as I'd start to slip into an uneasy sleep, the box would rattle and jolt.

One day, the box began to shrink. Slowly, inch by inch. My arms and legs contorted against the sides. As my bones snapped and popped, my joints dislocated, and my veins burst, the box disintegrated into dust.

I crawled into the sunlight, eyes burning. My hands shielded my face against the severe blue sky and intense sun. Eventually, my hunched body adjusted to the light, and I looked around. Nothing. White sand stretched as far as I could see. No matter how far I walked, the day never ended, the sun never moved, the horizon didn't change. No mountains. No sea. No end. Mile after mile, I dragged myself forward on the infinite landscape.

It . . . it was too *open*. Too exposed. The vast emptiness was worse than the confines of the box. I curled into a ball in the sand and tried to bury myself. I yearned for darkness. I yearned to be back in my box, surrounded by comforting metal walls. Safe walls. Walls with no way in or out. At least it would be shaded. At least the sun would be gone.

"You're here too, huh?"

I raised my head. A man crawled toward me, clothes tattered and sun bleached. He seemed familiar, but in a terrible way. The sight of him made my insides writhe in shame and guilt. I squinted at his leathery cracked face and moved my parched vocal cords.

"Leo?" I mouthed. My throat barely made a noise.

"Yes."

"What're you doing here?"

He clawed at the sand and dragged himself forward. "You sent me here."

"No," I moaned. "You're dead. You're *dead*."

"You're right."

Tears leaked from my eyes and soaked the sand. "Does that mean . . . Am I dead, too?"

Leo shook his head. "Not yet."

We stared at each other.

I sucked in a sob. Sand coated my throat, but I didn't care. "I didn't want to kill you. You know that, right? Please. You have to believe me. If there was another way . . ."

Leo continued his crawl forward, hatred mounting in his gaze. "I don't care. I don't want to hear your excuses. I'm stuck here, and it's your fault. You did this to me."

I reached for him, but he crawled away.

"Leo, come back!" I screamed. "Don't leave me here!"

He ignored me, pulling himself out of sight. I tried to follow, but he was already gone.

Fresh sobs and shrieks escaped me. The pain of my broken body was nothing compared to the agony inside me. I thrashed and cried. I tried to drown myself in the sand, but it wouldn't work. I tried to suffocate myself, but I couldn't. The sun sat high in the sky as I lay there, exhausted, dazed, and empty.

The sand shifted, swallowing me whole. My sobs of relief stopped as I fell again into darkness. Images flashed through my head, settling on a green blur. It focused into—

—*a hallway made of a billion twitching eyes stared back at me. Rushing fluid sloshed into the narrow floor, gathering mounds of errant floating eyeballs with each new swell. Sticky liquid swept around my legs as I walked down the corridor. The eyes followed me, just as I knew they always had, and always would. They saw everything. They knew everything.*

They knew me.

I looked down at myself. My arms clutched something. A book. The Book of Bones, its thick, pale cover crisscrossed with brittle white shards and tarnished

bronze. I tried to drop it, but it stuck to my skin. It was a part of me. I couldn't
exist without it. Somehow, that made sense.

At the end of the hallway stood a black form wreathed in darkness. I
couldn't tell if it was a creature or a human or something in between. A trail
of fumes reached out for me, fingers spreading wide. The sight sent waves of
terror through me.

A laugh of pure joy bubbled out of my throat. It turned into screams and
back to a laugh. I loved it, the fear. I couldn't get enough of it. I needed more;
the pumping of my heart was an addiction, now. I needed to feel alive. My
slow steps slogged toward the figure, but it only seemed to get farther away.

"Come," it told me. "Stay."

I reached for the smoke—

My body jolted as the Table slowed. The pain, the thirst, the hunger, and the unyielding terror lingered in my brain, but I'd stopped screaming. Breaths came in gasping waves. The stretched leather straps of the chair were the only things keeping me upright.

The Spinning Table slowed to a stop. A small buzzer sounded nearby. I sobbed, though I wasn't really sure why. Where was I? What was I doing here?

A man leaned over the chair. His eyes looked funny. He smiled. "You see what I mean now, Lily? Much too weak."

Lily? Who was he talking to?

"My head . . ." I slurred. "It's open. Is it open? It hurts."

"Allister, maybe we should—"

"Give her another turn."

"What? Look at her. She can't do another—"

"Fine! I'll do it myself."

There was a moment of silence before the table hummed in rhythm. My ears warped with the sound of my own screams.

The pain was back.

The flashing images were back.

I didn't want to look at them, so I clawed out my eyes. It didn't matter. They were in my mind now, pasted onto the razor blades dancing around my skull.

—trees made of skinned arms and legs. Acid-green monoliths of flesh. Checkerboards of Tears in the sky, inverted oceans, desert plains that oozed blood from the cracks in—

The Table stopped spinning.

"I *told* you she couldn't take more than one turn at a time!"

"She needs to be ready. If she's not, then that's her fault."

"We don't have another chance at this! You're going to kill her! Are you—"

"*Don't say that word!*"

Oh, I could breathe again. That was nice. Breathing felt *so* nice.

"Lily? Can you hear me?"

Who were they talking to? Who was Lily?

"You're being too easy on her. She's fine."

"No, she's not! Now she might be damaged beyond repair."

Someone undid the straps holding me up. I slumped onto something cold and smooth. My eyes were open, but I couldn't see from them. That was fine. Whatever.

I was still trying to figure out who they were talking about. Lily. That name seemed vaguely familiar, but why? Those words felt important. They kept repeating themselves in my head.

Name. My name. Were those important words? I felt like they should be.

Years. Twenty-one of them, actually. That was important, too. I knew it was, but it was so tantalizingly out of reach that I couldn't quite grasp it. What did it all mean?

Pounding. My head . . . it throbbed. But that was how it always felt, right? It always hurt like this.

Breathing. I was . . . still breathing.

My eyes focused on the golden gears beneath my face. My breath had fogged up the glass of the tabletop. A faint reflection stared back at me. My eyes widened.

My name was Lily Masters.

I was twenty-one years old.

My head was pounding.

But I was still breathing.

"My name is Lily Masters," I croaked. "I'm twenty-one years old. My head is pounding, but I'm still breathing."

". . . Lily?"

"My name is Lily Masters." I cackled. "I'm twenty-one years old. My head is pounding, but I'm still breathing."

I laughed, repeating the phrase over and over. I couldn't stop laughing. The pain was funny, really, because everything hurt so *much*. It all hurt so much. Was there a person mixed in with all that pain? There couldn't be. They'd drown in it.

I laughed until a sharp sting on my neck stopped me. I was tired. So sleepy. The feeling intensified, and my head slumped forward.

I had a dream I talked with God.

"Do you know who I am?" he asked.

I blinked and looked around. There were clouds everywhere. Lots of clouds. Orange clouds. Puffy clouds. God sat at a desk hovering in the clouds. He wore glasses and tweed clothing. Somehow, I always thought God would look different. Maybe a white robe or something.

"Sorry?" I shook my head. "I don't believe we've met."

The man rose from his chair, face stricken. He walked on nothing but air, and that didn't seem to bother him. "Now, now, Miss Masters, don't tell me you've completely lost yourself?"

I tilted my head. "Masters?"

"Yes, that is your name."

I narrowed my eyes. It occurred to me that the man might not be God after all. Better ask just to be safe.

"Are you God?" I asked.

The man chuckled. "No, but I shall gladly remind you of this later. Come now, Lily, after everything, are you going to let these people take your mind away from you?"

"People? What people?"

He put both hands on my shoulders and looked over my face. His eyes were the color of hazelnuts. He pulled me into a hug. I wasn't sure why, but it seemed an odd thing for him to do. "They may be many, but you are stronger."

That hurt. Those words hurt.

"It . . . h-hurts," I cried. "It hurts!"

"Good," he said. "That's how you know you're still alive."

I stood still. I was crying, but something inside me felt different. Solid. Something within my disjointed insides hardened.

Flashes of faces, places, and things flooded into my head. My mom. My dad. Ollie. My childhood. Years of school, holidays, and warm summer nights, and everything in between. Alice, Roger, Cliff, Henry, Bea, even Margot. Everything in the last few months seemed sharper than the rest. I recalled every conversation, every encounter, every emotion.

Every memory.

They didn't hurt. They extinguished the pain. The more I remembered, the less the pain consumed me. I gasped and stumbled backward into the air as the memories came rushing back.

The man leaned back against the desk with his hands in his pockets.

"J-Jerry?" I asked.

Jerry's mouth twitched. "Welcome back to the Collective, Miss Masters."

"My . . . my name is Lily Masters." My voice wobbled. "I'm twenty-one years old. My head is pounding, but I'm still breathing."

"Again."

I used the squishy red armchair to pull myself to my feet. "My name is Lily Masters. I'm twenty-one years old. My head is pounding, but"—I laughed—"I'm still breathing."

"Metaphysically speaking." He took a seat back at his desk. "Your incorporeal form does not contain lungs, so you might have to change that one."

I smiled. "I missed you, Jerry."

"Welcome back to sanity, Miss Masters."

"What happened?"

"Your mind was shattered, but you pieced it back together," he said, picking up a book. "I think this Allister fellow has bit off more than he can chew."

"But the Table, it—"

"The Table broke you, yes, but as you have just found out, broken things can be repaired, to a point. Another turn might be the end for you, so try to avoid that."

I rubbed the side of my head. Though the pain was gone, the memory of it wasn't far away. I doubted it ever would be. "What did it *do* to me?"

"In simple terms? It pushed you. It pushed you right off the edge into insanity." He turned the page. "Try pushing back next time. You might be surprised what you can do."

I folded my arms. "*You* gave me a hug."

"*You* thought I was God."

We stared at each other.

I held out a hand. "Call it even?"

He reached over the desk and shook it. "Even."

TWENTY FOUR

Misplaced

Muffled voices reached me from another level of consciousness. I knew I was awake, but I was reluctant to open my eyes. The pain from the Table was still fresh. Horribly fresh.

Eventually, I cracked open my eyelids. The fuzzy form of an old desk and strange painted runes on the walls sharpened into view. I was still in Reginald's room, lying on the cold stone floor. My hands were tied to the leg of a table. The bindings were much looser than they had been before, at least, so my wrists didn't ache. I furrowed my brow at the old coat draped over me in a small effort to keep me warm. Someone had even placed a leather bag under my head to act as a pillow.

"You can't disturb him now. He's with the book."

"He told me to wait, and I have. I need to collect. Now."

"You shouldn't—"

"I said *now*."

Someone huffed an annoyed breath. "Fine. Wait in there."

The metal door screeched, sending a jolt of pain through my head. Margot walked into the room and froze when she spotted me.

I rested my head back on the bag. "Look who it is: the traitor."

She closed the door behind her and faced away from me.

"What are you even still doing here?" I asked.

She folded her arms and leaned against the desk. "They haven't paid up yet."

"And you're surprised . . . why?"

She ignored me and stared at the door.

I sat up slowly and leaned against the leg of the table. Every muscle in my body felt overworked. My throat was raw, so I swallowed. It didn't help.

"Who else have they got here?" I asked. "Besides Roger, Cliff, and me?"

"I don't know," she said. "You were my only job."

I huffed a breath through my nose. "And how long have I been your job?"

She shrugged, arms tightening across her chest. "Legion contacted me after I came to help with cleanup. After October. They needed a package delivered to them in exchange for . . . what I needed. I didn't know who you were until the day you started training. I didn't know what they wanted you for."

"Pete and Tinker never called you, did they?"

"No."

"Do they even know you're here?"

"No. I doubt they even know I'm still alive. As far as they know, the rest of their family is dead, myself included. I'm fine to keep it that way."

My teeth ground together. "You didn't have to involve Roger in this. If I was your only job, you should've left him in Rome."

"He would've looked for you," she said. "He would've raised the alarm. I couldn't have that."

We stared at each other for a moment. She chewed on the side of her cheek, facing away from me. She turned back and uncrossed her arms. "They wanted to kill him, you know. He was just another loose end, and they wanted him gone. I convinced them he was more useful as a hostage."

"Wow, what a great person you are."

"At least he's alive," she snapped.

We waited in silence. Mumbles from the other side of the door grew and shrank in volume as someone passed by.

I shook my head. "I don't get you, Margot. You're not like these people. I know you're not. Why did you do it?"

She turned her head toward the black reflective glass. "I told you; they had something I needed, so I got it. I don't expect you to understand. It was important."

"More important than Laura or the research camp? More important than all those innocent people in Rome? How could you help them do it? You killed—"

Margot whirled around. "I had *nothing* to do with the research camp, or Laura, or Rome!" She drew a shaky breath. "I didn't know about Rome. My job was to bring you to a rendezvous point after a distraction was set. I never helped with anything else."

"Maybe," I said, "but you sat back and allowed it to happen."

She stared at the floor.

I gave a humorless laugh. "Rog was right. Doing nothing *is* worse."

The door screeched open. My head throbbed at the noise, and I closed my eyes until the pain subsided. Reginald entered and spotted me awake. His eyes flicked to Margot as he grabbed his black bag and approached me.

"Do you remember who I am?" he asked.

"Yes," I said.

"Do you remember your name?"

"Unfortunately."

His mouth twitched. "You had me worried. I thought your mind was broken."

"It was," I said. "But a good friend helped put me it back together."

Reginald turned to Margot. "Allister should be here in a few minutes. Wait elsewhere."

She sighed and gave me a side glance as she walked away.

"You're smarter than this, Margot," I called as Reginald pulled the old electrodes off my head. "Whatever they promised you isn't worth this, and you know it."

She paused and turned her pained gray eyes to mine. "It is to me."

Margot closed the door and left Reginald and me alone.

"Can you stand?" he asked.

"I don't know."

Reginald untied my hands and helped me up. My legs didn't give out, so he kept a hand under my arm and steered me toward the desk.

I sat in the chair opposite him. "How long was I gone?"

He took my pulse with one hand and held a stopwatch in the other. "Less than a day. Do you feel dizzy, lightheaded, or disconnected?"

"All the above."

He pulled a cuff around my arm to check my blood pressure. "That is normal."

The cuff expanded around the top of my arm until it released. I felt my heartbeat as the blood rushed back into my fingers.

"So . . . that Table." I swallowed. "That's how you did it, isn't it? That's how you got Allister to hear the Collective."

He paused and studied the floor. "Yes."

"Why? What did you need him for?"

Reginald sighed. "It was Declan's idea, almost forty years ago. We were roommates at university when Legion sought us out. Both of us excelled in academics—him in history and me in science—and we were ambitious. A little too ambitious, perhaps."

He pulled off the blood pressure cuff and stowed it in his bag. "We were next in the long line of members tasked with locating the Book of Bones."

"For what? To destroy the planet?"

He chuckled. "Is that what they told you? That the *Ossabrium* is going to end the world?"

I didn't answer.

"In a way, they're right. The world won't remain as we know it; it will be reshaped. Reconstituted. The Book of Bones has incredible power, yes, but it's also a map. A map to where the Ones are sealed. A map to where He is sealed. To wake them up, we have to find them first. The Book of Bones is both the key and the summoning bell. Without it, we have nothing. Without it, the world will never be truly free."

"Free from what?"

"Ourselves. Humanity is a mistake, you see. A fluke. We were never supposed to be here in the first place. The One's return will correct that mistake. Only those who choose to follow Him will remain. We'll create a new world. A better world."

"Do you really believe that? That humanity is a mistake?"

Reginald paused, looking down at his callused and wrinkled hands. "I did when I joined Legion. It just . . . made sense when they recruited us. Humans are violent, selfish, brutish creatures. We've overpopulated and overharvested our world out of greed. No other animal has done that. No other animal could. Our very existence is an abhorrence against nature. But . . ."

"But?"

He looked up. "After a lifetime of pursuing the book . . . after a lifetime of traveling the world, I don't know what to think. I've seen horrible things, yes. I've done horrible things. But I've also seen beauty. Forgiveness. Sacrifice. Courage in the face of overwhelming odds. Duality. It puzzles me."

He rummaged around in his bag again and pulled out another set of electrodes. "As we searched for the book, Declan and I hit one dead end after another. No matter how hard we tried, the *Ossabrium* eluded our grasp. It was always one step ahead of us. We always seemed to arrive too late. It was a maddening chase, one that Legion had been engaged in for hundreds of years.

"One day, at a curiosity shop in Germany, Declan stumbled upon something . . . different. Something that no one had tried before. He discovered blueprints for a machine that could give the user infinite knowledge. A machine that could connect you to the Collective, if you survived the process."

"The Tillinghast Papers."

He nodded. "Precisely. We dug deeper, discovered the paper's whereabouts, and Declan organized an operation to recover them. But when we got there, we learned someone had taken them first. So he . . . improvised. Declan has . . ." He sighed. "Declan has changed over the years. The search for the book has hardened him. It has consumed him. He's not the same man he once was."

Reginald produced a new cotton swab stained with fresh disinfectant and scrubbed off the old adhesive on my skin. "We recovered the papers from Los Angeles, and I began building the machine. It took decades to get it right. Countless failed attempts. Countless setbacks. In between it all, I had a son. His mother died in childbirth, so he grew up down here, surrounded by my research. He loved it. He wanted to be a part of it.

"At first I kept him as far away as I could. It was dangerous, I knew that, but over time . . . I relented. We had hit so many dead ends that I couldn't take it anymore. As you know, the ability to hear the Collective is either passed down genetically or learned over a lifetime, but we . . ."

His face paled. "We didn't . . . we didn't have a lifetime to wait. Allister became our test subject."

The brief memory of the little boy screaming at the Table flashed across my eyes.

"Oh my God," I whispered.

"The machine—" He gestured to the other room. "It speeds up the process of a Discovery by breaking down the walls in your mind. It allows your perception of reality to be shattered beyond repair. Humans are funny; whatever we can't comprehend, we just block out. Ignore. But when those walls break . . . you can see and hear things. Terrible things. Things like the Collective, and the beings associated with it.

"Recently, Allister had a breakthrough," he said. "He located a researcher who found the book's location. She knew *what* it was, which was interesting. It's an incredibly slippery thing to search for, the book. For some reason, you can't track it in the Collective. It's a blind spot, like all humanity wants to forget its existence. You can't search for it directly, but you can find people connected with it."

My stomach sank. "Laura."

Reginald nodded. "We found her. We got her to tell us where it was. Then her friend came looking for her, and Declan formed a plan to 'kill two birds with one stone,' as it were. We knew they'd come after the book, and so would you."

I exhaled slowly and looked down at my hands. "You did that to your own *son*? You drove him insane to find the *Ossabrium*. You made him like this."

Reginald glanced at the rusty door. "I as good as killed him. Because whatever monster is out there, it's not my son."

"But what do you need me for?" I asked. "You already have someone who can hear the Collective. You've already found the book. Why do you need me too?"

Reginald lowered his gaze. "Because, to locate beings of unknowable power, you need help. And to make a deal with one, you also need a bargaining chip."

Twenty Five

Penance

The door banged into the wall as Allister strode inside. "Is she ready?"

Reginald eyed his son with apprehension. "This is incredibly risky, Allister. I doubt if she can take another turn and keep her mind intact. If you'd only wait—"

"I *said*, is she ready?"

Reginald shakily placed another electrode on my head. "Almost."

"Good. This is taking too long as it is."

I watched Allister as he paced about the room, trembling eyes flicking back and forth. How had a normal child turned into this? What kind of person would he be if they had never subjected him to the Table? What would I turn into after doing another few turns? Could I even handle it?

I already knew the answer to that, and so did Jerry: no. The next turn on the Table would be my last. At least, my last turn as Lily Masters. My mind would be so far gone, I wouldn't know *who* I was. I would be as good as dead. Just like Allister.

"Where are the others?" I asked. "What's happening to them?"

Allister smirked. "Are you sure you want me to tell you that?"

My chest tightened, and I glared at him.

He laughed and petted my hair as I struggled to scoot away. "Aw, c'mon, don't be like that. You'll forget them soon, anyway."

I swallowed.

The metal door shrieked open again, and Margot entered the room, colorless eyes sweeping over me. "The job's done, and you owe me."

Allister sighed and reached into his pocket. "I suppose a deal is a deal. Here." He pulled out a crumpled envelope and handed it to her. "That's all I could find."

Margot's eyes widened as she snatched the envelope and tore it open, scanning the small note inside several times. Her eyes watered, and she looked back up. "He . . . he was there all this time?"

"For the last five years, as far as I could see. Safe and sound. Well, mostly."

She shoved the paper in her pocket. "We're square. I'm out."

Margot turned to go, but Allister blocked her path. "Since you're here, why don't you stay and watch this turn? I bet you'd like to know just what this piece of information was worth."

"No," she said shortly. "Get out of my way."

She tugged open the door. Allister mumbled something to the armed guards outside, and they shuffled in front of her, rifles at the ready.

Margot's eyes flicked to the two burly men. She chewed on the side of her cheek and folded her arms. "Why do you need me here? You got what you wanted."

Allister flashed a wide, almost hungry grin. "Because I want someone to see what this thing can do. It's almost an art form, the Table. The way it . . . changes you. Shapes you. There's something beautiful about it." He let out a wistful sigh, returning his shifting irises to Margot. "Stay for a few minutes. I insist."

Margot glanced at the armed guards again. "Fine. Make it quick."

Reginald escorted me to the back room, Allister and Margot in tow. I took deep breaths to slow the beating of my terrified heart. Reginald gave my arm a comforting squeeze as he felt me shaking.

A strange feeling settled in my stomach as I realized I was about to die.

It hadn't hit me until now, but that's what sitting at the Table would mean. My body would still be here, but whatever was inside . . . it wouldn't be me. Somehow, that seemed worse than outright death. Maybe I'd get lucky and have a heart attack or a stroke or something.

I walked to the chair slowly and sat, waiting as Allister buckled me in. Struggling wouldn't do any good, and I didn't want my last conscious moments spent crying and begging for my life. Margot stood by the wall, and we made eye contact as Allister cinched my hands onto the Table.

I swallowed. "I believe what you said before. That you didn't know about Rome. I believe you, Margot. I hope whatever you got from them was worth it."

Her eyes widened, and her breath caught. She looked like she wanted to say something but stopped herself. Her hands tightened into fists by her sides.

Reginald spun several dials and flicked some switches, and the Table hummed to life. Taking a few steadying breaths, I didn't stop the tears from falling down my face.

I wondered how long it would take my mom and dad to find out I was dead. Would I just be missing forever? Maybe Henry or Bea could tell them, if they hadn't already. Maybe they'd do me the kindness of destroying my body before Legion had a chance to use me. Who would they send to do it? Someone who didn't know me, probably. Maybe Roger would volunteer for the job. In a strange way, I hoped it was him. At least he'd get a chance to see that I wasn't there anymore. If he was still alive, anyway.

My heart squeezed as I thought about Roger. I hoped he'd escape without me, and I hoped he'd forgive me for all the things I never told him out loud.

Hope. All I had left was hope.

Because what else could I do?

The Table hummed loudly.

Reginald pressed three large buttons on the control panel, hand hovering over the switch. He stared at me, his tired blue eyes pained and conflicted. He shot a glance at Allister, who watched me with obvious pleasure. Reginald nodded to me, and I clenched my teeth together.

I took one last breath as he pulled the switch down.

I had vague thoughts about trying not to scream; they perished when the Table started spinning. I shrieked as my hands stayed welded to the glossy surface. My arms and legs strained against the straps as every nerve in my body wailed in pain. Bronze coils and golden gears blended together with silver wires until it was one blur of moving pictures.

My mind slipped downward into the Table. Once I fell inside, there was no coming back. Not this time.

I needed to breathe.

I needed to ground myself.

I needed to push back.

My name was Lily Masters.

—bright hordes of chameleon-like creatures scuttled grotesquely over a pink ocean floor. Revolting piles of tentacles stretched to reach for screaming humans. A sky pouring blood from the clouds like rain—

I was twenty-one years old.

—venous clots of stringy vegetation choked out once thriving cities. Picturesque streets were now craters of smoking earth—

My head was pounding.

—red tidal waves of chemicals swept through homes and vaporized everything in its path. Winged spiny creatures flapped through the sky with horrible screeching noises—

But I was still breathing.

—the metal box shrank against my struggling body, snapping bones and crushing muscles. The great white sun burned my skin—

My name was . . .

—agony. Breathing was agony. Years of suffering condensed into mere moments in time. There was no escape from it. There was no relief. In the darkness of a thousand wretched nights, a figure spoke to me. It whispered—

My name . . .

The hallway built from a billion eyes—

My name . . . my name was Lily Masters.

Smoking tendrils of vapor reached out for me—

I was . . . I was twenty-one years old.

"Come," they whispered—

They may be many—

"Stay."

"But I am stronger!" I shouted.

The Table wobbled in its eternal spinning. Sparks sputtered from the machine, and smoke leaked from the table as the pulsing hum ceased.

I stopped screaming, shutting my eyes against the sparks raining down on the room. Margot and Allister ducked away from the machine as Reginald hurried to shut it down. Trailing vapor leaked into the air as the whirling hum of electricity sputtered to a stop.

It was quiet except for my ragged breathing.

Allister stared at the Table in disbelief before turning to me and yanking my head back. "What did you do?"

I laughed.

He jerked his arm and ripped out a chunk of hair. I laughed some more. Any pain seemed so insignificant after what I just experienced. It was funny, really.

"*What the hell did you do?*" he screamed.

"I pushed back." I laughed. "And you can't do . . . *anything* about it."

I kept laughing as he unstrapped me from the chair and dragged me into the next room by my wrist. The laughter ebbed as he threw me to the cold floor.

I looked up, staring down the barrel of a gun covered in tally marks. He cocked it.

"You just lost your *one* use in this world, you know that?" Allister trembled. "The *one* reason I kept you alive, and now you're useless, you understand me? *Useless!*"

I used the desk to claw myself to my feet. "I may be useless, Allister, but you know what I'm not?"

"*Don't say—*"

"Crazy."

He yelled and backhanded me across the face. "*Don't call me that!*"

My ears rang with the cracking noise. Margot and Reginald followed us, watching in shock as I stumbled back into a bookshelf full of glass beakers.

Reginald tried to approach his son. "Now, Allister, just calm—"

"That was our *one chance* to get her strong enough to bargain with me! This will set us back *years!*" He took better aim, his finger shaking on the trigger. "We don't have years to wait for her. She passed her expiration date hours ago. She's done. I'll find somebody else."

"Allister, if you'll just—"

Static. A wall of it. Both Allister and I straightened to hear the crackling static swimming through the air.

T . . . r . . . a . . . i . . . t . . . o . . . r . . .

My eyes widened. Allister's gaze turned to his father.

"You did this, didn't you?" he said, his voice dangerously calm. "You weakened the Table so she could break it. You betrayed me. You betrayed us."

Reginald's face paled. "N-no, of . . . of course not. I-I-I . . ."

His voice faltered.

Allister nodded thoughtfully, his pupils twitching. "Frankly, I'm surprised you lasted this long."

He turned the gun on his father and squeezed the trigger. I clamped my eyes shut and turned away, but that didn't stop the sound. I covered my mouth with my hands and held back a scream. Reginald's feet poked out from behind the desk. A spatter of blood covered the painted wall behind him.

Allister returned the gun to me. A faint wisp of smoke rose from it.

"I should've known you weren't worth the trouble," he spat.

My body froze in place. I couldn't move, breathe, or think.

Allister stared at me for a long minute. "What a waste of time."

My eyes widened as he pulled the trigger.

Another bang shattered the silence, but there was something in front of me. A shape had lunged into the path of the bullet. The shape jolted with a choked noise. Margot crumpled to the ground.

"Huh." Allister cocked his head with an amused smile. "Interesting."

Shouts and muffled gunshots came from outside as a guard banged open the door and shouted something. Allister turned to me and raised his arm again. He fired, but the gun just clicked open. He pulled the trigger again. Nothing happened. Glancing at me and Margot, he ran out the door as the nearby shots drew closer.

My body broke from its frozen position, and I stumbled forward. "M-Margot?"

I turned her onto her back. She shook uncontrollably, her hands clasped over her chest as she stared at the ceiling. Dark red leaked between her fingers, blossoming across her shirt.

"I better get . . . a *damn* good statue for this," she gasped, choking out a laugh. "And . . . and those better be my last words."

I pried her hands away from her rib cage, recoiling at the wound beneath. The hole ripped through her was inches wide, the surrounding bones shattered from the impact. I pressed down on the wound. Her chest compressed with a sickening clicking noise.

"Why did you do that?" I asked.

She struggled to focus. "Because y-you were right. Doing nothing is worse. And I . . . needed . . . to do . . . something."

My stomach tightened. I pressed harder on the wound, but I knew it was useless. A puddle had already formed on the ground beneath her.

I tried to keep my voice steady. "Hang in there, Margot. I-I-I'll find some help, and we'll get you patched up, okay? You're going to be fine."

Margot choked out another laugh. "You're a terrible liar, flower girl."

More shouts and gunshots from outside the door echoed back at us.

"I'm-m-m s-sorry I was so hard on you in t-training," she wheezed, "but I didn't want to get attached. Guess I sh-should've tried harder."

With tremendous effort, she reached into her pocket and shoved the envelope Allister had given her into my hand. "P-please, you need to find him. I know you don't have a single reason to help me, b-but p-please find him."

"Find who?"

"M-my brother." Her eyes spilled over with tears. "I wanted to give him a b-better life, so I"—she sucked in a sob—"so I joined up and wiped his memory so he wouldn't look for me. I planned to c-come back when I had enough money for us to . . . to make it on our own, but . . ." She sobbed again and convulsed. "When I came back, he was gone. I've been searching ever since. I've t-tried other ways, b-but no one could find him except Legion. Not even that cr-crazy witch in the forest."

Tears stung my eyes. "*That's* why you started all of this? Why didn't you just ask me?"

She gave a shuddering laugh. "You said it yourself. It could've taken y-years."

The shouts grew closer.

Margot's labored breath came in violent gasps, and she reached for my hand. I clutched hers, the envelope crinkling between our blood slick palms.

She stared at the ceiling. "Tell him I'm sorry. Tell him I'm so sorry for everything." Her eyes focused on something I couldn't see, and she squeezed my hand. "I'm sorry for leaving you alone, squirt. I was selfish. I never should've left you alone. I'm s-so, so sorry, squirt. I'm s-s-so . . ."

She exhaled a wet, rattling cough. Margot's hand fell slack, her silver eyes emptying as her body sagged against me. A last wheezing breath left her throat, and she didn't move again.

Twenty Six

Escape

I couldn't let go of her hand.

"Margot?" I whispered. I shook her to keep her awake. Her head lolled to the side. "Margot, come back. Please don't . . ." I shook her again. "*Margot!*"

Shouts behind the door grew louder. Someone grabbed me from behind. I couldn't stop myself from screaming and thrashing as they pulled me away from her lifeless form.

"*Lily!* It's me!" a familiar voice said. I stopped thrashing. I knew that voice.

Sobbing for air, I turned in time for Roger to shove me behind the door. The doorway cracked into powder as bullets struck the edge of the wall. Roger ducked around the corner and returned fire with an unfamiliar pistol, leaning back as more pops of powdered stone flashed into the air.

There was screaming in my head. I wasn't sure whose it was, but the wails and shrieks inside my skull echoed so violently, I almost passed out. I clamped my hands over my ears. It wouldn't stop.

"*That's the sound of your friends dying. Those are the sounds they'll make when you have lost everything.*"

"*Get out of my head!*" I sobbed, my voice lost in the cracking of gunfire.

"When I say go, we're going to make a run for it, okay?" Roger yelled over the constant banging. I nodded and tried to ready my shaking legs.

He ducked around the corner and grabbed my bloody hand. "Stay close to me."

Roger pulled me out of the room, leaving Reginald and Margot behind us.

I tried to stay close as we ran down the hallway and skidded to a stop around a corner. The unbearably straight corridors provided little cover. Roger continued to pop into the line of fire, finally leaning back.

He slammed a new cartridge into the bottom of the grip and panted. "This is my last one."

A loud metallic bang echoed down the hall. The shouting stopped. So did the gunfire. We looked at each other, and Roger inched his head around the corner. He raised the gun at someone approaching.

"Calm down, son," another familiar voice said. "Just me."

Roger lowered the gun and leaned on his knees, his entire body shaking. "Holy *shit*, Henry!"

I peeked around the corner. Henry approached us, his blue-green broadsword at his side. A smoking metal husk of a force bomb lay nearby, the unconscious bodies of a dozen guards next to it.

A wave of relief passed over me. I tried to keep my voice steady. "I've never been so happy to see you."

Henry flashed a small smile. "You too, both of you."

Roger coughed, wobbling on his feet. The left side of his face was swollen, deep gashes and welts circling his wrists. Dozens of burn holes dotted his shirt. Cigarette burns. A trail of blood leaked from a circular gouge on his neck.

"How'd you get here?" Roger panted.

Henry checked over his shoulder and waved us forward. We followed. "Oh, come on, you didn't think we were just going to abandon you, did you? We've been working to locate you all since the attack in Rome. We got lucky and tailed a suspected member to Venice a few hours ago. She led us right here." His head jerked to the side as more shouts and gunfire echoed from farther down the tunnel. "I brought the cavalry. We gotta move."

We sprinted down the tunnel, feet slapping against the cold stone. It seemed like the corridor would never end. Eventually, it bent, leading to a series of crank-operated doors. I glanced behind us. Three men rushed down the hallway, spotting us at the end.

Roger slammed into the door and tried to crank it. It was stuck.

"Come on," he huffed. "*Move!*"

I backed into the wall. Henry stood in front of me, sword at the ready.

A flash of red whipped in front of the guard's feet, and they tripped spectacularly forward. Dancing out from an open doorframe, a woman twirled her spinning red disk like a giant yo-yo and took out the three men in a matter of seconds.

Bryn straightened out of her defensive pose and smiled at me. "Hullo, Lily. Nice to see you again."

One man moaned. She thumped him on the back of his head.

I gasped for air, giving a half-hearted wave.

Henry frowned. "I thought I told you to stay as backup."

Bryn flipped her scarf over her shoulder. "Whoops."

The metal crank finally gave way. Roger spun the wheel and yanked open the door. We darted through it. Another endless tunnel stretched into darkness.

"We can't get back to the front, Henry," Bryn said as we ran. "There's too many. We're going to have to find a spot close to the outside and teleport out. Irene has a signal booster. Where are the others?"

"They're getting Cliff," Henry panted.

Roger ran lopsidedly as he pulled two Teleporters from his pocket. He shoved one into my hands. "Here, Lil, I swiped these when I left."

I clamped my blood-covered hand around the small silver disc. It dug into my palm, but I didn't care. If it was a way out of this hell, I was never letting it go.

"Henry!" someone shouted off to our left. "Go! Go! Go! They're right behind us!"

Irene, Chelsea, and Artemus sprinted down the intersecting hall, waving for us to turn. We skidded around the corner as they caught up to us.

"I would say good to see you," Artemus shouted, "but I'll just save it until it's actually good to see you!"

"Where's my dad?" Roger asked the new group. "I thought you were supposed to get him?"

"He should be out by now!" Irene gasped. "Snuff was the only one strong enough to carry him, so we caused a diversion and let them make a run for it. But we didn't know they had—"

Vicious snarls echoed behind us.

"Dweller hounds!" Chelsea finished for her. "They've been breeding dweller hounds down here!"

"*What?*" Bryn squeaked. "That's impossible!"

The barking grew closer.

"Well, don't look now," Artemus shouted, "but I think they'd disagree with you!"

I glanced behind me. A horde of strange scaly dogs bounded toward us from the opposite end of the tunnels, getting closer every second. It was enough to give my shaky legs a reason to keep up the pace.

"Is this tunnel ever going to end?" Roger gasped.

"Doesn't look like it, does it?" Henry huffed. "You think we're close enough, Bryn?"

"How should I know?" Bryn snapped. "*I* was supposed to stay as back-up!"

The humid, stale air burned my throat with each breath. I wiped some sweat from my eyes. The domed stone tunnel just kept going, its many small ponds of water disturbed as the seven of us ran for our lives. In my hand, I felt a small buzz from the Teleporter. I'd inadvertently made a connection. At least we were close enough to the outside for that to work.

Angry shouts rounded the corner in front of us as we slid to a stop. The dweller hounds still closed in behind us, as did the group in front. Allister was one of them. We locked eyes. He smiled.

"*You think you can run from me?*"

I clamped my hands over my ears. "Shut up! Shut up! *Shut up!*"

Irene yanked out a small metal rod from her jacket. She unfolded it and slammed it into the old stone wall. After a few strikes, it stuck in. A series of lights flickered feebly on the shaft. The hair stood up on my arms, a tingling sensation rippling across my skin.

Roger held the Teleporter close to it, his eyes widening. "I've got a signal!"

Crack!

Bullets pounded the wall. Chelsea stumbled forward as a shot crashed into her arm, a fine mist of blood sprouting from it. Irene pulled her to the ground. We ducked as Roger opened a flickering portal beneath us.

"Everyone in!" he shouted.

Shots rang out as we dove into the weakening portal, leaving the dank, stale air of the tunnel behind us.

I slid on the smooth wooden floor until my feet hit a bookcase. I stared up at the towering rows, marveling at the chandelier above me. Nearby, the infinite expanse of stars shone through the windows of the viewing bay. Giftshop had never looked so beautiful. The quiet had never sounded so good. No screams, no gunshots, just ringing silence.

"Everyone alive?" Irene called.

The group moaned, slowly rising from the ground.

"*That*," Chelsea wheezed, clutching her arm, "was way too close."

"No kidding," Artemus agreed, plopping onto his back. "I'm never moving again."

"Those bastards . . . they had . . . dweller hounds," Bryn gasped. "*Unbelievable*. Where'd they get them?"

Henry hacked a cough. "No idea."

I leaned against the wall and unclenched my Teleporter from my blood-stained hand. Seeing the caked-on red brought everything back. Rome. Flashes from the Table. Reginald's feet poking out from behind the desk. Margot's empty eyes. I bit the top of my wrist to keep from screaming.

"Lily? Are you hurt?"

I couldn't look up. My entire body shook.

"Lily, can you hear me?"

I clamped my eyes shut.

"Lil."

A hand pressed against my shoulder. The simple touch pushed me over the edge. I buried my head in my arms and sobbed. I wasn't sure if I was screaming or crying, but I didn't care. It was too much. Everything was too much. I wanted it to stop. I wanted to erase the last few days from history. *I* wanted to be erased from history.

Someone tried to pull me into a hug. I thrashed away.

"Did . . . did she say she—"

"Just give her some space, Rog."

"Do you think she was—"

"Artie. Not right now."

Roger let go of my shoulders. Eventually, I calmed down enough to hear the surrounding conversation.

"I'm staying here."

"Rog, you've already lost a lot of blood."

"I'll be fine. I've stayed standing for this long, right?"

"It's just the next room. You both aren't going anywhere. It's safe now. And you won't be much use to anyone if your arm gets amputated."

It was quiet.

"Fine."

There was shuffling as the presence next to me disappeared. It became silent again.

Something touched my arm. "Lily?"

I jumped, half expecting to see insane golden eyes staring at me. But it was just Irene, peering kindly with blue ones. Chelsea and Artemus stood behind her, keeping their distance. Bryn, Henry, and Roger had left already.

"Let's get you off the floor, huh?" she said.

The kindness in her eyes hurt to look at. The sun-cracked face of Leo crawling through the desert forced itself into my mind. I knew it was a hallucination from the Table, but it didn't matter. The guilt, before choked by fear, was back. I couldn't take it anymore.

I scrambled to my feet. "What is *wrong* with all of you? How can you even look at me? Don't you know what I did?"

The three of them seemed confused. Irene stepped forward. "What do you mean?"

"Don't you . . . don't you know that I—" I clenched my fists together. "Don't you know I'm the one who killed him?"

"Who?"

"Leo!" I shouted. "I killed him! Your teammate! Your friend! I've seen his life, his memories. *I've lived all of it!* I know what he meant to you, so"—my breath caught—"why are you all so nice to me?"

Chelsea clutched her arm. "Lily, you've been through a lot, I think you need to get some rest—"

"No!" I sobbed. "I *killed* someone you cared about. I dropped him into the goddamn *sky*! Don't you hate me? Don't you hate me for taking him from you?"

"Lily, we don't hate you," Artemus said. "We've known since October."

"W-what?"

"Henry told us what Leo got involved with, back when The Bound almost came through." Irene sighed. "And . . . we knew what had to be sacrificed to stop them. He was so broken after Anna died that I'm pretty sure it was the kindest way for it to end for him. We're just sorry you had to be the one to do it."

"But . . . but . . ." I stuttered. "How can you look at me and not see the one that killed him? How can you do it?"

"Because you didn't kill him," Artemus said. "The Bound did. Simple as that."

My legs wobbled. I grabbed onto the bookshelf behind me to keep from falling.

Artemus reached for me. "Here, let's get you cleaned up—"

I jolted away from him, blood pumping loudly in my ears. My body screamed at me to run. To hide. To fight.

He shot a glance at Irene and Chelsea, who nodded.

"Lily?" Irene said. "I'm going to do a medical check on you. Is that all right? It's standard procedure with hostage victims."

Chelsea and Artemus walked to the door and closed it gently behind them.

I swallowed. "Why did they just leave?"

"Just to make you more comfortable. I can have them come back, if you want."

"No, it's fine. Can I sit down?"

She nodded and stepped out of my way. "Of course. Can you take your jacket off?"

I tugged my jacket tighter around me. The thought of removing any layer of protection made my skin itch. Eventually, I shrugged it off and sat on the table. I looked down at myself. Deep red cuts wrapped around my wrists, the rest of my arms covered in fingerprint-shaped bruises where Allister had pushed and pulled me around. The thick rectangular bruises were from the straps of the Spinning Table. Just the sight of them brought back the pain. I shoved it away.

Irene retrieved an orange medical kit that appeared on a nearby table and unzipped it. She glanced at my arms and cleared her throat. "Lily, when you were taken, did they . . . do anything to you?"

"They tortured me into insanity and back again, if that's what you mean."

"No, I mean, did they . . . assault you? Did they force you to . . . do anything?"

"Allister hit me a lot, and . . ." I trailed off, realizing what she was asking. My stomach clenched. "I . . . I don't think so. There were a few times I thought he would . . . I thought he'd . . ." I closed my eyes. "But I don't think he ever went that far."

She nodded and unwrapped a few packets of disinfecting wipes. "Did they give you anything to eat? And drugs or injections that you can remember?"

"When they kidnapped me, they used something on a rag. And I think Reginald gave me a sedative after the second . . . the second . . ." I stared at the ground. It was so hard to talk about it. Why couldn't I talk about it?

Irene dabbed at the cuts on my wrist. Despite Giftshop's warm hum, they stung. Irene continued asking me questions, and I answered them, trying to convince myself I had escaped from the tunnels. Was I sitting in Giftshop, or was this all just a dream? Was I still hooked up to the Table? Was this all one big hallucination? I didn't think I could handle that.

The door opened quietly a few minutes later, but I still jumped. Henry and Bryn peeked into the room, their faces solemn. Irene finished wrapping my raw skin in fresh, sterile gauze and nodded for them to enter. "Any word from Snuff?"

"Nothing yet," Henry said. "I have a connection back in Venice, and so does Roger, but I don't think we should risk going back. Snuff might've made it out, just not to Giftshop. Any ideas, Irene?"

"His apartment in Portland." She shrugged. "But why wouldn't he just come here?"

"Maybe he panicked?" Bryn offered.

"Snuff doesn't panic," Irene said confidently. "If he's not back by now, that means he didn't make it out. Neither did Cliff."

I swayed on the table when static ruffled past my ears. It felt different. Louder. The whispers were clear, accompanied by a faint image in the back of my mind. I couldn't see much, only fuzzy shadows.

C...a...p...t...u...r...e...d...

"He's been captured," I repeated.

"Is he still alive?" Henry asked. "Are either of them still alive?"

I closed my eyes and listened again. The fuzzy shapes sharpened into two men locked in a room. It faded quickly.

H...o...s...t...a...g...e...

"They're alive," I said. "I think Legion is counting on us coming back for them. They'll be ready this time."

Henry held his head in his hands.

"What're we going to do?" I asked. "We can't just leave them there."

"No, we can't. And we can't leave the book there, either."

"So, what now?"

Henry was speechless. His eyes shone as he slumped onto the table. "I don't know. I truly don't know."

TWENTY SEVEN

Ventriloquist

We sat in tepid silence.

"You and Rog need to get some rest," Bryn said. "You've been through enough."

"What about Cliff? What about Snuff?" I asked. "What are we going to do about them?" I glanced at Irene. "And where's Jack? Didn't he come with you?"

She bit her lip, clearing her throat to keep it steady. "Jack is . . . in the hospital, in critical condition. He . . . he didn't make it out of Rome in one piece."

I put a hand to my head. Rome . . . that felt like so long ago now. "Who . . . who else did we lose in Rome?"

They all looked down.

"Thirty-three people died in the explosion," Bryn whispered. "Fourteen were ours."

I leaned on my knees.

"Get some rest, Lily," Henry said. "We'll take things from here. You've been through enough. Rog'll be here in a few minutes, and you two can head back to Stars Crossing. We'll keep in contact once we know something."

"But wait, we can't just—"

"Give yourself some time," Irene soothed. "Even if it's just a few hours, give yourself some time to process. There's nothing else we can do right now."

The door opened again, and Chelsea and Artemus hurried through. Chelsea's arm hung in a sling. Artemus held up an open Chatterbox, his face white. "Irene, it's the hospital."

Irene's eyes widened, and she looked at Henry. He nodded. "Go. I'll keep you in the loop."

She jogged to her ever-shrinking team without another word and closed the door behind her.

"Where's Rog?" I asked.

"Getting a med check," Henry said, grimacing. "That boy sure can take a beating."

The door creaked open for a third time, and Roger entered. His swollen face had lessened, the cuts and scratches cleaned and taped. Someone had replaced his blood-soaked and cigarette-burned T-shirt with a clean one. The uneven bulge under his clothes showed that his injured shoulder had been freshly bandaged.

He barely glanced at me before turning to Henry. Even in that brief glance, the betrayal in his eyes was evident. My stomach sank.

"Any news on my dad?" he asked.

Henry looked down. "As far as we know, Snuff didn't get him out."

Roger's jaw clenched. "Is . . . is he . . ."

"Lily heard he's still alive," Bryn said. "We're guessing they're holding them hostage, hoping we'll come back for them and the book."

"And we are, right?" Roger said. "Going back for them? We can't just leave them there."

"They know we're coming this time." Henry sighed. "There will be twice as many guards. Anyone who goes down there won't make it out alive."

"I don't care." Roger balled his hands into fists. "We've got to get him out of there! He'd do the same for me. He'd do the same for any of you! I've got a connection. I . . . I'll go back there alone if I have to!"

"If you do that, we'll be in a bigger mess than we are right now. You know he—"

"I can't lose him again, Henry!" Roger shouted. His voice broke. "I *can't* do this again. God, not again."

Henry put a hand on his good shoulder. "I know. But there's nothing we can change about it now without putting more lives at risk. They know we'll come back for them, so they'll keep them alive."

It was quiet.

Henry cleared his throat again. "You need rest, both of you. Get home, get some sleep. I'll come get you in a few hours."

Roger stared at the floor.

Henry sighed, waving for Bryn to follow him. "Till again."

Roger and I mumbled departing words as Bryn and Henry walked out the door.

We stood in silence. Neither of us seemed to know what to say.

"Do you have a connection to the house?" he finally asked.

I shook my head. "I think I accidentally made a connection when we were escaping. Down in the tunnels. I'm not sure, though."

He shuffled a few steps to the door. "Let's not risk it. Can you—"

He broke off as his gaze fixated on the fingerprint bruises on my arms. His eyes widened. I tried to cover them up with my hands before tugging on my jacket. He reached forward but stopped himself.

Roger swallowed, his jaw clenched. "Did he . . . did he touch—"

I shook my head slowly. "Not like . . . not like that."

His body shook. The veins stood out on his arms. "I'll kill him. I swear to God, I'll kill him."

"Rog, he didn't—"

"I don't care," he said. "After everything he did, I'll . . . I'll . . ."

"Please, don't let them win," I whispered. "Don't give them the satisfaction of making you into one of them. Don't let them turn you into a killer, too."

He hunched, shutting his eyes tight. He let out a rushed breath. "Let's just go home."

We shuffled through Giftshop after signing out. I didn't have a pen, but the cut on my head had opened again, so I dotted my initials using blood.

"Who fixed up your head?" Roger asked. "That looks like it was sterilized a few days ago."

"Reginald."

"Who?"

"Allister's father. Or he . . . he was. He . . ." I closed my eyes. "Never mind. How's your shoulder?"

He shrugged and winced. "I'll live."

"What about . . . everything else?"

He hesitated, tugging his shirt away from his skin. "Let's just say I'll never take up smoking."

We didn't pass another person the entire way to the Connector room. Roger tugged open the door to the Roseland Connector and stepped through. We squinted at the bright pink and orange light as we trudged through the familiar landscape. The last time we walked this trail was after my parents had called, informing me they were selling the house. How was that only a few days ago? It seemed like years had passed since then.

"Was . . . was he lying?"

I turned. Roger had stopped walking.

"What?"

"Was he lying? Allister. When he said you knew about my mom?"

I swallowed, staring at the spongy vegetation below me. "No," I mumbled.

"What?"

"No," I said louder. "He wasn't lying."

"And you . . . you didn't tell me? You just . . ."

He trailed off and stared hard at the ground.

"It was an accident," I said. "I wasn't—"

"How long have you known?"

"Since the morning after Bonfire."

He turned away from me.

"I triggered a residual memory from the Collective," I tried to explain. "I . . . I wasn't looking for it on purpose."

"But you found out and kept it to yourself." He shook his head, his eyes flicking back and forth. "You knew *all* this time?"

"I didn't . . . it wasn't my place to tell you. It wasn't—"

"Then whose job was it?" His voice shook. "My dad's? Some stranger? Why did no one tell me? Why did they lie to me my entire life?"

"Because you would've gone after them by yourself. You could've gotten yourself killed! You could've gotten other people killed!"

"Oh, are we talking about me now, or are we talking about you?"

My breath caught.

"You lied, Lily!" he shouted. "You knew something bad was going on, you *heard* it, and you kept it from everyone. You kept it from me! That's not what we do! That's not how this is supposed to work! Now people have died, and it's your f—"

The color drained from Roger's face as the words died in his throat.

My eyes stung. The guilt that I'd tried so hard to push off choked me, twisting my insides into knots. But he was right. He was so painfully right. I should've said something the minute I heard the voice at the sparring ring, but I didn't. It was my fault things had gotten this far. All of it.

His eyes widened. "I-I'm sorry, I didn't mean to say—"

I turned back toward the trail. "Let's just go."

A hand was on my shoulder. "I didn't mean that."

I jolted away. Tears streamed down my face. "Don't touch me," I whispered. "Please."

"Lily . . ."

I walked toward the Gate. After a moment, he followed, and we approached the pole in silence. I wasn't sure how he was going to manage climbing with his injured shoulder, but he wordlessly mounted it and shuffled up. I followed, my shaky arms barely managing the task. Every part of me was exhausted. Every part of me felt drained and dead. I was more tired than I had ever been in my life, but somehow, I was still moving forward. I had to keep moving forward.

Because what else could I do?

We clambered out of the Gate, descending the stairs of the barn and stepping into the icy rain. The gray sky was getting dark, droplets pelting the muddy ground. I had no idea what time it was, or even what day it was.

How long had we been down in the tunnels? A few days? For all I knew, we'd been there for weeks. A lifetime.

We trudged up the stairs and pushed open the creaky door. The house was cold, almost as chilly as the outside. The air seemed staler, too. I flipped on the kitchen light. The old bulb flickered to life, revealing the cozy kitchen. It was strange, being somewhere so normal. So familiar. The lack of threat was unsettling, somehow.

We stood in silence.

Roger seemed like he wanted to say something but stopped himself. He cleared his throat. "I think some of my stitches popped. I'm going to stop the bleeding."

He disappeared into the hallway, shutting the bathroom door behind him.

I closed my eyes and leaned against the counter, stopping another sob from working its way out of my throat. Gripping my elbows, I crossed the living room and climbed the stairs to the loft, not bothering to turn on the light. I just needed to be alone. At least I needed to be away from Roger. Seeing the betrayed hurt in his eyes would be more than I could handle right now.

On the last step, static rattled through my head. My heartbeat skyrocketed.

B . . . e . . . h . . . i . . . n . . . d . . .

I almost had time to yell before a hand covered my mouth and jerked me backward.

"Ah-ah-ah, no screaming."

I tried to struggle, but the cold hard feeling of a gun jammed into my side. Allister leaned me back against him, my feet barely touching the floor. I choked as I tried to breathe, horribly aware of the gun in my rib cage.

"You scream, you die, understand?" He pushed it further into my side. *"Any trouble from you, and you're done."*

I nodded, and he released his hand from my mouth. He clamped his arm around my waist and pulled me closer.

"H-how did you get here?" I whispered.

He jolted me. *"You don't need to talk to me like that. C'mon, let's make this quieter."*

My eyes burned, but I complied. *"How did you find me?"*

Allister shuffled us closer toward the stairs leading down to the living room. *"Tracked your Teleporter when you escaped. Locked onto your energy signature and took a shortcut here when you got back to Earth."*

I glanced down at his wrist. *"You said those were short-range transporters."*

"They are. When you don't have an organic coordinate to connect to. And fortunately for me"—he squeezed his arm around my stomach so hard my ribs ached—*"you're an organic coordinate."*

He moved us down a step. *"Now, we're going to tiptoe downstairs, wait for him to leave, and then use that little Teleporter of yours to get us back home."*

"I don't know what you're talking about."

He pushed me forward. *"Don't lie to me! I know you have an energy lock at the edge of the electromagnetic field. They told me you do."*

I closed my eyes as I felt blood coming from my nose. *"Please, just let me go. You don't need me anymore. You already have the book."*

He nuzzled into the side of my neck, and I gagged. *"Don't be like that, Lily. Just because you upset me doesn't mean I can't have a use for you. You might not be able to bargain with me, but you can still be a peace offering to Him. An appetizer, if you will."*

The bathroom door opened downstairs. I felt the color leave my face as Allister chuckled softly in my head.

"Showtime," he said. *"Now you're going to do exactly as I say, or he dies first."*

We walked together down the stairs until he pushed me on the last step. I lost my balance and fell on my hands and knees. Allister gestured with the gun to the kitchen. I obeyed, peering around the corner.

"Exactly as I say."

I turned toward the stairs with my back to the hallway and the front door. The thumping of my heart made it hard to breathe. I tried to keep from shaking.

Roger's footsteps entered the kitchen. He sighed. "Lil, I'm . . . I'm sorry. I didn't mean it, what I said before."

"I don't think this is working out."

"I just lost my head. I don't blame you for what happened. And I . . . I'm sorry for yelling at you. That wasn't okay."

I tried to move my mouth, but the choking pain inside me made it impossible to breathe.

"Lil?" A hand pressed softly to my shoulder. "You all right?"

"Say it."

"I don't think this is working out," I repeated. My voice wobbled.

The hand lifted. "What?"

"This thing between us. I don't think it's working out."

I sniffed back the blood dripping from my nose. "This . . . this thing between us. I-I don't think it's working out."

It was quiet.

"It's been a long couple of days," he said after a moment. "I don't think now's the time to—"

"This isn't going to get any better, Rog."

"This isn't going to get any better, Rog."

"And I think it's time you moved out."

"And . . . and I think . . ."

"*Say it.*"

"I think it's time you moved out."

I heard him shuffle back a step. "What? I . . . I don't understand."

"*I think it's time we stopped seeing so much of each other. I don't want you here. You need to leave.*"

"I-I-I think it's time we stop seeing so much of each other. I don't want you here. You need to leave."

It was quiet. I closed my eyes.

"But I thought . . ." He took a breath. "But I thought that we . . . I thought that you . . ."

"*I could never love someone like you.*"

I bit my lip so hard it bled.

"*Say it.*"

I couldn't breathe.

"*Say it, or he dies.*"

"Lil—"

"I could never love someone like you."

Silence.

Minutes passed, and I shut my eyes tight, hating myself for every moment of it.

When he spoke again, his voice was unsteady. "Lily—"

"Please, just go," I whispered.

After another moment, I heard the front door open. It stayed open for a long time, letting the cold air fill the house.

It closed, leaving me alone as I sank to the floor and sobbed.

Twenty Eight

Colosseum

I stared at the floor, my hand clasped over my mouth.

Allister waited a few minutes before hopping down the stairs. He heaved a contented sigh, an enormous smile plastered on his face. "I think that went well."

My shaking body hunched closer to the floor. The things I'd been forced to speak seemed to echo in the cold room. Those words would never leave my mind, just as I knew they would never leave Roger's. My chest ached with every shuddering breath.

Allister kicked my side. "Get up."

I flinched, glaring at Allister's insane golden eyes. The twitching fibers of his irises grew more intense as he watched me. I tried to find any semblance of feeling, remorse, or emotion in them. I failed.

I stood, wiping my eyes. "I don't understand you. You hear the Collective. You're connected to all of humanity. You, of all people, can empathize with every single person who has ever lived." I clenched my hands into fists. "How can you be like this? How can you enjoy putting people in pain? How can you throw away life when you know the value of it?"

Allister laughed for a long time. He pulled me close and cradled my head with one hand, caressing it with the gun in the other. The cold metal of the barrel passed over my cheek. I bit back a scream.

"Silly, that's *why* I do it," he said. "Because when you know someone's hopes and dreams, fears, favorite song, most embarrassing moment, favorite ice cream flavor, first love, last thoughts before they go to sleep, perfect day . . ." He trailed off with a rapturous sigh. "And you know you can take that all away so *easily* . . ." His hand trembled on my face, and his breath caught. "That's the feeling of true power. That's the feeling of being *God*."

I leaned away in disgust.

He tugged me close and pulled the Teleporter from my pocket, poking the gun into my stomach. He shoved the small metal disc into my hands. "Let's get out of here, huh?"

I clutched the Teleporter, glaring at him as I opened a flickering portal. The dim, humid tunnels lay beyond it. A ripple of fear ignited inside me.

I couldn't go back down there. I couldn't do it again.

Allister shoved me through the portal. I splashed into a puddle of lukewarm, grainy water. The portal closed almost immediately when Allister stepped through, and I sat staring at the blank stone wall.

I closed my eyes as the hope of escape vaporized. My grip tightened around my Teleporter as I willed for it to take me back to Giftshop, or home, or anywhere else. It didn't.

"Don't get your hopes up," Allister drawled. "I've expanded the electro-magnetic interference. There's no way you're using that thing down here now."

Allister jerked me to my feet and dragged me down the hall. I cried silently, not bothering to struggle. What was the point? By the time anyone noticed I was gone, it would be too late. I'd be dead, insane, or worse.

And Roger wasn't around to save me this time.

After stumbling down several identical hallways, Allister turned next to one of the many doors lining the side of the tunnel. An armed guard outside it nodded at Allister as we approached.

"Can't say you're going to like what happens in there," Allister said. He leaned in to nuzzle my neck. "Unless you'd rather just come with me?"

I jerked away from him. He chuckled, nodding to the guard, who opened the door. "Try not to make her pass out. I need her awake."

Someone behind me grabbed my arms and pulled them behind my back. I watched Allister walk away as they tied my hands and closed the door.

They tugged me backward, wrapping plastic ties around my bandaged wrists. I turned, recognizing him. He was the man who had asked Margot to dance at the gala. Instead of a suit, he wore a black rubber apron and dark clothing.

"I don't have you for very long, hm?" He sighed, surveying me. "Why he never gives me a schedule, I'll never know."

He shoved me into the wall. My head cracked against the stone, and I slid to the ground. Everything went blurry while the man connected my arms to a hook at the base of the wall. At least I could sit down.

He crossed the room to examine a surgical metal tray. From my vantage point on the floor, I couldn't see what it held, which was probably a good thing.

I stared at the grainy ground. The man hummed a little tune while he snapped on some stained gloves and held up a small metal patch with wires sticking out the back. Grabbing a scalpel, he approached me.

"Right." He twisted my head to the side by my hair. "Don't move."

He lifted the knife. I closed my eyes.

There was a knock at the door, and the man leaned back. Sighing again, he stood. "What now?" he mumbled, opening the door. Conversing with someone quickly in Italian, he seemed irritated and tugged off the gloves.

"I can't get *one* minute's peace around here," he grumbled. He tossed the gloves onto the tray, slamming the door on his way out.

I let out a few deep breaths and slumped against the wall.

"Lily!" someone whispered.

My head jerked up, heart lifting when I spotted Cliff tied to the wall on the far side of the room. Even in the darkness, he didn't look good. His swollen face was tinged blue and purple, his left arm a bloody, lacerated mess. But he was alive.

"Cliff!" I whispered back. "You're okay!"

He chuckled darkly. "Mostly. What're you doing here? I heard you escaped with some others? Did they all get caught?"

I shook my head and explained what happened.

He scowled. "Damn transporters. What a cheap way of getting around. Did Rog make it out?"

I nodded as my heart twinged with pain. "Yes, he's out. Who else is here?"

He shrugged. "For sure? Me, Snuff from Irene's team—"

"Hullo, Lily," came a voice to my right. Snuff hung by his hands at the other end of the room. He no longer wore his hat or eyepatch, displaying the scar tissue of his empty eye socket. He flashed a lopsided smile, and I nodded back.

"—Payton and Max from the recon team, and you. I haven't seen Payton or Max in a while. I think they . . ." He shuddered. "I think they got put in the Colosseum."

"Colosseum?"

"It's . . ." He shook his head and refocused. "I'll explain later. Before he comes back, can you reach that scalpel? It fell off the tray when he left."

I swept my eyes around the room and spotted the small scalpel under the instrument table.

"I don't think I can reach it," I said.

"You're anchored to the wall, but you can pivot. Use your feet," Snuff said. "But don't get caught. I tried something like that, and now I'm . . . hanging out."

Nodding to Snuff, I twisted my body so I was on my side. My foot inched closer to the small scalpel. I heard voices outside the door, and my mouth went dry. I stretched and felt the metal shift under my foot. Sweeping it toward my hands, I finally snatched the small instrument. I tucked it into the sleeve of my jacket just as the door opened.

The man strode in again and turned his eyes to me as he tugged on his gloves. He picked up the metal patch and twisted the wires between his fingers. "Right, where were we?"

He frowned at the tray, looking around the room. "Where did I put that?"

I tried to look confused. "Put what?"

"My—you know what. That was one of my best instruments," he complained, looking around.

"You put it back on the table," Cliff called. "You losing your memory or something? Don't feel bad. Age comes to us all."

The man clicked the remote hanging from his belt. Cliff arched against the wall. The small metal patch hummed as he mostly held back a scream. The man released the remote. "What have I told you about talking?"

Cliff blinked a few times and tried to look thoughtful. "Are you asking me? Maybe you really *are* losing your memory."

The man kicked him in the stomach, turning his attention back to the metal tray. Cliff coughed and wheezed. He glanced at me, flashing a slight smile.

The man clucked his tongue and picked up a much larger scalpel. He pulled my neck to the side by my hair. I squirmed as he lifted the knife once more.

"Again," he said, "don't move . . ."

The metal door screeched open. The man threw his hands up in exasperation. "*Honestly*, Allister! How do you expect me to work under these conditions?"

I jerked my neck back to the side. Allister stood in the doorway, face flushed, eyes wide. He smiled. "My apologies, Lorenzo, but sometimes you just can't predict these things. I need her *now*."

He pulled a velvet-covered package from under his arm and inclined it toward me. I froze as a smattering of images strobed across my eyes.

—darkness lit by torchlight. Dozens of hands reaching upward toward the sky. Enormous bonfires fueled by emaciated corpses. Ink blots on paper. Arcane writing swirling around yellow stained pages made from stretched skin—

The Book of Bones.

"The book," I whispered. "You really did get it."

"Actually, *he* did." Allister gestured to Cliff. "Led us right to it and, as a bonus, got it out for us."

Cliff looked away, still recovering from the sparking metal disc.

Allister tucked the book more securely under his arm. "You know what? These two have been bait for long enough. Now that we have her, we don't need them anymore. I think it's time for another tournament, don't you?"

Cliff's and Snuff's heads jerked up.

Lorenzo smiled. "I'll say."

Allister waved out the door, and three guards entered. Our hands were still tied as they jerked Cliff and me to our feet. Snuff crumpled to the ground after he was released. He rose, staring at the guard with his scarred socket. The guard backed away and instead grabbed Cliff, who struggled to keep standing.

"Get them to the watch room," Allister said. "I'll inform everyone the Colosseum is open for another show."

"Cliff, what's the Colosseum?" I asked.

The guards led us down a long sloping tunnel, tripping us if we didn't walk fast enough.

Cliff paled. "Back when . . . back when they attacked our facility in Los Angeles"—he stumbled as a guard struck his leg—"a number of specimen samples were stolen. Among them were highly aggressive creature eggs. They—"

He broke off as an echoing roar shook dust from the ceiling.

"They've been experimenting on them," he whispered. "They made me watch one of these with some of their other prisoners and . . ." He shook his head. "It wasn't pretty."

I swallowed the dryness in my throat as we neared the door. Another roar erupted from behind it, and one guard cranked it open.

Snaking pipes, tubes, and gauges covered the room, a dirty window taking up one side. A door sat next to it, leading to a solid stone balcony. It overlooked the enormous, oval-shaped cavern, a football field in height and three times in length. A sand pit filled the center, surrounded by slick stone walls. Dark blotches smeared the sides. Rough seats had been cut into the stone, lining the high walls to create a colossal amphitheater. Hundreds of people filled the seats. They screamed and laughed at the occupants below them. A huge banner hung over the sides of the wall: a single black circle painted on bloodred cloth.

There were . . . so many. There were so many people. I never dreamed Legion had this many followers.

"Look," Snuff hissed. "Max. Payton."

Cliff stepped forward. I watched in horror as a huge bounding creature chased two tiny figures around the pit. The creature's six legs stuck out at awkward angles, thick sickly toned skin folding and tightening with each ripple of muscle. Its spine retracted out of its elongated back. A dozen eyes covered its bearlike head, patches of fur sticking from its body in tufts. Great streams of sizzling fluid spewed from its gaping maw.

The two tiny people ran in circles, ducking behind gouged chunks of stone littering the sandy pit. One figure tripped as they rounded a boulder. The creature pounced. I looked away, but even from behind the window, I could hear the screams.

Cliff turned. "Oh, God."

The other figure bolted from their hiding spot and sank their spear into one of the beast's many legs. The creature flicked its tail and sent him flying into the slick stone wall. He didn't last long after that.

"Ah, and another one gone," Allister remarked wistfully. "Didn't put up much of a fight, did they? Pathetic."

"You want to see pathetic?" I seethed. "Look in a mirror."

He chuckled, tracing the outline of the velvet-wrapped book. "You're going to hurt my feelings, Lily."

A guard pulled me to the other side of the room and tied my bound hands to one of the many pipes. I clamped onto the end of my sleeve as the scalpel wobbled.

Shouts echoed from behind the door. It banged open, a person shoved through it. He stumbled to his knees, his hands already tied behind his back. Declan entered behind him and kicked his side.

"Here, found this one snooping around in town. You expecting more company, Allister?"

My stomach flipped. "Roger?"

Roger jolted, eyes growing wide when he spotted me. "Lily? What're you—"

"I'm so sorry!" I blurted. "He made me say it! I didn't want to, but he said he'd kill you if I didn't—"

Allister slapped me. "Shut up!"

Roger's eyes brightened. "You didn't . . . you didn't mean any of it?"

I half laughed, half sobbed. "Not one word."

He gave a tired smile. "Neither did I."

I smiled back.

"God, I'm so tired of you getting in my way!" Allister shouted. He jerked his head to Declan. "Get him up. He's going next."

"*No!*" Cliff yelled, struggling against the restraints. "No!"

"Put them on deck. They're after him."

"Do you want to give him a sporting chance?" Declan asked.

Allister grinned. "Sure, why not? The others hardly put on a show at all. Get him his stuff. We'll see how long he lasts."

Declan crossed the room while the other guards pulled Cliff and Snuff to the balcony. It took two men to drag Cliff out the door.

"Roger! Roger, I'm sorry!" he screamed. "I'm so sorry for everything, sport! I love you!"

"Dad?" Roger's voice cracked as he tried to stand. "Dad!"

Declan tucked a hand under his chin as he surveyed a table near the window. An odd assortment of things lay on it. My insides jolted as I spotted Margot's bloodstained lilac dress among them, and my long-range weapon. I recognized other things the longer I looked. Things from my emergency pack from Rome. Roger's, too, and Margot's, and others from the ground team.

Everyone they killed. They kept them like some sick trophy.

I swallowed. Declan sifted through the table and pulled out Roger's leather bracers, holding them to the light. He smiled, nodding to the door Cliff had gone through. "How poetic. Like mother, like son."

Roger stared at me while a guard cut his hands free. His mouth moved like he wanted to say something but couldn't get the words out. He swallowed and clenched his jaw.

Allister put a hand on his shoulder. "You know, usually, these tournaments bore me. No art. No elegance. Just primal gladiatorial combat. But this time—" He slapped his arm. "This time I'm going to enjoy myself."

Allister chuckled and headed to the balcony.

Declan and the other guard grabbed either side of Roger, shuffling to the corner of the room. A curved door was there, attached to a cylindrical tube that disappeared through the floor. The door had a window studded with iron rivets. Dark smears spotted it.

I watched helplessly as Roger neared the strange door. He stared at the floor before throwing himself sideways into the wall. The guard stumbled and lost his balance while Roger elbowed Declan in the face.

Shaking free of their grips, he bolted across the room and kissed me.

I didn't have much warning before his lips pressed against mine. My arms pulled against the bindings as he cradled my face. I kissed back. Everything faded away as we stood together, an untouched island of safety and happiness in a sea of horror.

He pulled back, leaning his forehead against mine. Declan recovered and tore him away toward the door. I leaned forward as he left, every part of me wanting him to stay as he got thrown into the metal cylinder.

His brown eyes stared at me until the window fogged over, taking him out of sight.

Twenty Nine

To Hell and Back

I stared at the empty window, tears streaming down my face.

Declan wiped some blood from his nose and turned to the guard. "I want to watch this out front. Keep an eye on her."

The guard nodded and stood watch by the door. Declan clutched Roger's leather bracers in his hands as he entered the balcony. He glanced back at me before standing with Allister at the edge.

Even from my vantage point, I could still see most of the arena. In the pit, the giant creature paced impatiently, flexing its spine through its patchy skin. Its great fanged mouth opened wide, letting out an ear-splitting roar.

The crowd screamed as a small figure entered the pit. Roger stood waiting with his arms at his sides, shoulders squared.

"Hey!" Declan shouted, waving the leather bracers above his head. "Run!"

He chucked them into the pit below while Allister cackled maniacally. Roger sprinted for them, but so did the creature. I strained against the pipe and clenched my teeth as he ran, breathing again when he'd snatched the bracers and hidden behind a rock. The creature roared, shaking the room. Dust rained from the craggy ceiling.

A glint of light on the table made me tear my eyes away from the window. The lamps above me shook, swinging over a small metal object. It flashed again. My stomach lifted when I saw the Post-it-Note-sized piece of uneven metal.

A Glider.

Roger had packed a Glider.

I glanced back at the guard. He leaned against the window, craning his neck to watch the arena. I carefully reached into my sleeve for the scalpel, almost dropping it. Making sure the guard was still watching Roger, I positioned the blade against the cords and sawed, slicing my skin when I missed or pushed too hard. That was good; that meant it was sharp.

I watched Roger's progress as I worked, keeping an eye on the guard. He didn't seem the least bit concerned about me, because why would he be? I obviously wasn't going anywhere. And even if I did, where would I run?

Roger evaded the creature for longer than I thought possible, but after a while, he began to tire. All it would take was one slip up, and he'd end up just like Max and Payton, whose bodies still leaked into the sand.

I kept sawing and pulling at the straps. Just a bit further. I was so close.

My stomach dropped as the inevitable happened. Roger turned too slowly, and the creature clipped him. He flipped end over end before the creature caught him in its clawlike grasp, holding him near its fanged mouth. There was a flash of pink. The creature recoiled. Roger fell to the sand. I heard a muffled scream as he landed, clutching his right leg. He crawled under the nearest rock as the creature bounded around the pit. It crashed into the sides, tearing out huge chunks of stone from the slick walls.

Finally, after one last tug, my wrists came free. The guard glanced back at me, but I held my hands behind my back and pretended to stare out the window. He turned back to the scene, much more interested in what was happening in the arena.

I glanced at the Glider and my long-range weapon. I would only have one shot at this. If I messed up, I wouldn't get another chance. What if I tripped? What if I fumbled? If I screwed this up, Roger, Cliff, Snuff, and I would be dead, not to mention the rest of the world. Allister already had the book. It was only a matter of time before they found Him. Before they woke Him up. There'd be no stopping them after that.

My eyes closed. I inhaled slow, calculated breaths. Scenes from the last few days played out in my head. I thought of the training sessions with Margot. The things she taught me. Her face dragged itself to my mind, replaying all the conversations we had until the end. Her end, when she gave her life to save mine.

I opened my eyes. Allister and Declan stood on the balcony, engrossed in the Colosseum battle.

"Make a decision, flower girl."

I waited until the creature gave another deafening screech and darted to the table. I grabbed the Glider first and clicked it open, snatching my long-range weapon. The guard turned, taking one moment too many to realize what was happening. By then, I had already stepped on the Glider.

He shouted and grabbed at me, but I had already leaned forward. The Glider hummed as I accelerated through the balcony door. Declan and Allister turned at the shout, faces uncomprehending as the Glider zoomed toward them. Declan tried to reach me, but I jammed the scalpel into his arm. He screamed and stumbled into Allister.

And then I was free.

The stale wind rushed around me as I swooped in a high arc. I grabbed my weapon and pulled it onto my hand, buckling it tight.

The Colosseum seemed so much bigger from above, and so did the creature. The stands were in an uproar as hundreds of angry people shouted at me. The creature reared on its hind legs as it saw me approach. I swerved to avoid the massive beast, its spiny claw swiping mere feet away. Trying to keep my hand from shaking, I aimed my weapon in its general direction and fired three purple discs.

The first two shots missed, but the third sank deep into the creature's flank. It started, turning around. I fired another succession of discs. They all hit their mark, but they seemed to just be an annoyance. No more than a pinprick. I held my arms steady again and fired. By sheer luck, the disc pierced one of the creature's many eyes. It thrashed, bucking and kicking across the arena.

On my second pass around the pit, I spotted something move from behind a rock. Roger. He gaped at me, mouth open, eyes wide. Above him on the wall were Snuff and Cliff. They hung by their hands on a cantilever platform, attached to wooden frames. Roger waved for me to get them first as he crawled to a new hiding spot.

I swerved upward and slowed next to their platform. They pulled their hands as far apart as their bindings would allow, scrunching away as I approached. I didn't have time to worry about hitting them before they were already off the stands, disappearing into the next room.

I circled back to Roger. The creature gave a deafening roar as it spotted me. It pounced in short bursts and bounded into the air. It soared higher than I thought possible, almost reaching me. I wobbled as I swerved to avoid its claws. It missed again, its leg crashing deep into the stone wall. It tugged and pulled its massive body, but it couldn't come free.

Debris flew everywhere as it thrashed. I pointed the humming board toward Roger. He pulled himself to his feet as I neared. Getting as low as I could, I reached out. We grasped hands, and he swung himself onto the board. The Glider buckled under the additional weight.

"You okay?" I shouted over the wind.

He grimaced and tried to balance on one leg. "Not . . . really. I-I think my leg's broken. Did you get my dad and Snuff?"

"I got them down, but I haven't seen—"

The creature wailed as its leg came free from the wall, taking massive chunks of rock with it. The people in the stands scrambled away as their benches became rubble. The giant red banner was soon reduced to swatches of shredded cloth as the creature slashed its claws.

A bubbling noise emanated from the creature, and Roger squeezed my arm. "Turn! Now!"

I leaned to the side and crouched forward as a boiling stream of acid coated the wall behind us. The rock disintegrated almost instantly.

"What even *is* that thing?" I shouted, making another loop.

"I don't know. I've never seen anything like—" He squeezed my arm again. "It's coming back!"

I heard the sizzling stream gurgle from the creature's mouth behind us. A horrible acrid smell burned my nose and throat. I stepped back, and Roger clamped onto my shoulders as we sputtered upward. The spewing acid coated the stalactite-covered ceiling.

The rock buckled. With a great cracking sound, the ceiling collapsed, letting loose thousands of gallons of seawater.

Chunks of rock fell with the gushing waterfalls. I swerved left and right to avoid being knocked out of the air. The people in the stands ran for the exits, most of them disappearing in flashes of light. The creature erupted in a mighty roar before chunks of the ceiling covered its flailing body. Briny water filled the pit in moments.

"I see them!" Roger shouted. "My dad and Snuff! There!"

He pointed to the watch room. Snuff held back a few guards while Cliff struggled with Declan inside. Allister fiercely tried to enter from the balcony, but someone had locked the door. He wouldn't set down the *Ossabrium* to free up his other hand.

Something inside me tightened. The book. He still had it. Now might be our only chance.

"Can you fly this thing?" I asked. "With your leg?"

"I-I think I can do it if I'm on my hands and knees. Why?"

"The book! I need to get the book!" I picked up speed and shuffled to the side. "Hold it steady for me. I'm going to jump for it!"

"*What?* Are you insane?"

"Rog, this whole place is coming down!" I yelled. "We need to get out of here! If Allister escapes with the book, there's no telling where he'll go. Now hold it steady!"

He pressed his lips together but didn't argue. We switched places on the Glider as carefully as we could. He dropped to his knees and looked back at me. "I'll come back around for you! Ready?"

I nodded and kept my eyes locked on Allister. He turned as we approached, eyes widening as I launched myself at him.

We tumbled onto the balcony and rolled into the wall. I made a grab for the book, but he kept his hands clamped on it. We struggled until the velvet casing came off, and the book went flying onto the other end of the balcony.

Scrambling to my feet, I splashed toward it. Allister grabbed my arm and twisted it hard. I screamed and tried to throw him off, but he clawed me back.

I pulled us forward and reached for the book. It was huge, bulging at the seams, and buckled around its middle with leather strips. Delicate splinters of bone and strange jewels adorned the cover. The pages fluttered against the straps. Like it was breathing. Between the din of rushing water and the screaming of people in the Colosseum, I heard it.

It . . . *whispered* to me.

Allister yanked me backward and threw me to the ground. He pulled himself on top of me, hitting me in the face. Again, and again, and again. My head cracked against the stone over and over, my vision blacking out every few moments. Something snapped in my nose.

"It's mine, it's *mine!*" he yelled. "I've worked too hard to lose it to you!"

My arm came up. His fists hit the top of a purple disk before I raked the edge across the side of his cheek. He screamed and fell back, clutching his face. It gave me a chance to roll away and stumble after the book.

My fingers closed around the nauseatingly smooth leather. Something hit me from behind. Allister's bloody hands latched onto the book, and we tugged against each other. Grainy water rained from above as we stood in knee-deep green foam. A gash spanned across Allister's face, dripping blood onto his already soaked clothes.

"*You can't stop us!*" he shrieked. "*We're more powerful than you know! We'll win no matter what you do!*"

"*Get out of my HEAD!*" I screamed.

I pulled with everything I had. The leather bindings of the book split open. We fell onto opposite sides of the balcony, the book landing between us. Allister and I stared at each other as yellow stained papers fluttered into the air.

The ceiling gave a terrible rumble as the entire cave system collapsed inward.

"Lily!" someone yelled.

Water covered my face before I knew what to do. I cracked open my eyes. Things had gone strangely quiet, almost peaceful. Through the murky water, Roger reached for me, his eyes scrunched closed. Allister held on to the edge of the balcony, trying to turn the device on his wrist.

It seemed we floated for an eternity, unmoving, sitting in stasis with no inclination for survival.

My body jolted. I blinked through the gritty water. I grabbed Roger's hand and kicked off the wall behind me to reach Allister. Everything moved so slowly. My lungs ached for air. Allister twisted the device on his wrist the moment before I grabbed his shoulder.

The world compressed. A horrible jolt shook me from the inside out, pulling apart everything in between. I squeezed Roger's hand. He squeezed back. I choked on a mouthful of water and convulsed. For all I knew, we were still underwater, drowning while waiting for the hope of air.

The pressure released. The bubble of water we had taken with us popped, and we fell onto something hard. I gasped for air, staring at the alarmingly bright shade of blue above me. Puffy trails of white floated across it. Dark triangle shapes crossed overhead. Birds. Seagulls.

I blinked and turned my head. We had landed in a sloping drainage tunnel opening into the ocean. The water lapped against the sides as small ripples flowed from the darkness of the tunnel. Across the sea sat a beautiful city: colorful buildings built on the water, boats large and small, traversing its waterways. Music drifted across the gentle waves.

I coughed out some seawater, flexing my hand. Roger squeezed back. He turned to me and gave a tired smile, his chest rising and falling with broken rapidity as he gasped for air.

"Hey," he said.

I smiled back. "Hey."

Another flash of light accompanied the two coughing noises farther down the tunnel. We sat up as Snuff and Cliff stumbled into the light.

They spotted us lying on the ground. Cliff gave a strangled noise of joy and stumbled to his son, wrapping his arms around him.

"I thought I lost you, sport," Cliff whispered.

Roger hugged him back, his eyes shut tight. "I thought I lost you, too. You know, *again*."

Allister stirred, coughing out a mouthful of seawater. He rolled to his knees and heaved a few breaths before looking up. His eyes widened at the four of us, and he scrambled to his feet. Snuff grabbed him by the shirt and twisted his arms behind his back.

"Oh, no you don't, you little weasel," he growled. He took off his belt and wrapped it tight around his wrists.

Allister struggled for a moment before sinking to his knees.

"How did you guys make it out?" I asked.

Cliff held up a short-range transporter with a grim look of triumph on his face. The band was torn and stretched. "It took almost twenty-five years, but I did it." He took a shallow breath and looked up at the sky. "Got your six, Amy."

Roger looked down.

"What do we do with this?" Snuff asked, jolting Allister forward. I found myself holding back a smile. It felt strangely satisfying to see him with his hands tied.

Cliff surveyed him, glancing at us. "Whaddya think?"

Roger sat up, carefully straightening his broken leg. He stared at Allister, who, for the first time, looked scared. Roger's jaw clenched.

I put a hand on his shoulder. He relaxed and looked away. "I guess we should keep him close until we know what to do with him. The Quiet Room?"

Cliff nodded. "By all means. Giftshop will be thrilled."

Snuff chuckled and pulled out a Teleporter. "The Quiet Room it is."

"Oh," I breathed, and pointed. "Look."

We turned our attention to the end of the drainage pipe. A large square object sat at the edge, the water tugging it slowly out to sea. The yellow pages flapped in the wind now that the straps had ripped, and they fluttered in rhythm. Even though we were sopping wet, the book wasn't. The pages were bone dry. Ink and blood covered both sides of the pages, depicting strange creatures and ritual practices. The whispering I heard earlier had intensified.

I knew that whispering.

It was the whispering of a billion eyes.

Allister lunged for it, but Snuff held him back. It didn't stop Allister from inching toward the book with all his might, his golden eyes bulging.

I covered my ears to stop the whispering, but it didn't.

"Close it," I begged. "Please, someone close it."

Cliff limped over and shut the cover, picking it up. The whispering stopped. I closed my eyes. Silence. Finally.

"Well, well," Cliff mumbled, turning the book over in his hands. He tucked it under his arm and looked around. "We need to get this back to Giftshop. I hope Henry hasn't done anything stupid since I've been gone."

Roger chuckled. "Course he has. Why do you think I showed up to get you?"

Snuff nodded to Cliff. "You ready to get this slimeball back too?"

Cliff glared at Allister, looking him up and down. "Definitely."

Snuff opened a portal and shoved Allister through it.

He glared down at me as he passed. *"You think you can hold me? I'll always be with you, Lily. You'll never be able to get me out of your head. Whatever it takes, whatever it does to me, I'm going to make your life a living hell."*

I glared back. *"I'm not scared of you."*

"You will be."

Snuff led him away from the portal as Cliff helped Roger to his feet. I supported one arm as we stumbled into Giftshop, leaving the lapping waves of the sea behind us.

THIRTY

A Rearrangement

We lasted exactly thirty minutes in Giftshop before collapsing from exhaustion.

Snuff deposited Allister in the Quiet Room while Cliff, Roger, and I contacted Henry and Bea. They sat in stunned silence as we explained how we escaped, breathing a sigh of relief for the first time in almost a week. Immediately, Bea left to warn the Southern European community to watch for fleeing Legion members in the area. I wasn't fooling myself; even though many had drowned in the Colosseum, more had escaped as we had. It wasn't comforting to know Legion was still around, but the fact that we'd thrown a wrench into their plans helped ease the anxiety.

Henry had taken the Book of Bones deep into Giftshop, where its fate would be decided at a later date. We all agreed that it was too dangerous to leave on Earth, but no one wanted to destroy it yet. We didn't know what would happen if we tried, and frankly, the thought struck fear into me. I couldn't shake the feeling that the book was somehow . . . alive. I worried it had the propensity to fight back against its own destruction.

Snuff had sent a message to his team, followed minutes later by Irene, Chelsea, and Artemus bounding through the viewing bay door. There were tears, laughs, and a solemn silence as they informed Snuff of Jack's condition. He had lost a leg in Rome but, fortunately, had awoken from a coma. The doctors said his progress looked good, but he'd never walk the same again. Their broken team left to return to the hospital not long after, Chelsea leading the way.

After everyone had been caught up, and the *Ossabrium* and Allister secured, Cliff, Roger, and I collapsed on various chairs and couches in the viewing bay. Giftshop (metaphorically) rolled up her sleeves and began healing our numerous injuries, the warm hum coming in waves as we slumped in our seats. Cliff slouched into a cushy armchair, his swollen face lessening by the second. He was fast asleep within minutes.

Across the room, Roger rested his recently set broken leg on a table. I sat by him, clutching his hand as we waited for our respective pains to subside. Neither of us seemed to want to let go of the other.

Wrinkling my nose, I heaved a sigh of relief. The clicking, crackling noise had stopped. I probed the bandages on my wrists. No pain, only a little soreness. I unwrapped them and flexed my hands. The deep cuts and burns from the restraints were now only light pink lines. Under my sleeve, the bruises were already fading to yellow. The fingerprint-shaped ones lingered a deep purple.

Roger ran his fingers gently over my wrists. "Those look better."

I exhaled a sigh. "They feel better."

His eyes flicked to the bruises, and he pulled back. "Is . . . this okay?"

"Is what okay?"

"That I'm touching you. Are you . . . okay with it now?"

I chuckled softly. "Yeah, I'm okay."

"Because, if you aren't," he continued, his eyebrows knitting together, "if it makes you uncomfortable after everything, it's okay. I can—"

I grabbed his hand and placed it back on my wrists, giving a reassuring smile. "I'm okay, Rog, really. It helps. It helps to . . . forget everything."

He returned the smile. "Just checking."

"Thank you. How's your leg?"

He shifted his weight on the table and winced. "Still a little tender. When that thing grabbed me in the Colosseum"—he blew a breath through his teeth—"I thought I was a goner."

I looked down. "Me too."

"That was some crazy shit you pulled, by the way." He shook his head. "That business with the Glider? You could've gotten yourself shot."

I shrugged, giving him a sideways glance. "Something had to happen. I wasn't about to let you die down in that pit. And you know . . ." I cleared my throat. "You pulled some crazy shit yourself."

Roger swallowed, his face flushing pink. "Well, I . . . in my defense, I thought I was about to die. And you were just . . . standing there, and, um, I didn't know if I'd get another chance to . . . not that I didn't have, like, a *thousand* opportunities before then, but it never seemed the right time, and I . . . I didn't—"

I kissed him so he'd shut up.

He seemed startled, but recovered. He kissed back, pushing back my hair and pulling me closer. I wrapped my arms around his shoulders. He tightened his around my waist. With every passing second, we found a way to get closer.

He broke away, glancing to the side.

"What's wrong?" I asked.

Roger nodded to the other side of the room, where Cliff was still fast asleep.

"We have a chaperone," he grumbled. "I guess he's making up for the last ten years."

I stifled my laughter behind my hand. Roger laughed too, and we tried our best to keep our giggling quiet. It was so good to see his eyes light up again. It was so good to see him smile. The horrors and despair of the last few days subsided, just for a moment. They'd never disappear, I knew that, but just for a moment, we were two normal people, lying on a couch holding in fits of laughter.

Roger wrapped his arm around me. I buried my face in his good shoulder. The steady pump of his heart lulled me to sleep, accompanied by the wafting scent of cinnamon and hot chocolate.

My feet inched toward the end of a cracked stone ledge, the wind whipping at my hair. I squinted at the dizzying drop. Grotesque creatures floated below me, screaming and wailing as they swam in undulating waves. I covered my ears. It didn't help. Far in the distance, flashing pops lit up the swirling clouds like colored lightning.

"You think this is over for you, Lily?"

I turned. Allister stood a few yards away, glaring at me, his golden eyes twitching.

He shook his head, a slow smile creeping over his face. "You destroyed everything we worked for. And now you're going to pay."

"Let it go, Allister!" I shouted over the wind. "You've lost! It's over!"

"It's never over!" he screamed. "Our cause remains immortal! Only the strong will survive the rise!"

The creatures below screeched and groaned in agreement.

"You've lost!" I shouted. "There's nothing you can do about it!"

His smile grew wider, splitting open the gash across his face. "I still have you. We're two sides of the same coin, Lily. You're meant to be by my side at the end of everything. It's already in motion."

My hands clenched into fists. "I don't care what happens. I'll never help you!"

He chuckled. It turned into a wild cackle. "We're connected, Lily Masters, more than you know. I'm coming for you, and you can't stop me."

The ledge beneath my feet cracked and shattered. I fell backward into the sea of waiting creatures as Allister laughed himself further into insanity.

I jolted up as fanged mouths ripped me to shreds. Minutes passed before I stopped screaming enough to hear Roger's voice or feel anything other than agony.

"Lily! Wake up!"

The pain ebbed. My eyes opened. I blinked at the dark wooden walls and hanging chandelier. Giftshop. I was still in Giftshop.

"Lily? Can you hear us?"

I twisted my head. Cliff and Henry stood nearby, faces pale, eyes wide.

A hand brushed some hair away from my face. Roger wiped the tear streaks from my cheeks and helped me sit up. "Lily? What happened?"

I coughed, catching my breath. "A-Allister. It was . . . it was Allister. He's trying to—" I held my head in my hands. The pounding in my head was back, but so much worse than before. My stomach sank.

"Allister?" Cliff said. "He's still in the Quiet Room. He shouldn't be able to do anything."

I shook my head, and the pain worsened. "We're still connected through the Collective and"—my eyes watered—"we always will be. There's . . . there's nothing you can do."

"*I want to make a deal.*"

I clamped my eyes shut. "Please, just *stop*!"

"*Tell them I want to make a deal.*"

"He . . . he says he wants to make a deal."

"*Now.*"

"N-now."

Cliff, Henry, and Roger glanced at each other. Roger shook his head slowly.

"*Either I talk to you now, or this never stops.*"

I winced as my vision spotted.

"*Tell them.*"

"He . . . he says either we talk to him now or"—I sniffed back some blood—"or this never stops."

The pounding in my head peaked. I almost passed out.

"Please," I whispered. "Leave me alone."

Cliff stepped back. "Let's go hear what he has to say."

Roger did a double take. "What? We can't negotiate with him!"

I put my hand to my mouth to keep from sobbing. I wanted to agree with Roger, but if I could just make the pain stop for a moment . . .

"*Ticktock, Lily.*"

Tears fell from my eyes.

"I'm not saying we're negotiating," Cliff said, "but we can hear what he wants. Can you stand?"

Roger heaved himself onto his good leg before gingerly testing his other. He stood on it for a moment before nodding.

Roger helped me stand, too, and we limped forward together. It was hard to walk. It was hard to breathe. It was hard to do anything but focus on the pain. It was so much worse than before. This wasn't the kind of pain I could ignore. I couldn't even *pretend* to ignore it anymore.

"Now you're getting it."

They led me through a series of unfamiliar doors and down a long set of stairs. Eventually, we came to a stop at a large metal arch carved with swirling patterns. It led into a small hallway with a single white, splintery wooden door at the end. A card reader sat where the knob was supposed to be. It seemed out of place.

Cliff fumbled with a ring of keys on a peg and pulled out a single black keycard. "Don't engage with him, Lily, no matter what he says. All right?"

I nodded and inhaled a shuddering breath.

Cliff slid the keycard into the reader. The door clicked open, and Cliff pushed it forward. Roger's hand found mine. I clutched it tightly.

The stark room was shocking compared with the rest of Giftshop. The seamless white walls almost hurt to look at. Dividing the room in half was a strange jiggling substance. It wobbled as we got close, spanning from one wall to the other to create a holding cell. A fly buzzed through the air until it hit the clear wall. It vaporized in a flash.

Allister stood on the other side, leering with a confident smile. The gash across his face was no longer bleeding, but no one seemed to care that it wasn't patched.

His eyes traveled over me. "Nice to see you again so soon, Lily. Too bad this has to separate us. You look so *soft* under this light."

Roger stiffened. I gave his hand a comforting squeeze.

"What do you want?" Henry asked, folding his arms.

"I want to make a deal."

"You're not in the best position to be making deals."

"Aren't I?" Allister said, glancing at me. A tidal wave of pain and nausea ripped through my body. I doubled over. Roger caught me before I hit the floor.

"S-stop," I choked.

He chuckled, attention returning to Henry and Cliff. "I want the book. And I want to walk out of here."

"No chance in *hell*," Roger seethed.

Allister raised an eyebrow. I coughed up some blood.

"It's your choice." He shrugged. "Make me a deal, or this never stops. How long do you think she can hold out? A few days? Probably less."

"You—"

"We're connected in ways you can't imagine." He sneered. "I've been training my whole life while she had her gift just *given* to her. All those years I spent building all that muscle memory gives me an advantage she'll *never* have. All those years learning how to navigate the Collective has armed me with enough experience to kill her slowly. Methodically. From the inside out."

The room was quiet.

"And I know you won't kill me," he said with another smile. "It's against your oaths. So, you have a choice: Which do you value more, her life or mine?"

My vision swam and warped. Roger was the only thing keeping me standing. He pulled me gently away from the clear wall and helped me sit against the door.

Roger nodded for Henry and Cliff to join us.

"I . . . might have an idea," he said.

"Roger, we're not killing him."

He shook his head. "No, no, no, didn't you hear him just now? He said he built up his ability over years of *muscle memory*."

Understanding bloomed behind Cliff and Henry's eyes. They glanced at each other.

"Do you think that would work?" Henry asked.

Cliff nodded, rubbing the back of his neck. "I . . . I think it might. If we hit enough core memories. It would take a while."

"We have time," Roger said. "What have we got to lose?"

"If it doesn't work, it'll probably fry his brain."

Roger shrugged. "Can't really say that bothers me. But I don't think it would. We'd just need to do it slowly. We need to at least try."

They nodded, and Cliff fiddled with some buttons by the door. The clear wall evaporated instantly. Allister watched them, his confident smile wavering.

Henry clapped him on the shoulder. "Let's take a walk."

I'd never been down this hallway before.

It was long, longer than any other hallway in Giftshop. Doors branched off at regular intervals, each marked with a map of different areas of the world. We had exited through one with a carving of the Pacific Northwest of the United States.

Roger kept me steady as we journeyed down the hallway. No one had spoken since leaving the Quiet Room. Even Allister had gone silent, both out loud and in my head.

The door at the end of the hallway loomed. It was made of plain dark wood and set with a shiny bronze handle. We neared, and the door swung open.

It was a circular room with a circular carpet lined with low-set circular bookcases. A fire crackled in the fireplace at the far side, bright lamps illuminating the space. At the center of the circular room sat a large squishy armchair. It looked well used but clean. A crocheted doily adorned the table next to it, a thin vase with a single flower resting in the middle. The complicated tubing system suspended above the chair connected to a set of computer monitors nearby.

We entered. Roger closed the door behind us and locked it.

Allister laughed. "What's this? Are you going to read me a bedtime story?"

Henry walked him to the chair. "How much do you know about nanotechnology?"

The blood drained from Allister's face. He threw himself backward.

Henry and Cliff latched onto his flailing arms and pulled him to the center of the room. Roger made sure I could stand on my own before helping them secure him in the chair. Straps buckled around his arms and legs, torso, and head.

He thrashed as Cliff turned on the computer screen, and Roger donned some disposable blue gloves. My legs gave out as a wave of nausea, pain, fear, and anger slammed into me. Henry crossed the room and grabbed me before I hit my head.

"Stop!" Allister cried. "You . . . you can't do this!"

"Oh, I think we can," Cliff said, entering something into the computer. "You said it yourself, you monster; we don't kill people. But you do."

Roger grabbed a tube above the chair and attached it to a large-capacity syringe. He set a new needle to the end, staring down at Allister as he ripped open an alcohol wipe. Allister tried to break free of the straps, jolting, pulling, and twisting, but they didn't budge. Roger swabbed behind his right ear and stepped back, picking up the syringe.

"What do you think, everything to do with Legion, the Book of Bones, and the Collective?" he asked his father.

"I think that's a start."

"No! No!" Allister shrieked. "I've worked too hard for this! You can't take this away from me!"

Roger bent down and put an arm around the back of his neck. Allister stopped struggling, his breathing irregular.

"I want you to remember this feeling," Roger said. "This feeling you're having right now of being alone, scared, and helpless. Having the knowledge that I can do *whatever* I want to you, and you can't do a *damn* thing about it."

The hate in Allister's eyes rose to new levels. Roger patted his shoulder with a smile. "Remember this feeling."

Allister turned his frantic gaze to me as Roger readied the syringe on the back of his neck, "This isn't over, Lily Masters. You hear me? I'll find you! I'll find all of you! I *will* come back! *I'll come back for you!* I'll . . . I'll . . ."

His voice faltered as Roger pressed the plunger down. Allister's twitching golden eyes glazed over, and he slumped forward.

We waited in silence. Slowly, like a snake unwrapping from my brain, the pain behind my eyes faded. The tremendous weight pressing on my skull had moved out, taking the pain and fear with it. I sank to the floor in relief.

Roger snapped off his gloves and tossed them in a nearby trash can. "You okay, Lil? Do you feel any different?"

I nodded and closed my eyes. Silence. Silence had never sounded so good. I couldn't help but smile. "He's gone. It's over."

Roger limped across the room and helped me stand. Cliff typed a few more lines into the computer and joined us. Allister remained immobile, eyes staring into the distance, mouth slack. The twitching in his irises had disappeared. His glazed eyes looked more hazel than gold. Sitting unresponsive, he almost seemed . . . normal.

"What'll happen to him?" I asked.

"It'll take a while for his memories to be rearranged," Cliff said, "but when it's done, he won't remember any of us, the book, Legion, or how to access the Collective."

"All of it? Will there be anything left?"

"We're not taking anything away from him," Henry said. "We're just . . . shuffling what's already there. He'll be a different person, if this works."

"We might even reinstate him somewhere," Cliff said. "We'll keep tabs on him, of course, but we could give him a chance at a normal life. Out east, maybe. Somewhere quiet. Somewhere he can live out the rest of his days completely unaware of . . . everything."

I turned away. "It seems too good for him. To just be able to walk away after everything he did."

"Maybe," Henry reasoned. "But I'd sleep better knowing we took this path rather than the alternative."

"What about Legion?" Roger asked. "What are we doing about the rest of them?"

Cliff heaved a sigh. "We've certainly disrupted their plans by destroying their central base and taking out a few of their leaders, but they're a big operation. We've put out word to the rest of the Jumper communities. They can't hide forever."

"And we now have the book," Henry added. "That gives us a little peace of mind. As much as we can hope to get, anyway."

"So . . . what happens now?"

"We do what we always do," Cliff said. "We pick up the pieces. One day at a time."

We watched the computer flick through fresh lines of code before exiting the room, leaving Allister's vacant gaze behind us.

EPILOGUE

<u>Promise</u>

"Miss Lily!"

I turned. Two figures ran down the trail behind me, the darkness of the forest parting at the beam of their flashlight. They weren't the first people I'd seen at the outpost, but they were the first to approach me. After the events of the last few weeks, the Northwestern community needed a pick-me-up, and Rhonda was the first to shout for a redo Bonfire, as the last one didn't go so well. Most of the outpost was deserted as everyone was already at the gathering, but there were a few stragglers. Myself included.

I'd taken the long way through town, still unsure if I should go. There would be a lot of remembering, not to mention sounding off tonight. I wasn't sure I was ready for that.

Squinting through the trees, I tried to make out the figures. I brightened as I recognized a rumpled suit and a bobbing, messy bun.

"Nicholas? Addy?" I called. "Is that you?"

Adeline didn't slow down when she neared, tackling me into a hug while Nicholas stood back and laughed. We hadn't seen each other since Rome. Part of me was too afraid to ask if they had made it back.

"You guys are all right!" I exclaimed. "I haven't seen you around, so I thought the worst."

"And *we*, dear Lily," Adeline said, "are *so* happy to see you! We would have been included in the rescue team. But, well"—she sighed and smiled—"I was unconscious, and Nick couldn't bear to leave my side."

Nicholas inclined his head in a bow. "My apologies, Lily. I was otherwise occupied."

"We were, however, briefed on your daring escape!" Adeline nudged my side with her elbow. "It seems you have a habit of saving the day."

I looked down. "Well, I wouldn't say that—"

"Ah, yes," she said, eyes twinkling. "But *I* would."

The sounds of singing echoed through the woods. Adeline bounced toward it. "Come now, I shall race you to the Bonfire, Nicholas."

He shuffled his feet. "Adeline, you know you would best me"—his eyes glinted—"but I'll wager I can best you at this new game of 'hacky-sack.'"

Her eyes narrowed. "You wouldn't dare challenge me."

"Watch me, my dear."

She took off running toward the music. "You fool! A Masters is never beaten!"

My stomach jolted.

Nicholas smiled, watching her run into the dark. "What an extraordinary woman."

"W-what did she just say?" I asked.

324

He sighed. "I was rather hoping you'd never find out."

"Wait, then she's . . . we're—"

"Related? Yes, I believe so. By marriage, anyhow. Her husband's name was Preston Masters, and he was a very cruel man. He used his power and influence to manipulate people, and his gifts of psychic prowess to gain wealth. He was renowned for his strange abilities. He could . . . how do I put this . . ." Nicholas thought for a moment, tucking a hand under his chin. "He could see things with his eyes closed, almost as if his soul hovered above his body. Very peculiar."

My eyes widened again.

Nicholas frowned, his usually calm eyes flashing with anger. "He led our expedition into the Gateway that day. He led us right to those infernal beasts. He offered Adeline to test their strength, and she agreed. Never steps down from a challenge, that one." He chuckled. "Not once. But . . . things went wrong. I tried to intervene, and two hundred years later, here we are."

He looked down, shifting a mound of pine needles with his foot. "I apologize if I have seemed short with you. It shocked me when I learned Preston survived and took a new wife. I can only hope he never did to her what he did to Adeline."

"Nicholas!" Adeline called far up the trail.

He smiled and shook my hand. "I must bid you adieu. I have a challenge to beat. Farewell, Lily. I'm sure we shall meet again."

I shook it with a smile. "See you around, Nick."

He jogged into the darkness. I stood alone in the chilly night air and watched him disappear over the hill. Christmas songs danced through the forest, ranging from solemn old carols to upbeat modern tunes. I hadn't realized that Christmas was right around the corner until the dust settled, and I glanced at a calendar. To know it was scarcely weeks away left me feeling disoriented. I'd just moved to Stars Crossing only a few days ago, it seemed. At the same time, it felt like I'd been there for years.

I shuffled through the woods, pausing when I passed by the sparring ring. My heart tightened. How was it that just a few weeks ago, Margot and I were training here? We'd even stolen pudding together. It hurt to think about running through the streets of New York, laughing our heads off as our feet slapped against the concrete.

Everything seemed so normal then. Now it just seemed like a mess.

Six days had passed since we escaped from the Colosseum. I'd spent enough time in Giftshop to have most of my injuries healed, but I knew there were some things that would never be completely whole again. There were parts inside me that were broken beyond repair. The best I could do was try to keep myself running without them, like a damaged machine limping forward with stretched springs and unhinged gears. My new status quo changed every day, it seemed, but I tried my best to accommodate it.

When Roger and I returned to the outpost, Carl had bounded up to us, excited to see his best friend back in one piece. It was a joyful reunion until Carl looked around expectantly.

"Where's Margot?" he had asked with a smile. "She said she'd drop by after Rome, but I haven't seen her around. She get transferred back to the East Coast already?"

No one had told him about Margot. I still wasn't sure if that was because he never asked or no one had the heart to tell him the truth.

Roger had put a hand on his shoulder and suggested that they go for a walk. I waited on a stump while my eyes burned, only looking up to see Carl leaning against a tree with his head in his hands.

On the same day, I discovered Eli's wife was missing. No one had seen her since Rome, but the search party had recovered a note pinned to a tree made illegible by the rain. It was clear what happened, but they had yet to find a body.

The days following weren't any easier, as suddenly the Northwestern community was grieving sixteen of its members: Max, Payton, and the fourteen who died in Rome. I'd never spoken with most of them, but their absence was noticeable even to me. Giftshop had gone into a sort of mourning period, with the memorial hall still locked up tight. Another hallway had opened next to it to allow passage to the Guest Book, draped in black velvet and abundant with pictures of those who died.

I discovered my parents had called multiple times when I was gone. After I'd calmed down the initial "Why didn't you pick up? We were worried sick!" they informed me of some recent developments. Apparently, their buyer had reconsidered buying the property, and now it was back on the market, though I suspected not for much longer. A certain charitable organization had contacted my parents about the property, claiming that they wished to pay full price for the house and re-deed it back to the original owner.

When my parents expressed suspicion, the spokesperson (whose name just happened to be Henry) explained that he was part of a large-scale genealogical organization with an interest in keeping family homesteads with the original family. They couldn't fault them for the offer, but they still needed a few days to 'think it over.'

I'd asked Cliff if he had anything to do with the original buyer "reconsidering" the estate, but he shrugged innocently. My parents still planned on coming up on their scheduled visit tomorrow morning, but we'd come up with a story.

Now that Roger and I were actually a thing, we decided it would be best to use that as the cover story. We planned to tell them we met at the local grocery store when I dropped my groceries and had been dating since I got to town. I knew it was sappy enough for my dad to buy it, but my mom, as always, wanted every single detail. I spent many hours on the phone yesterday, telling them all about Roger and our completely fabricated love story.

All the strange friends and colleagues could be explained later, but for now, that was enough.

Roger had removed any evidence that he ever lived at the house, staying at the outpost until their visit was over. It left me alone for a few days, but I didn't mind. I had plenty of visitors to keep me company; Irene's team made a habit of stopping by daily.

I breathed in the frigid air, climbing on the railing of the sparring ring. The solar-powered floodlight on a nearby tree lit the world around me in a halo, scattering away the darkness.

I reached into my pocket and held the crumpled water- and bloodstained envelope in my hand. I'd already looked over it a thousand times, but I flipped it open again and stared at Allister's handwriting.

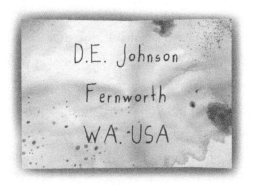

Fingerprint-shaped bloodstains covered the paper. I tried unsuccessfully to ignore the pain in my chest. Every time I closed my eyes, I could see it. I watched Margot lunge into the path of the bullet. I watched her fall. I watched the light leave her eyes. I watched it over, and over, and over again. So much death and anguish colored the last few weeks. Sometimes I thought I'd drown in it.

"You took the long way too, huh?"

I glanced up at the edge of the halo. Roger approached with a sad smile. He climbed next to me on the fence.

I returned the smile and shoved my hands back in my pockets with the note. "Yeah. I just needed some time."

"Me too. This is going to be a rough one."

We sat in silence. The wind rustled the barren branches overhead.

"You nervous about tomorrow?" I asked.

"Meeting your parents?" he said. "Oh yeah, terrified."

I cracked a smile. "Even after everything we just went through?"

"*Especially* after everything we just went through." He shook his head gravely. "It really puts things in perspective, how terrifying parents are. I'd almost have another go in the Colosseum."

I bumped his shoulder while he laughed. The woods were cold, but now that he sat near me, it wasn't so bad. I tilted my head back. The twinkling of a million glittering stars shone above us. The sky, the whole universe, really, was big, dark, and so far away. Even the stars couldn't light it all. How could all those stars even compete with the darkness? It didn't seem possible.

Wait. The stars . . .

Memories buried under the last few weeks stirred. My eyebrows furrowed. "Huh."

"What?"

"I just remembered . . . something strange. Something Reginald told me. He said . . ." I trailed off.

Roger leaned forward. "He said . . . what?"

"It was about . . . the Ones. I told you about them? He said there were people who sealed them away. Old enemies, he said. They were people of light. He said their power came from the sky. The stars."

"From the stars? What does that mean?"

"I dunno. I haven't really thought about it until now."

"Who were they? What happened to them?"

"Reginald didn't say. He didn't get into a full explanation before he . . ." I cleared my throat. "Before he and Margot—"

I stopped talking again. Music floated through the forest.

"Is it . . ." I swallowed. "Is it stupid that I miss her?"

"No," Roger said. "It's never stupid to miss someone."

I shook my head. "But she betrayed us. She got people killed. But somehow I . . . I really wish she was here right now."

I tightened my hand around the paper in my pocket. Roger grabbed my hand and took the note with it. It crinkled between us.

"Of course you do," he said. "Despite everything, she was still your friend, Lily. She put your life above her own, in the end."

"That doesn't make it right, what she did."

"No, it doesn't. But it helps us to understand."

My eyes burned, the hot tears stinging my face in the cool night air. I glanced down at the note between our hands.

"Hey." He wiped the tears from my cheeks. "We're going to find him. Wherever he is, we're going to find her brother and make things right. And we're going to do it together, okay? Promise."

I squeezed his hand and closed my eyes. The future seemed so rocky. Even though the immediate threat was gone, I couldn't help but feel something else loomed ahead. I didn't know what it was, or who, but something was coming. Something nobody had faced before. Something we couldn't handle on our own.

But maybe that was all right.

Because maybe we could face it together.

"Promise."

END OF BOOK TWO

Acknowledgments

This book was made possible by those who participated in The Otherworlds: Book Two Kickstarter campaign. For your support, faith, and patience, you will forever have my everlasting gratitude. I will strive to be worthy of your trust as my journey continues.

I'd like to thank Lisa, the wonderful editor at Enchanted Ink Publishing, for providing an incredible level of professional service. Arin Hanson, Dan Avidan, my favorite grumpy grumps, thank you for continuing to keep me company through long hours of work and fits of imposter syndrome. Many, many, *many* thanks to my parents, brothers, sisters-in-law, niece, and nephews for bearing with me all these years. And, consequently, keeping me sane through the painting of a thousand eyeballs.

And for Stewart, who wasn't able to see Book Two completed, I hope your new home has sailboats, that Leica camera you always wanted, eternal sunsets, and an absence of mayonnaise. Rest well, my love.

About the Author

RJ Kinner is an author and illustrator who resides in the beautiful California foothills with her overly enthusiastic Siberian Husky. Her hobbies include hiking, rock hounding, panicking over crippling self-doubt, and baking. In addition to her published works, she has illustrated a tarot and corresponding oracle deck (The Kinner Tarot, and The Echoes Oracle) from two successful Kickstarter campaigns. With questions or inquiries, contact rjkinner@rjkinnerart.com.

ALSO BY

rjkinnerart.com

Made in the USA
Monee, IL
30 April 2024

57699561R00193